AF430422

Empire

of

Mud

A NOVEL

JAMES SURIANO

WeavingGenesis
PUBLICATIONS

Copyright © 2020 James Suriano
All rights reserved.

Book layout by ebooklaunch.com

For Nosipho Mnisi

Your bravery runs deep in the blood of your son.

Also by James Suriano

Novels

Inbiotic

The Antarcticans

Dark

Aeon

The Cult of Mao

Truco

The Water Crown

Club Sunrise

The Sisters of Woo Magic

Short Stories

Finding Mr. Harikami

Revenge and Regret

Saved-ology

Trapped in France

Short Story Collections

To Catch a Breath

"We are not put on this earth to see through one another.
We are put on this earth to see one another through."

– Gloria Vanderbilt

MUD

Balapitiya, Sri Lanka, 2004

The wave was on top of me, swirling violently, heaving up and down, a type of schizophrenic tide. The latest swell of water pummeled at the back of my head, dragging debris over me, burying me in destruction. Clawing toward what instinct told me was the sky, I could not hold my breath much longer. I broke through, my head ramming a board and pushing to the surface of the watery mix with every possible piece of our village. I gulped air. The life that left me for at least a full minute crashed back, invading my mouth and lungs. The momentous impact of the wave left a hissing whine in my ears. There was a cow beside me, with its nose packed full of mud and in the last spasms of life. Ruka, my daughter, had been holding my hand and Mewan, my son, was standing in front of me when the tsunami hit. Our backs were to the ocean and smiles danced on our lips. I squeezed my hand, she was not there. Mewan had vanished in front of me like a cruel magic trick. I could only process what had happened in slow motion. I tried mightily to push my mind from one assumption to the next but they came in baby steps.

Until my eyes locked on Mewan. The red belt I'd tied around his waist a few minutes before the impact was the only remaining thing on his body. He was lying with his face in the mud, his back arched and lifeless. His hands were somewhere beneath him. None of this made sense. My mind deteriorated into a thousand pieces and memories as I imagined my life without him. I focused on him, and harnessed the fear that another wave might come, to propel every muscle in my body toward him. I leapt over the cow, a bathtub, and car door until I reached Mewan's small body and pulled him out of the mud. He was limp. The way he looked when I birthed him, until my neighbor had whacked him on the back and he wailed his way into this world. I hit him with the force of life and then sucked at his face, frantic to pull out the sediment. He was suffocating or maybe he was gone already, on to his next incarnation. I spit rocks, hit him again, and screamed his name through the grit of my mouth, commanding him to come back to me. His face was losing color.

"Mewan please. We need you."

His arm sputtered to life and he wiped at his face. He struggled with the uncomfortable condition of his body, coughing and then vomiting out the ocean.

"Mama's here." As I put one hand to my body to reach for my sari, I realized my clothes had been pulled from my body and I had nothing to wipe him with but my muddied embarrassment.

Where was Ruka among the jagged posts of painted bamboo, sheared-off palm trees, and thatched roofs flipped on end as if a giant wandering child had stampeded with abandon? The tourist shop we had been in front of, full of bright handicrafts, knitted fabrics, and small treasures made of palms and coconut husks, had slid into the ocean and was floating intact. Around us, drowned bodies lay like turned pebbles, tumbled repeatedly by the tremendous force of the water. I pulled Mewan close to my body. If another wave came, I would squeeze him to death before I let him go.

A single cry broke through the awed silence. I searched the faces of the people who were with me, immobilized in the mud, bewildered, and trying to process why so few of us stood over so many. Then there was a second cry and a third before a rising orchestra of small voices gurgled against the silent shock. I caught the sound of a breathy whimper, which I recognized as Ruka. My eyes swooped over the dead bodies. Ruka was there, bent backward over branches, themselves twisted and broken by the current, hovering above this display of hell. I pulled out my left leg; it was stronger than my right. The polio from my childhood had left my body as two different people sewn together in one. I willed myself closer to her, forcing my body through the liquefied earth. I took a few more steps, my heart pumping under a weight I was sure would collapse it into a flat piece of worthless muscle from the fear and exertion.

Ruka was upright, a strange angle inhabiting her dangling arm. When she saw us move toward her, she looked for a way down from her unnatural perch. A body lay impaled on a branch beside her, already gray, its fingers in a final grasp for safety. A sight a six-year-old shouldn't see. Mewan quieted. His head was on my shoulder, his breaths calmer in my ear. I reached the tree, the muscles in my legs burning. But an indefatigable intent drove me, I would save them both if it was my last act in this life.

"Ruka, jump. Jump to Mama," I urged her.

She looked at her broken arm. I saw a finger twitch. There was nothing to lose; I could see it on her face. Our world was fractured; our only hope was to advance beyond it. She jumped and splattered in the mud. Ruka was strong, stronger than any six-year-old girl I knew. She pushed back her wet, black hair and strained until her hand was in mine. Some miracle had assembled the puzzle of our lives.

We reached the end of the muck by sheer will. The villagers stood at its edge, some with their arms out, pleading with the mud to return their loved ones. Others were digging aimlessly, and a few frantically ran from spot to spot, unsure what do to. Female elders touched us as we walked past them. I felt a piece of cloth draped over my head, hanging down to cover my body. The air held a tight weave of moisture and heat, and insects began to congregate. I didn't want to imagine what would be here in a day. Ruka tried to pull away and walk ahead, but I held her tighter. I was not ready to separate from my children. I'd felt in that minute the sensation of losing both of them, an agony which shredded me. She ground her teeth in frustration of being restrained. I would not let her go, not yet.

Someone called her name. Ruka didn't turn. She kept going, mud flaking off her legs and feet, her torn orange sari dusting the ground. She pumped her arms like a determined rhinoceros. My vision began to open up, and I could see outside my immediate surroundings. My brain gave a reprieve from the protection of devastation; I could handle this. The small lanes and houses now gone, we charged into an obliterated landscape. The forest still stood but at an artificial height on the hillside. Our house stood above the line the greedy ocean had reached. I was grateful.

I had survived the first of many attempts the gods would make on my life.

OFFER

Two Years Later

I walked the lane we stood on when the tsunami had enveloped our lives. I imagined even my husband, Pramith, might walk up to me and nuzzle his face in the back of my hair, as he always had done. This was the last place I'd seen him, and the trick of my mind was that he was somehow still here. The mud had been cleared, and the buried coconuts now sprouted into small trees. The buildings made of palm boards and thatch roofs were built to look like tikis; a fresh woodsy smell emanated from the shops. They sold trinkets to tourists and food to locals. Baked goods, vegetables from the ground, but the busiest of all of them was empty, with people lined up for Ravantha and his son to come in from the ocean at five o'clock to sell their catch from a splintery board with dried fish guts. There was an earthenware pottery store and an artist selling photographs of our everyday life. No one minded playing the exotic destitute local if it meant money came to the village from far away. Tourists were gold, and one of the small blessings of the disaster was that it brought more of them.

Mewan ran ahead, bumping into people, tumbling backward among the milky-white people. They arrived like gods, with their stacks of luggage and shiny accessories strapped to their body. We were happy to sell them even more at ten times a reasonable cost; they gobbled up everything my people set in front of them. The money never did more than enrich the person selling, though. We needed Sri Lanka to give us electricity and clean water. We always heard a familiar refrain answering our calls: *In time.*

Mewan toddled into a man in a white robe. His skin was light, but not like the other tourists, and his hair and beard were as black as my hair. I noticed his white leather shoes with a green crocodile on them. He looked impeccable. He picked up Mewan, held him in the air until Mewan giggled, and set him back down. Although it was unusual for foreigners to pick up children, it wasn't completely unheard of. I raised my hand at the man, and his eyes looked in my direction. Holding Mewan's hand, he approached me.

"What a nice young boy. But he looks hungry." He looked me up and down. "As do you. I'm Khalid." His hand was out, ready to embrace mine.

He spoke Sinhala, which was very unusual for a foreigner.

"We don't have much," I said. "It's been hard since the tsunami. Only they have been lucky to rebuild." I gestured to the new business. I was hoping he would offer me money or food, both of which we could use.

"You should come work for me." Khalid pulled glossy images from his bag and waved me closer to him. The first page was a map. I recognized my island nation and a green line with an airplane arcing over the waters between my country and India, then a long flight line arriving at a country jutting into the Red Sea. He tapped his index finger on the starred destination, then opened the pamphlet. Inside were pictures of gleaming towers and rooms filled with polished stones, precious metals, and furniture covered with the skins of exotic animals. Apartments with expansive views of the city appeared below: more towers, more sparkle, crystal-blue water in the distance.

"These are common apartments of the people you could work for. They'll pay you handsome wages, give you a place to live, provide you with as much food as you need."

"But my children …"

"Yes, think precisely of them and the money you could send home. They would be provided for, finally. You could offer them a life you'll never be able to achieve if you stay here, selling—" He pulled at the masks, made with plastic straws, hanging from my body. My mother had taught me to make them in better times, when she would step away from the business of the tea plantation and construct crafts with me. Years later, when she and my father died from cholera, I made them to remind me of her. This was long before Mewan was born. I wanted to be of use, so I asked the other women to teach me their skills, but they didn't want the competition. In our village, I was the only person to sell masks. Ruka had the brilliant idea to attach rubber bands from the supply deliveries to them so they could be worn. The tourists' children loved the way they trans-formed their faces into tigers, ostriches, and monkeys.

"It would only be for one year, and then you can decide to continue working or come home." Khalid tilted his head down to catch my gaze.

He pulled out another pamphlet and showed me how much money they would pay me. A number in an unfamiliar currency, dinars. I saw a picture of a small house, with a few rooms, the walls sturdy and even, brightly painted. The roof was intact to keep out the drenching rains. It was in the style of my town, but a home I could never have dreamed of living in. A house with an indoor toilet and kitchen where water ran from the sink. "If you're smart with your salary," Khalid said, "you'll be able to buy a modern home when you return."

I imagined myself living there, Mewan running on clean hardwood floors rather than packed earth where worms and mites wiggled their way to the surface and crawled over him at all hours trying to burrow into his skin. I saw Ruka with piles of books around her, reading and smiling with a cooling breeze coming from the elevated windows, rather than the stifling wet air seeping from the mountainside that our shack was built into.

"Other mothers from your village are going," Khalid said. "I've already booked their tickets and found them families." He flipped to the next page in the brochure. A room, with a single bed and a dresser, a bathroom behind it. A white toilet, a sink and shower, all indoors. "This is a typical room where you might stay. You'd have your own bed, your own bathroom."

"Could I bring my son and daughter? We can happily live in that room. They would be no problem, I promise."

"Oh, no." He shook his head and stroked his beard. "That's not possible. Only you can go."

My insides felt heavy, while my mind swirled with the highs and lows on the way to the possibilities he was presenting.

"When do I need to tell you by?" I asked. Mewan wrapped around my leg like a snake. He was patient but wanting.

Khalid put away the glossy packet and twisted his hands. "I'll only be here for a few days, so make your mind up quickly. Many women want these jobs. Many women want to provide for their families."

I felt the pressure of when there were only three fish left for sale and four people behind me. If the decision wasn't made, it would be made for me. "Can I tell you tomorrow? I'll meet you right here."

Khalid sucked his teeth; they were white and in a neat row, his lips red and full. "Yes, but I hope there are still spaces available." He tickled Mewan's belly and patted his head. "He'll be fine." He gestured around us. "Look at all the kids he has to keep him busy. And when he's grown, he'll thank you many times over."

He was right; there were many kids who had survived, more kids than parents, their young bodies able to come back from the ocean's trauma. They ran barefoot, most with shorts emblazoned with advertising from the city. Mewan had been spared the scars; the mud had cradled him.

Khalid bowed and floated off; he seemed light and airy, with no weight of worry. His freshly washed white thawb swayed with him.

...

I ran my fingers over mangoes lined up on a coconut mat, sold by a boy Ruka's age. She would beam at the purchase, even though she'd know it would cost me three days' wages. I smiled at the boy. In my head I felt like my mother, who had scoured the markets each day for a boy to marry me to. The possibilities of Ruka's and Mewan's futures were stacking up in my head, making me dizzy. I pried Mewan from a root he had fixated on and hurried to our house.

Ruka was on the front three steps, sweeping dirt that trickled down from the mountainside. Occasionally, rocks would fall and strike our metal roof. There were enough dents to remind me of the times my heart had stopped in the middle of the night, fearful another wave was coming. It would be a lifetime before that fear would abandon me.

"Ruka, can you come sit with me? I have to ask you something." She put her broom down. Calluses on her eight-year-old hands hid behind the stick. She swept wherever someone would pay her. She climbed up the trees at night to pluck fibers from the palmyra tree to retool her broom, readying it for the next job. I was proud of how hard she worked to help Mewan and me.

She sat on the steps and looked up at me. An orange bandana held her hair out of her eyes while the salt of her sweat crisscrossed the paisley pattern like starbursts in ice.

"I was offered a job." I thought I would present the best news first. For us, being offered a job—picking tea or rocks, shoveling sewage, cleaning anything—were welcome words.

Ruka put her palms together and smiled. She tilted her chin up to me, waiting for the rest of the good news.

"But the job isn't here." I put a mango in her hands when I said this.

"We would have to move?" She immediately filled in my hesitation with glee.

"*I* would have to move. You would stay here with your brother."

"To Dubai?"

How did she know the name of this city? I didn't know where it was; I only had seen the pictures and knew it was somewhere only a plane could take me.

"I—I don't know. Maybe. Where did you hear of that city?"

"Kiyoma's mother is going. She told me a man in a white dress came to her this morning and promised her riches and her mother said yes."

Kiyoma was Ruka's best friend. She lived higher up the mountain and picked tea for a plantation. This was good; maybe Kiyoma could live here or Ruka and Mewan could stay with her family.

"She's going for sure?" I had met her mother in passing. I'd heard she'd stopped talking after the wave, her voice lost to the ocean, along with her husband.

"Yes. She can't stand it here anymore, and she thinks Kiyoma is fine to take care of herself." Ruka put her hands on her hips. "We are eight, you know."

I squatted in front of her and handed her Mewan. "And you're ready to take full responsibility for him too?" Mewan grabbed for Ruka, rubbed his face on her arm, and gave her a playful nibble.

"I already take care of my brother. But who will take care of you?" Ruka patted Mewan on the back, then pulled a string from her pocket, quickly twisted it into a ring, and slid it onto his finger.

"Don't worry about me, sweetie. The man in the white dress tells me everything will be just fine."

...

The next day, Khalid was pleased I accepted the offer. He gave me a piece of paper and asked me to fill in the blank spaces between words. Many of the words were foreign.

"I can't read all of this," I told him.

"That's fine. Bring this with you when you meet me in three days at the dock. A boat will take you to Colombo."

The next two days were filled with my asking Ruka, "Who will watch Mewan while you sweep? Who will swat the jaguars away when food becomes scarce for them and they prowl the mountainside shacks? What if the gangs come and try to rob our house?"

"I'll do what you've always done: I'll tie Mewan to my back. I'll look the jaguar in the eyes and swat at him with my sturdiest broom. If the gangs come, I'll go find shelter with Kiyoma. I'll do everything you've taught me and so I'll go on."

I wanted to know I had given her everything. If I was honest, though, my everything wasn't reliable armor. New lessons were thin lately, and if I stayed here I'd likely spend the next years just making sure what she already knew stuck. There were girls on their own only a year older than Ruka. I saw them hustle harder than I did.

On the third day, I woke before Mewan and Ruka. Mewan was sleeping between my body and arm, his head lodged into my armpit. Ruka had spun herself into a ball at the bottom of a mat on the floor of our house. I wriggled away, careful not to wake Mewan. I leaned over his face, closed my eyes, and felt his warm breath. I pressed my lips to his forehead and held them there, savoring the sweet smell of my little boy and forgetting everything but the feeling of him in this moment. In the days to come, I knew I would return to this memory for comfort when I was gone. I wanted to make sure it was vivid.

Hours passed, and I approached the dock—Ruka behind me, Mewan running ahead. A long line of women, swatting at bugs and drinking from disposable teacups, waited. A shop front stood where the wooden dock slats nestled into the sand. The interior was filled with small tables, more men who looked like Khalid in their strange clothing, busy smoking and filling out forms for the women who stood in front of them. Women I recognized, women like me. They had stacks of blue pocket-size books with a gold eagle on the cover. On the exterior wall of the shack a sky-blue covering had been hung, and one of the men ushered the line of women into place to take their pictures. Each of us ended up with a book of pages with the name of our country stamped in gold on the front. My picture was inside, with many words and numbers covering the rest of the page. A picture of a man was on the opposite page.

Ruka looked over the book. "Who is this?" She tapped at the man.

"A prince," said the woman standing behind her, waiting to get another cup of tea and her share of fresh dates.

Khalid had his hand on my elbow. "Do you like those? They're"—he pointed to the dates—"like coconuts in Dubai. Everywhere." He looked me in the eyes in a way Mewan might when he wanted to get my attention. "Shula, you're going to a better place, I'm certain."

The boat sounded its horn as it came into view from behind the mangrove trees. Mewan was playing with a girl his age at the base of a tree, peeling the delicate layers of bark away and laughing, then handing them to her. Khalid positioned my body toward the boat, let go, then began to line up the other women who had received their book.

"Mewan," I called to get his attention. I wasn't sure I should leave my place in line. His head tilted in my direction. I knew he heard me, but he decided to continue. He didn't know I was leaving, after all. In his mind, he would fall asleep with his head on my chest, this night no different from the last.

Ruka appeared. "You're going?"

"It's time. Can you—"

She was gone before I could finish the sentence and returned with Mewan, who was crying, having been pulled from his game. "Mama is leaving, Mewan. You have to give her kisses and hugs."

"No." He was defiant.

"Yes, Me-Me. Mama is leaving for a long time."

"No." Mewan butted his head into his sister's shoulder.

I couldn't help but smile at the two of them standing there. It was better this way. I didn't have to pry him off me. I kissed his head, hugged them both, to which Mewan squirmed and whined, then stood up straight.

He looked up when I was on the boat. There was worry in his eyes now, and Ruka held him back from trying to run to the boat. I had to push against the other women for one last glimpse at everything we were leaving behind. Mewan was in tears. It was a moment I hoped he wouldn't remember.

CITY LIFE

I remembered Colombo from a trip as a child. My parents had brought me to Mount Lavinia, a hotel on the ocean's edge with long outdoor porticos overlooking a pool. My mother had stood at the end of the portico, the ocean behind her, smooth and orange from the sunset. There was more to the picture then, the reason for being there, the others who attended, but I couldn't remember. The boat passed the hotel. The water between us was choppy, the skies dark green. I felt the first drop on my hand as I held the bamboo rail of the overloaded boat. We were all quiet. Khalid and the other men working with him shuffled through the thin spaces between our bodies. Stories of these boats sinking were common enough to have made their way inside our fears.

"When the boat docks, follow the yellow line to the waiting vans," Khalid told us. "They'll take you to the airport."

I stood behind a woman who was slightly taller than me, with a pink-and-green knit bag hanging from her shoulder. I wanted to touch it. The color made the texture look spongy;

I wanted to see if that was the way it felt. I'd brought only one sari, which created a bulge in my pocket. The pictures Khalid showed me had maids in uniforms; he'd said everything would be provided, and I took him at his word.

We followed the yellow line to the bus, a line into the airport, a line into the plane. We were obedient line followers, a trait my schoolteachers had drilled into all their students and that stayed with us long after the other learning had faded.

...

The aircraft door opened into the dusty heat. I felt delirious from the long flight. Two boats of women and four teenage boys from my village occupied the back half of the plane. As much as I hadn't liked the experience of flying, I was hesitant to leave the safety of the group. We had exchanged stories during our hours in the air. It was enough to keep our minds off our families, and for some, off of the pain, which still seared from that day two years ago. The flight attendants had passed around books with translations from Sinhala to Arabic. I found the book unhelpful; I was never good with languages.

Kiyoma's mother walked up the aisle. When she reached my row, she put out her hand to let me advance in front of her. "Our daughters will be fine," she said. "Sometimes I feel like Kiyoma is raising me. The girls are strong and know so much about the world."

I was surprised to hear her speak. She was trying to make me feel better, and I knew what she said was true. Ruka was extraordinary and beautiful too; she would be okay.

When I stepped out of the plane onto the stairs that led to the tarmac, there were two white tents with men in uniforms looking at our small books, scribbling and stamping them. The sun pelted me without relent; I felt like I might wither under its brutal weight.

Under the tent, a man talked to me in his language, shook his head, wrote symbols in my book, and banged a rubber stamp of power. I'd only seen one once before at our public village building, where I registered Ruka's and Mewan's births. I tried to say thank you, but the sand rode the hot winds down my throat and made it painful to talk. It didn't matter; I could tell I was on my way.

After boarding another bus, we drove through the city. Everything was stacked in neat order: the roads, buildings, people, and the trees lining the roads looked lonely and contrived. Nothing was natural; the ground had given birth to steel and glass, children it didn't recognize. Eventually we stopped at a building that vanished into the clouds. Khalid pointed to Kiyoma's mother and a woman at the front of the bus. "This is you," he said.

This wasn't any of us. We were more than animals, herded from one pen to another. I could see my father's eyes looking at me. *Shula, don't worry what anyone says. Focus your mind.* I waved to Kiyoma's mother and gave her a smile of hope. I would focus my mind on her well-being, on her happiness, on her success with her new employer. Those were useful thoughts.

The bus pulled away, conquering the long boulevards under its massive wheels. Such power, to transport us. We swayed side to side over humps in the road, through gates, which, gliding back on their own, were operated by an unseen force. Then came rows of individual, identical houses, neatly lined with white barred fences and desert shrubs. Three more women left the bus; I didn't know who they were.

We left the neighborhood of sameness and headed for the coast. The busy roadways met the glittering sand and azure water. Everything was new, and glitzy cars zoomed past the bus. We crossed a bridge, leaving the mainland behind. The other side of the road was planted with lush flowers. Sculpted forms had been placed for anyone driving to admire, date palms planted in precisely designed cutouts of the concrete streetscape. Roads on each side jutted out from the strip we were on. Groups of men who looked like the men of my country, with hard hats and bright work gear, roamed like wild herds. The question of who had done all this bounced in my head as we moved through the city. Now I had an answer. My people. We had built this oasis in the desert. A bubble of pride welled in me.

When we turned right on Al Hilali, Khalid stood and waved me forward. I wanted to watch through the window. I'd been recording each turn in my head, along with chosen landmarks I knew I would remember. I stole one more glance—two glossy, black light posts with pointy crowns on top of them. I put my hand on each seat against the aisle of the bus as I moved forward, the passengers looking up at me. I could tell they were more worried about their destinations than mine. When the bus stopped, Khalid put his hand on my elbow to guide me outside.

"Put your hair up and put this on." He handed me a head covering. "No one here will appreciate that thick mane."

"When will you pick me up?" I asked.

He looked bewildered by the question. "I don't understand what you're asking."

There wasn't malice in his response, but maybe he didn't remember telling me. "This is for one year and then I go home, right?"

"If it's what you want. Look at your house. Do you think you'll want to go back to your village after living here?" He directed my attention to the villa we had stopped in front of.

There was a break in the box hedges lining the property. There was a locomotive-statured car with two letters gleaming on the front grille and an ornament of a silver woman with billowing clothes leaning forward. The house was two stories, with two shiny brown doors. The place seemed so quiet; I wasn't sure if I should approach it.

Khalid nudged me forward. "They're waiting for you."

My foot touched the ground, and I headed toward the doors, which cracked open. I tried to see who was in the darkness. They opened farther. I heard the bus pull away behind me. I wanted to turn and tell them not to go, but I couldn't be rude to my new employer. A man appeared. He had a freshly cut beard against his rigid jawline and eyes like the black night. He was also athletic and his shoulders and arms filled out his coat, tailored with persimmon-colored embroidery and a starched high collar. His white pants were wide, his black leather sandals showing pale manicured feet.

He waved me softly toward him and smiled. "*Marhaba.*" A word I didn't know. When I didn't respond, he said, "Hello." I knew some English from the tourists and aid workers who had come to our village. "Hello." I smiled and bowed, then climbed the few stairs to the door. He opened it wider, and I stepped inside.

There were no houses like this in our village. I saw my reflection in the milky veins of the brown floor. Upward, the ceiling was impossibly tall, the rooms above overlooking the space I was in buttressed by railings of polished wood and spiraled metal. There were paintings the size of me on the walls, along with pedestals where statues of things I couldn't identify stood proudly. Pieces of furniture, all with deep-purple upholstery. A color that reminded me of the dead bodies I'd witnessed after the tsunami. I pushed the memory far away from me. The wrong thought to have in this masterpiece of a house.

The man held his arms wide and welcomed me to his house. Then he brought them in tightly toward his body and said, "Mohamed."

I took it as a welcome to tell him my name. I brought my arms in as he did and said, "Shula."

Then he began talking quickly in his language. I understood nothing he said. I followed him through the house. Along the way, we passed a room with a long table made of twisting red glass that rose up out of the center and connected with the ceiling behind the stairs where the ceiling came to a normal height. It was a sitting area, lined with couches and chairs and low tables. It reminded me of a lobby. The wall of windows beyond looked out onto a covered patio, a small putting green, and a pool that bordered a blue waterway. I could see the other homes on the opposite side, but we were far enough away to maintain privacy. The home was beautiful and clean—unlike anything I'd ever seen. I wondered what part of the house they lived in. Still, the home had a sterile feel, as if it were built to wall its occupants in solitary confinement.

A shadow moved behind a door at the end of the room. I ignored it, thinking it might be a boat passing on the water. Mohamed kept talking, pointing to the windows, the sills beneath them, the chairs, and the surfaces where the decorative molding covered the walls. He whacked with his palm and pointed out the dust that rose from them when he did. I understood what he was getting at. He wanted perfection, everywhere. Through the doors at the end, we arrived in the kitchen. It was half the size of the sitting room and equally dense in fine materials. Stone countertops, a gleaming steel stove that never looked to have been used. Mohamed came to me and held out his hand. I reached for him and touched it, unsure what he wanted. He jerked his hand back, wearing a look of disgust, and fled to the sink to scrub his hand.

The heat of embarrassment blossomed from my chest. He came back to me and said, "Passport." I didn't understand the word. He reached in his robe and pulled out his passbook, tapped on it, and jabbed his finger at me.

I understood. He wanted my travel document. I pulled the blue book from my pocket and handed it to him. He squatted and opened a cabinet. I saw a metal box inside, along with a keypad. He punched in a code, pulled the lever, threw the book inside, shut the door, and engaged the lock.

My father had a safe; he had kept my grandmother's three gold rings and important papers inside. But he never told me how to open it; he never told anyone. Which meant when he was gone, so was everything inside it.

Mohamed led me to the back of the kitchen. There was a small hallway, with a door on the left. He opened it and showed me that it led to the dining room. He stopped there and gestured for me to continue. There were three more doors. The first was a closet with cleaning products, mops, brooms, and a tall machine. The second door opened into a very small room with two machines as big around as me, as well as a sink, with what I think were soaps. When I opened the door to the third room, I stood staring into the darkness, wondering if my eyes would adjust. I took one step in, hoping the lights might turn on as they had in the other rooms.

There was a female voice behind me now, talking with Mohamed. I rubbed my thumb and forefinger together rapidly, as I always do when I'm nervous. Footsteps came toward me. They would think I was useless. Light flowery scents fluttered my way, and then a soft click. My eyes adjusted, and I turned to face a woman. Her face was wrapped in the purple of the chairs, with black eyeliner and drawn lips. Her visage looked full and it glowed. She smiled kindly. Her hand went to her stomach, and she rubbed the bump, which didn't belong on her slight frame. Mohamed left.

"Your room. Welcome. I'm Ousha," she said in Sinhala. I couldn't believe she spoke my language.

I turned back to see a single bed against the wall with the width of the door space next to it. At the end of the bed was a dresser with a television mounted on the wall above it. I walked farther inside to find a closet with several uniforms hanging inside and an open door to a bathroom. I was so excited I wanted to jump. This was all mine? It didn't seem possible that someone would give an employee such an extravagance.

I turned to thank them. The doorway was empty, though, so I walked back into the hall. The lights in the kitchen were off.

I shut my door and went into the bathroom. There was white tile, the sink was white, and I looked at myself in the mirror. A yellow happy-face sticker was in the center of the mirror. I ran my finger over it, and the mirror popped open. I pulled on it. There were small shelves inside. A few new toiletries and a piece of paper. I unfolded it. Letters and words in my language, letters and words that told me scary things.

•23•

SLICE

Hammering, drilling, loud breaking. I opened my eyes in the dark room. The sounds shook the walls. My feet sinking into the carpet, I groggily reached for the light switch. When I opened my door and stuck out my head, the sunlight from the kitchen windows assaulted me. Clearly midmorning. *I should be up and working.* I shut my door and hurried into my shower. The soaps caressed me and left my skin feeling soft and full. The soap back home, when I could get it, was harsh and made my skin tight and dry. I wanted to stay under the warm massaging water longer, but I knew it would be something to look forward to at night. The unsettling words from the paper in the mirror spoke over and over in my head: *I can't watch him do this any longer. I love you too much.* Who was the note to? And who had written it? I pulled out one of the uniforms from the closet. A black shirt with white-banded short sleeves, a white collar, and white buttons down the front, along with black pants. There were two pairs of black shoes. They were both too small, but one pair was broken in more than the other so I wore them. I combed my hair.

It fell onto my shoulders, and the soap had made it shine like glossy paint. I smiled at myself in the mirror and imagined walking through my village in these clothes. Then I saw Ruka and Mewan, and my spirits fell to the earth.

A few minutes later, I was in the kitchen. It was empty other than the smell of tea. It had been picked too early, and the acidity lingered. Before, in the life before my children and husband, I had worked on a tea plantation for many years. My father had owned it, and I wanted to show him how much I could do. My brother would scoff and tell me I should learn the finances, not the art of picking tea leaves. But I wanted to know where our money came from; I wanted to feel the heartbeat of my father's business.

I pushed through the swinging door into the sitting area. The pictures from the wall had been carefully laid on the floor; two construction workers were building shelves. They were Indians and stopped to look at me when I walked in. The older one said something to the younger, and they both leered at me. Mohamed and Ousha were absent.

"Where is Mohamed?" I politely asked the older man.

I don't think he completely understood me, but he pointed to the front of the house and then, in a gesture I recognized from home, spun his hand around, meaning he could be anywhere outside the front door. I walked past them and wandered through the house. I opened doors to figure out where things were. Closets, toilets, small rooms full of plates and silver. A few doors were locked. Eventually I found a dusting mop and ran it over the heads of statues and the sills of windows. The last maid must have been beloved; she seemed to have kept the house spotless. At the bottom of the staircase, I looked up, unsure if I could go upstairs. The workers were laughing at something, their voices echoing through the house. I opted to open the front door and clean the small porch. Two benches and small plants in rectangular pots ran the length of each side of the space. Some dust, a thin layer of sand maybe, coated everything, and it felt satisfying to have something to clean. I looked up and spotted a woman in the same outfit as mine walking by on the sidewalk. She quickly looked away, then looked back and nodded at me. I waved, which gave her permission to look longer until she was beyond the hedges. I was happy to know there were other women like me working close by.

The train-like car pulled in the driveway. Mohamed was driving. He stepped out and looked at me without acknowledgment. Ousha came next, holding an umbrella to shield her from the sun. Her purse was as big as a shopping bag. When she saw me, she looked surprised, hurried to my side, led me indoors, and pushed me up the stairs. There, the sterile, hard feel of the first floor turned velvety warm. The browns got deeper; the accents were cool blues, with plush carpets instead of tiles, and the paintings weren't behind glass. The texture of the paints was close and accessible. Ousha's black-and-cream pants rippled in the air and draped over the floor behind her as she walked. She sat me in front of a mirror; the vanity was filled with cosmetics and bottles of many shapes and colors. She pulled my hair back, took a brush, and kept combing it until it was all in her hand. Then she twisted my hair in a way I couldn't see and stuck three pins into it, creating a bun behind my head. She went to her closet and took out a sheer black hijab, settled it on my head, and pulled the folds of the neck into place. She found a burst of white feathers, from a baby bird, and attached it at my temple. I'd never felt so feminine and delicate. I touched my face to make sure it was me staring back.

Ousha patted the sides of my arms and whispered, "You should cover yourself. Mohamed is a very traditional man. But don't cover your beautiful face." She dipped her finger in a sparkly clear container then rubbed something on my lips. The sweet taste bounced off my lips and exploded in my mouth; with each caress of her soft finger, my lips felt more foreign. "Your teeth are perfect and white as coconut meat," she said.

"How do you know my language?" I asked.

She put her finger to her lips and nose, and gave me a smile. It was our secret.

"You can go anywhere in the house, expect Mohamed's office." She pointed to a door on the other side of the hall.

"Who will clean it for him?" I wanted everything to be perfect for Ousha and Mohamed. They had given me so much.

She held her palms toward me and waved them back and forth, as if to ask no more.

There were secrets here.

Mohamed's raised voice came from his office. Ousha looked at me, then pointed at the door. At first I thought she was directing me toward him, but then I realized she wanted me away from their bedroom. I heard him shout, followed by a thud against the office wall. A moment later, he barreled into the hallway. I took one look at his face and snapped my head toward the floor as I passed him and felt the wind of his furious momentum. A whimpering shriek came from Ousha, and then their heavy door closed, blocking any more noise.

I returned to the first floor. The men, now seated on the ground, ate meat wrapped in foil. With their mouths full, they snickered at me, pieces of their lunch visible in their mouths. I felt more dignified now after Ousha had groomed and dressed me. One of them stood up and blocked my passage to the kitchen. He reached for me and grabbed my chest, rubbing my breast roughly before I could avoid him. I'd dealt with men like this in my village. The only solution was to show them your strength. So I clenched my fist and swung. When my fist connected to his temple, his eyes rolled and he staggered back. The other two men laughed and pointed at him. Spotting a ceremonial machete on the wall, I lunged for it and lifted it off its hooks. I swung it at him as though I were cutting through the thick forest to clear more space for tea plants. I grazed his thigh and drew blood. The two seated workers stopped laughing and backed themselves against the shelves they were building. My attacker yelped and grabbed at this leg. I brought the machete up to his throat and threatened him: "I'll kill you next time." I knew he didn't know my language, but he knew what I'd said. He surrendered, blood dripping to the floor. I placed the machete back on the wall, took my feather duster from my belt and dusted it lightly, then walked my original path to the kitchen.

I heard loud feet on the stairs. Mohamed's voice boomed at the men. I pushed the kitchen door open a crack to see. They cowered as he lambasted them, pointing wildly. He was such a handsome man, his exterior cool and perfectly sculpted, but when his anger overtook him his face became sinister, his eyebrows looked like they belonged on someone else's face, and spittle flew from his mouth, showering the person he was yelling at. The worker I had cut was sent away, his blood leaving a trail marking his exit.

"Shula!" Mohamed screamed.

I straightened my back and pushed through the door. He pointed to the blood. I knew he wanted it gone from his sight. The sight of it likely sickened someone like him. I went to the closet next to my room, pulled out the mop and bucket, and added a green cleaner and water. A minute later, I was mopping up the thick blood. The men didn't look at me once while I mopped. I had made my point.

Family Expansion

Before I went to sleep, I opened the door to my room so the light would wake me and I'd be up before anyone else. I heard someone in the kitchen. Had I overslept again? I waited to see who it was. The footsteps were heavy but clumsy. Both Mohamed and Ousha had deliberate steps. A glass shattered against the floor. Something was wrong. I got out of bed and stepped into the dark hallway; a small light was on over the stove. It was a woman, her hair draped over her hands as she widely gripped the edge of the counter.

"Ousha?" I whispered. I wasn't sure if I was supposed to address her by name.

She held tightly for stability and turned her head to look at me. She was sweating; her black makeup around her eyes had run over her cheeks.

"What's wrong?" I went to her, watching the floor for glass.

"It's time," she said.

"The baby?"

She nodded.

"Don't move." I quickly retrieved the broom and cleaned up the glass scattered around her feet, then took her hand and sat her on the bench against the far wall. "Is Mohamed up?"

She shook her head violently, then wiped at her tears.

"Should I wake him for you?"

"No!"

I put my hands on her belly. Birthing babies wasn't new to me. I'd witnessed my brother's birth when I was five, and then a string of babies had come through my arms as the village women birthed them. Ruka was born on a boat halfway up the Madu River with my mother. It was very common for the women of our village to give birth wherever they happened to be.

Ousha clenched her jaw, grabbed my arm, and made a moaning sound. It was clear the baby was coming soon. Her legs and nightclothes were wet between her legs.

"What can I do for you, Ousha?"

"I'll be fine."

I didn't know what she meant; she was having a baby, whether she wanted it or not. I'd heard that women in rich countries went to hospitals to have their babies. Why was she not going? Surely she had the money. I went to the linen closet and retrieved towels. When I returned, Ousha was talking on her mobile phone. A few moments later, she hung up. "A medical team is coming. They will bring me to hospital."

"What about Mohamed?" As soon as I asked, I knew I shouldn't have.

"He has no interest in this." She looked guilty as she said it.

Ousha's body shuddered with birth pains. I helped her lie down on the floor and propped her head up with the towels I'd retrieved. Her hair was matted with sweat. She let out a gasp and grabbed for my hand. "I don't think I'll make it to the hospital."

I squeezed her hand. "I've helped with countless births in my village. The pain overtakes you, but the baby will come. Do what feels natural." When I had given birth to Ruka, my mother was at my side coaching me through it. This was what she had told me.

"It's coming," she said.

...

The medics were at the door, but the baby was almost out, so I couldn't step away. One more push and it came. I held it by the feet and whacked the baby's back until she cried. Then I tightly tied off the slick purple cord, grabbed a pair of kitchen scissors, cut, wrapped her in a towel, and handed her to Ousha, who had tears in her eyes. I remember the feeling as though it had only been a few weeks ago. But so much had happened since then.

I went to the door and let the medics in; they looked annoyed with me. I pointed them toward the back of the house. They examined Ousha, hooked a few machines up to her, and took readings. They looked at the baby, put a stethoscope to her chest, and shone a bright light over her body. When they were satisfied all was well, they said goodbye.

Ousha was now in a comfortable chair in the sitting room, nursing.

"What will her name be?" I asked.

"Don't talk so loud. We'll wake Mohamed," she scolded me.

I felt embarrassed for letting my exuberance get away from me. "Yes." It was all I could think of to say.

"Maryam."

"Mmm, sweet. Is that your mother's name?"

Ousha shook her head as if I'd offended her. She pulled Maryam from her breast and the baby whimpered, then cried. Ousha extended her to me. "There's baby milk in the cabinet above the stove."

I took the baby, confused why Ousha wouldn't continue nursing her. In the kitchen, I found a bottle with a small nipple. I removed the cap, filled the bottle with formula, and stroked Maryam's cheek. When she latched on to it, she was happy to drink, then fall asleep.

In the sitting room, Ousha pushed herself into a standing position and moved from furniture piece to furniture piece until she was at the bottom of the stairs. I watched her, unsure what was happening. "I'll check on her in the morning," she said, then climbed the stairs and bled into the darkness.

I looked at Maryam, who wasn't sleeping; rather, she was blowing small bubbles of leftover milk on her lips. I grabbed two more premade bottles of milk and brought her into my room. There, I propped myself up so my back was against the wall and made sure she was swaddled tightly. When the lights were off, I imagined Mewan was in my arms. My sweet boy, who I hadn't let go of for his first few months.

...

There was yelling in the kitchen. Then I heard the washroom door swing open and the top of the washing machine slam shut. Mohamed was screaming in his language, and Ousha was pleading with him. Maryam was asleep under my bed. I wanted her out of the way if someone decided to come into my room. Fortunately, she had woken up only once in the night. I got up, flicked on the bathroom light, and got down on my hands and knees to see how she was. She purred like a cat when she slept.

I pushed my hair back, washed my face, put on my uniform, and appeared in the kitchen a few minutes later. I caught Mohamed's back as he left; Ousha was there with her arms held up in question.

"Why did you leave all the bloody towels out? Mohamed was disgusted."

I lowered my head. "I didn't know you wanted me to clean them."

"Shula, you're the maid. Who else is going to do it?"

I wanted to say, "I was taking care of your baby," but I knew she didn't care, and it wasn't my place to speak back to her. She was my employer. "I'm sorry," I said instead.

Ousha went back to fixing her tea and faced out the kitchen window looking to the water behind the house. Maryam began to cry. I waited a few seconds to see if Ousha would react. Her only motion was to take another sip of tea. I rushed to my bedroom, scooped up Maryam from under the bed, and patted her back. Then I brought her into the kitchen, secured a bottle in her mouth to soothe her, and walked to Ousha's side. "Would you like to hold her?"

She looked down at the baby, then up at me. "She kind of looks like you," she said, before turning her attention to a boat as large as the house passing through the water. "I think

I might like to take a holiday after this. Sail away some-where." She stood up and picked a tea biscuit from the breadbox. "Someone will come today to install a crib for the baby. There should be room at the end of your bed if we move your dresser." With that, she left the kitchen.

Maybe she wasn't feeling well. There had been women in my village who temporarily had lost their minds after birth. Eventually they would come around and reclaim their children. It was a hard feeling to come to terms with. I was tethered tightly to Ruka and Mewan the second I laid eyes on them.

The deep grain wood and glinting of the steel appli-ances was harsh. Maryam needed natural light, so I brought her to my bathroom and rinsed her with warm water, removing the rest of the dried blood and mucus from her. I used my fingers to push her hair into place. She had black hair and dark eyes, and her skin had a brown tint and was slightly furry. She looked like a baby from my country. Emiratis were light and had a distinct look, like Mohamed.

The sun was ticking up in the sky. I walked the side-walk, to the end of the street, where it met the road. All the houses were white, with almost identical plants and palm trees. The only differences were the doors and the cars in the driveways. On the walk back, I passed some of the other workers. A few women stopped to look at the baby. They'd look at me, then at the baby and smile, with some worry.

"Are they sending you back?" one woman asked.

"No. This isn't my baby."

"Of course it is. Look at it." She pointed to my hair, then Maryam's.

"She's the baby of the family I work for." I was insistent.

Two of the women from Sri Lanka as well shook their head, then wagged their finger at me.

Back at the house, I opened the front doors softly; I had a feeling Ousha was sleeping. Instead, Mohamed was yelling at the men who were building the bookshelves. He seemed to be in a constant state of distress. So I kept to the front of the house, singing lullabies to Maryam. She was a calm baby, only crying when she was hungry. A few minutes later, a van pulled into the driveway, and the driver was soon at the door. Mohamed zoomed past me, lightly pushing me out of the way. I stood next to a tall marble column, with a stone statue of a robed winged woman playing a harp. A small light no bigger than the tip of my index finger illuminated it.

Mohamed was talking in his language, showing the man, who was dressed in a dark-blue uniform, into the house. He and a helper were carrying a crib. They brought other boxes to the back of the house. None of them looked at us while we stood there. When they were done, Mohamed showed them out, signed a paper, and shut the door. I moved closer to him, thinking he might want to see his daughter. He pointed his finger at me and firmly said, "No" in my language. He then pointed to the back of the house, as if he wanted me to return to my room. His face was stern and cross; the gentle look he had presented when I'd first arrived had vanished. His bare feet were silent as he walked through the house, inspecting the ledges of the paneling on the wall, running his finger across them, then looking closely at what had come off. He found a nook, a small shelf with a crystal elephant on it. When he ran his finger across it, it left a mark in the dust, and he held it up to me as incriminating proof, then made a sound of disgust and stormed off.

I opened the door to my room. The crib was where the dresser had been at the end of my bed, and the boxes were stacked on top of the mattress. Diapers, wipes, bottles of formula, clothes, and a few baby toys. My dresser was in front of my bathroom door, which prevented me from entering it. I laid Maryam on the bed and pushed the dresser into the bathroom, where it fit behind the door. I unpacked the boxes and stored the supplies under my bed. Maryam slept while I organized the room. I moved her to her crib, then pulled the door almost closed so I could clean the kitchen. The house felt uneasy, as if it tilted with worry. I ran a mop over the floor, polished the quartz counters, hunted for specks of food I knew Mohamed would find. I'd only been here a few days, but I wanted to avoid running into him. I cleaned the outside of the cabinet where the safe was, where my book was. I wondered why he had locked it away. It didn't feel right.

. . .

Ousha lay outside next to the pool, a green umbrella overhead, bathing her in hot shade. Mohamed had left. The shelves were finished, after which he counted off bills of money, like I might rifle through a stack of leaves, to pay the men. A flood of new workers had invaded the house, carrying tables and food, shimmering decorations, and lights. All of them were dressed in white uniforms with a palm frond of rainbow colors over each of their right chests.

They chattered among themselves, again in a language I didn't understand, shuffling around me as though I were a piece of furniture. I tried to clean, but they shooed me away. I opened the glass doors to the pool area and quietly approached Ousha.

She was reading and she looked up at me. "What is it?"

"Can I get you anything? Would you like to see your baby? Your husband is gone."

"I can't now. It's too hard."

"But I know about this. I have seen this before. It's best to see your child."

She pulled her sunglasses down. Her left eye was swollen and purple. She let me take an extended look before she pushed them back up. "There's a party tonight. It's for Mohamed's father. His birthday. You should make yourself useful wherever you can. Keep the baby in your room."

"Is there something else I should know?"

"Not now."

"I want to send a letter to my children," I said. "Can you help me?"

"Not now." Her eyebrows rose from behind the dark lenses; she seemed surprised I had children.

THE PARTY

In every family, there's a hierarchy. In this family, I was at the bottom. I heard the first guest arrive. Hearty greetings and laughter outside the kitchen door. It reminded me of the days when my parents were alive and they'd invite the entire family to the house to celebrate special occasions. The lights twinkled outside the kitchen window; the other homes were starlit wonders. I wanted to bring Maryam out, but Ousha had warned me not to bring her into sight.

Earlier in the day, when I was washing laundry, behind a stack of filled storage crates I noticed the back wall of the room had a cutout and a flat metal handle that popped out when pressed. I twisted and pulled the handle; the door opened a few inches before it pressed against the crates stacked in front of it. Maryam had begun crying and needed attention then. But now, discouraged from showing myself, with the baby fully fed and asleep in her crib, I went back into the laundry room.

With the washer, dryer, sink, and cabinets on the right, I pulled the crates and pushed them against the door so no one would walk in. When I got the door open, it was dark inside. I worried about scorpions or spiders as I reached my hand inside, trying to find a light switch. My fingers ran over a button on the wall, and I clicked it. Pipes and electrical wires were neatly tucked into the wooden framing of the walls. I stepped into the narrow passageway. It was much warmer than the crisp coolness of the house. From the lightbulb, I could see every few feet between the mass of wires. The floor was bare concrete, and there were building tools, extra tiles, and stacks of paint cans along the wall. Everything was covered in thick dust; this room hadn't been disturbed in some time. I spotted a door at the end of the hall, where a silver knob caught the light. I walked through, looking up; the space must have gone up the full height of the house, because I couldn't see where it stopped. As I got closer to the door, I heard pumps working, and the passageway got wider. Machines sat inside the space, hooked into the pipes and wires of the wall. Some of the pipes went into the concrete floor, while others snaked back into the walls. Wondering what each of these boxes of technology did, I unlatched the bolt on the door and twisted the knob. The heat from the outside air rushed in, and I was facing the water behind the house. A hedge about chest high surrounded the pool area where Ousha had been laying earlier. Round stone pavers formed a path from the service door to the seawall. When the glass doors from the main sitting area pivoted open, I ducked back inside, closed the door, and secured the bolt. I could hear sounds now, from the other side of the wall, which must have been the kitchen. I studied the wall as I walked back, and then it made sense. Clusters of wires terminated at the places where the appliances were on the other side of the wall. This was the access hallway.

I returned to the laundry room. I hadn't noticed the cross pieces of wood that were nailed into the studs next to the door; they formed a ladder. I followed them with my eyes into the darkness above. I wanted to see what was up there, but Maryam could wake at any time. More than an hour had passed since her last feeding. On the other side of the door was a space I could fit into if I turned sideways between the wall of the laundry room and the exterior of the house. I sidestepped into it to see how far it went. I didn't know what I was looking for, but it didn't take long to first see there was a hole behind the shower faucet, and when I looked through, I saw the whole of my bathroom. I wondered if this was a standard feature of the building or if the design was intentional to allow spying.

I stepped to move back toward the opening; it was dark except for the light coming through the small holes. My bare feet touched folded pieces of paper. I remembered the note behind my mirror. I dragged my foot forward; there were a few of them. My nerves prickled. The darkness, the holes in the wall, the space I occupied made me feel as though I'd stumbled into a quiet yet nefarious place. Keeping my back straight, I picked up the papers and put them in the pockets of my uniform. I returned to the bright whiteness of the laundry room and shut the door to the hidden access hallway. The act of moving the crates into place calmed me.

When I opened the door into the kitchen hall, I heard Maryam crying. Ousha was in the kitchen, and when she saw me, she charged.

"Where have you been? The baby has been fussing." She glared at me.

"I was doing laundry." I didn't want to lie. She had been mostly kind to me. My hand instinctively went to my pockets and touched the folded papers.

A woman older than Ousha in a black suit with cut stones adorning every part of her body entered through the kitchen door. She spoke in Mohamed's language to Ousha and kept looking at me as she talked. Maryam cried again; the woman heard it, then pushed past me to look for the baby. Ousha shot me a scalding look and pointed to my room. I rushed to the woman's side.

"I'm sorry if the baby has disturbed you," I told her.

She looked at my mouth, but I could tell she didn't understand what I said.

Ousha quickly translated.

The woman said something else then pointed to Ousha, who told me what she'd just said.

"She wants to know how old your baby is."

I began to wave my hands and shake my head to tell her it wasn't my baby, but Ousha was directing me otherwise.

"Two weeks," I said. I'd thought I was beginning to understand what was happening in this house, but now the picture had gone fuzzy again. Why would anyone disown their baby in their own home?

Ousha spoke and pushed at the door to my room. I stood back, letting the woman invade my space. She turned the light on and pulled Maryam from her crib. She stuck out her lips, made baby words, then cradled her in her arms. I got a bottle and handed it to her. The woman fed her and walked by me. If she'd genuinely thought I was the mother, why would she act as if I weren't there when she was holding my child?

Another older woman, who looked closely related to Mohamed, came into the kitchen and beelined to us, doting on Maryam. The door opened a third time; it was Mohamed, and when he saw what was happening, he exchanged a look with Ousha that was nothing short of fury, but he said nothing. He merely walked around the island in the kitchen three times, appearing to have lost his way, then left.

Maryam was passed to the first older woman and then to Ousha, who seemed uncomfortable holding her. She thrust her at me, and they sauntered off, laughing and lightly touching one of the other women. I went into my room and closed the door. I sat on the bed; this dear baby was asleep again. I closed my eyes and thought about Mewan and Ruka. I wondered what they might be doing. I imagined them in our house, Ruka keeping it as clean as possible, or Mewan climbing the coconut palms. Something he'd taken a fancy to since I'd told him his father could climb to the coconuts in under a minute, and on our first date, Pramith had done just that and offered the rich fruit to me as a gift.

I set Maryam beside me on the bed and pulled the papers out of my pockets. The first one was written in Sinhala. It was a desperate love letter. Another was a picture, poor quality, of a young handsome Sri Lankan man, not even twenty, the next a copy of his passport; the words were in Mohamed's language. They were on the bed in front of me, with the fold and dust marks of having been behind that wall. When the party was over, I would ask Ousha; maybe she would know why they were there.

A knock came at my door. "Yes?" I called, not wanting to get up.

One of the workers from the party slowly opened the door and waved me out of the room to follow her. Maryam was dreaming, her eyes moving back and forth under her lids and her body twitching. She would sleep for at least an hour, with her full belly and clean diaper. The woman pointed to a stack of dirty dishes and cups next to the sink, pointed to me, and made a cleaning motion. I filled the first sink with soap and water and got to work. As the dishes kept coming, I imagined who the boy in the picture might be. I gave him the name Kasun and watched him walk around this house. He felt trapped; the more I thought about him, the more I felt I couldn't breathe, as though someone were squeezing my neck.

POST OFFICE

Mohamed left early the next morning. I'd watched through the front windows as he departed. A car was waiting for him and he had a suitcase.

When the car pulled away, the house immediately felt lighter. I was barefoot, standing on the deep-pile smoky orange carpet that extended under the dining table. I turned my feet side to side, the silky, sturdy fibers caressing the soles of my feet. It was a piece of divinity, and I allowed myself the pleasure. A few moments later, I went back to the kitchen and made the breakfast I knew Ousha would like. Strong tea, almost black, with a touch of cream, and then a fine pastry, warmed but not hot, with a dollop of strawberry jam. I put them both on a tray and took it upstairs to her room. I knocked and waited. She said something in Mohamed's language, but it was in a tone that told me it was okay to enter.

She lay in bed, her hair pulled back, a tank top exposing her arms. They looked shadowed, and I searched for what was casting the darkness over the top half of her arms, but nothing was blocking the light. I approached her, and she held her arms out to take the food and tea from me.

"Thank you. This is a very nice surprise." Her mood seemed relaxed.

When I was next to her, I saw her arms were the color of mine when I didn't go into the sun, and then it abruptly stopped. From half her forearm to her hands and also above her neckline, the color was gone. She had the color of an Emirati.

I reached out and let my finger hover above the transition mark on her arm. "What is this?"

I sensed she would be open to my question today. Mohamed's departure had released us from convention.

Ousha laughed, first at me, then at herself. "I bleached my skin."

I didn't need to ask why. I had seen women in Colombo powder their hands and faces white. An affliction of being human, always wanting something you don't have.

"I need to mail money home to my family." I struck while there was some camaraderie between us.

"Give me the money. I'll mail it for you when I go to the post office. You just need to tell me where it goes."

"What do you mail?" I was curious.

Her eyes squinted. "Don't think because we're from the same place that we're the same."

I played her words over in my head, trying to understand what she meant. *The same place.* Did she think I was from here? A servant class of this country? Then I looked at her skin again, and her nose, and the artificial way it pointed up, and the texture of her hair, and the smooth spots behind her ears, where a surgeon had hid his handiwork. I understood. She was my country's blood.

"I'm sorry … I was just … I didn't mean …"

Ousha reached out to me and took my hand. "We all have to play our parts or things will unravel." There was sadness in those words. "I'll go to the post office before Mohamed comes back; he's gone for two nights."

I had so many questions for her. It was better to sprinkle them on her one by one, though. I heard my mother say, *Shula, no one likes a nosy girl.*

I left Ousha to enjoy her tea and pastry and floated through the house. At the bottom of the stairs, a terrible thought stuck to me: *Where would I send the letter to?* My house in Balapitiya didn't have an address because it wasn't an actual house. It was something we had built on someone's land, a place no one had forced us to move from. If I sent it to the post office, Ruka wouldn't know to pick it up and they'd likely not give it to a poor village girl without charging her. What good was it that I was here if I couldn't send my money home to help? Ruka was resourceful, but would she think I abandoned her for this better life if she never heard from me?

As my mind ran away with unlikely scenarios, I stepped outside onto the patio. I looked first at the bushes that separated the small pathway from the place where I stood. It was unnoticeable; the hedge extended all the way to the seawall, blocking the path of stones. The door was painted the same color as the house with no exterior handle, and the bright-orange chairs, green umbrellas, and blue pool drew my attention only to the immediacy and luxury of this house.

Ousha was beside me; I hadn't shut the door. "It's beautiful, no? When we first bought this house, I thought Mohamed had made all my dreams come true. Did you know we have a boat too? Big, like that one." She pointed to one of the larger boats wandering over the blue water. "I have everything."

I found it odd for her to make the declarative statement. She did have everything—it was clear—but the way she said it sounded like she didn't believe it, a repeated mantra someone else had forced her to utter.

"Do you have family at home?" I asked.

Her arm was still extended, pointing to the boat; she wasn't done showing me what was in the distance. "When the gulf is calm, we take the yacht and leave the Dubai coast and sail to Kumzar. It's a different world there—the landscape, the people; we might as well be on the moon. I always imagine where the water would take us if we kept going."

I wondered if I would ever get to go on that boat.

She let her arm down and turned, with tears in her eyes, and went inside.

I wanted to tell her I was sorry for bothering her with asking about a letter this morning. But she didn't bring it up.

An hour later, she left the house. I checked on Maryam. I would bring her outside but while they were gone there was more I wanted to see in the passageway. I gathered up dirty laundry in a basket and brought it to the door of the laundry room, in case Ousha came back early. I left it outside the door, then moved the crates inside the room to expose the door I would pass through. I opened it, stepped inside, and clicked on the light; this time I also brought a flashlight. I shined it down the narrow space that went behind my room. Magazines were stacked at the end; I couldn't see what they were, but right now I was more interested in what was above. I shone my light up, following the cross-wood slats that formed a makeshift ladder. Then I put the flashlight between my teeth and climbed. When I was above the first level's ceiling, there was an opening I could reach my hands into and pull myself. It was unfinished, but the floor was a solid piece of wood I could stand on. The walls were the same as below. I saw the back sides of rooms, as well as wires and studs, and small lights flashing green, indicating the house's systems were working.

I stepped carefully, making sure there was more floorboard ahead of me. When I was at the end, the space continued to the left; I imagined I must be over the dining room. Between the studs, I saw shoeboxes. I bent down and took the lid off one of them. Dried leaves, rolled cigarettes, and money, held together with paper strips. I felt wary of touching any of it. I closed the box, careful not to disturb the contents. The passage zigzagged. In front of me now, a new door. I turned the handle and pushed. It moved heavily into the room.

The room had a carpet the color of summer tea leaves, and the walls were paneled in stained woods; it smelled of masculine cologne. A large flat television was set into the wall, and a leather couch had fur throws over the arms. The space was impeccably neat. My footprint disturbed the grain of the carpet, and I felt my legs wobble. I knew this was the room Ousha had told me to avoid. I backed out, wiping the carpet with my hand to pull the fibers back to perfection. I shut the door gently and stood in the darkness for a moment to catch my breath and regain my composure. I felt close to knowing something about Mohamed. And I didn't want to stop until I found it.

I pulled open more of the boxes inside the passage. More of the same, until I came to a box where magazines were rolled inside. I unrolled one; images of fit and handsome naked men. I paged through them; most of the men appeared to be from the West, with light skin and European faces. Why would these magazines be here? I put it back and arranged the boxes as they were, then traced my way to the ladder. Although I wanted to spend more time in Mohamed's office, I didn't have the courage.

When I opened the door to the laundry room and pulled the basket of dirty laundry inside, the house was still quiet. While the laundry was washing, I headed outside to feel the sun on my face. Everything in the house seemed designed to keep the sun and heat out, which had a depressing effect on me. I slept in a room with no windows and spent most of my time in the kitchen and hallway, where Ousha wanted the shades pulled so the sun wouldn't reach her skin.

It was midday, and I loved the way the heat baked through me. I walked the perimeter of the pool, then stepped down to the seawall. There was a dock connected to it, with a set of steel stairs folded up. When I reached them, I saw a boat secured under the seawall. The stairs would reach the boat if they were lowered. Ousha had pointed to a cluster of boats in the middle of the water, which were still there. Mohamed must have parked his boat away from shore for depth reasons. I headed back to the pool, slipped off my shoes, and put my feet on the top stair, which was covered by water. The house felt expansive, like each room or section was a new world to occupy.

"Shula?"

I jumped up. Ousha stood in the doorway with two bags of food.

"I'm sorry."

"Don't be sorry, but don't leave the door open either. You'll heat up the whole house. Come inside."

I ran inside and stood at attention next to her at the bar.

"Didn't you want to send something with me to the post office?" she asked.

"Yes, but …" I felt grateful she had remembered something that was entirely my problem, and I wanted to show her how grateful I was, but this wasn't an area where she would be able to help me.

"But?"

"There's no way to mail money, and it won't be useful to them." I thought about the dinars of my salary. The people of Balapitiya would have no use for the colorful bills. I hadn't thought of these complications when Khalid had sold me on dreams and a new house.

"What town are you from?" Ousha asked.

"Balapitiya." I looked down in shame.

"On the coast? Oh, how lovely." Ousha put the last onion in the refrigerator, then came to the counter and let her hands rest. "I think it's time we had tea. Why don't you make sure the baby is comfortable so we don't get interrupted?"

Maryam was still sleeping soundly. I put a fresh diaper out and a bottle of formula next to her, so I could tend to her quickly if she woke, but I wasn't going to disturb her now.

"She's still sleeping deeply," I reported upon returning to the kitchen. The electric teakettle was on. Ousha had two cups out with satchels of tea inside them, along with a miniature bowl of sugar cubes. She pulled out a stool, invited me to sit, and pushed a cup in front of me. She poured the water and put out a plate of the biscuits she loved, shortbread with pieces of candied ginger and lemon.

"It might seem confusing why you're here." She waited for me to respond.

"No. I came because we have nothing at home. There is nothing confusing about my poverty."

Ousha took a biscuit in her hand and waved it around. "But this … what is going on here …"

I thought about the narrow passageway behind the laundry room and wondered if somehow she knew I'd been in there, knew I'd been in Mohamed's office. Was she trying to get me to confess?

"Every family is different." The thought seemed to be a consolation for her, an offering that her life was normal.

"Mohamed doesn't love me and I don't love him. It's an arrangement for the sake of his honor. His family is very"—she looked around the room for the right word—"prominent. As such, their first son must be married, with children."

This was more confusing; neither of them had shown any interest in their child.

"I was born in the United States," she said, "but my mother is Sri Lankan and my father is Jordanian but of the American type. If you saw him, his look would be hard to place. When he's in Italy, people think he's Italian. When we're in Dubai, they think he's Emirati, and with his ability to speak so many languages, he's a bit of a chameleon. After the terrorist attacks in the US, the country changed, so my father moved here for a finance job. I went to school, then university and graduate school. When I finished my master's degree in mathematics, my father thought a woman shouldn't work, so while I was searching for career opportunities, he was searching for a husband for me. My father worked for Mohamed's father, and I guess they thought us meeting would be a good thing. We met. I found Mohamed cold, detached, and knew he had no interest in me. He confirmed that on one of our meetings, when he said, 'My father insists I see you, so I'm here.' Even so, we agreed to honor our fathers. We would see each other a few more times, then come up with an excuse as to why we had to break it off. In the meantime, Mohamed's father kept presenting women to him, and Mohamed kept lying and saying he was interested in me, not all of them. At the same time, my father thought that because we kept seeing each other, things were going well. He was pleased I had found a young man, and his employer, the provider of all we had in Dubai, was happy as well."

Ousha was telling me the story as if this were unusual, but arranged marriages were common in Sri Lanka, and my parents had chosen my husband. The love that came from an arranged marriage had evolved, over time, from familiarity and shared experiences.

"After a year of this," Ousha continued, "I was working in a hotel, managing the finance department, and Mohamed was working at his father's company. It was easier for us to keep the charade going, and before I knew it, I was seated with Mohamed's aunties around me, who were applying mehendi to my hands and feet in intricate patterns as I stared at the red-and-gold dress on a bust." She bit into her biscuit and shook her head in disbelief.

"How long ago was that?" I asked.

"Two years."

"But surely you fell in love after? You got pregnant."

Ousha's eyes narrowed, and the warm connection between us severed. I had crossed a line.

"Mohamed's father developed much of what you see when you drive over the bridge from the mainland and he gave us this house as a wedding gift." The story had lost its momentum, and she got up from her seat. "I think the baby is restless." She gestured for me to check on her.

Maryam was sleeping soundly. When I returned to the kitchen, the tea glasses and biscuits had been cleared and Ousha was nowhere to be found.

GOSSIP

"And how long have you been here?" I asked a woman, older than me, wrapped in black muslin with heavy eyelids. She was holding infant twins and watching a toddler run on the artificial grass.

"This time?" She was thinking it over.

I nodded.

"Five years. The first time I was here just over three, and then they sent me back to Sri Lanka to recruit other women. They give a few of us a good experience—what they sold us in the brochures—and then we return and rave about it, which creates a flood of women willing to come work. But when you come here, it's a whole different experience."

"Why don't you leave?"

"I can't. They have my passport, and they won't return it to me. It was issued by this country anyway, so I'm not recognized as a Sri Lankan citizen."

She set the twins down to wriggle in the soft green. The toddler was on a slide now. The woman leaned into Maryam and tickled her nose.

"Sure doesn't look like an Arab baby. She looks like you." She stuck her finger out at me.

I tensed. This is exactly what Ousha and Mohamed would want. Should I correct her?

"You and the sir been messing around?" She let out a cackle.

The other women got a whiff of an interesting story and sidestepped to where we stood.

"I …" I had no idea what to say.

"So it is. He must be a handsome man."

"Ooooh, are you talking about Mr. Alwadiya?" the woman I had first seen walking by the house said.

"She is. They had a baby together. You see right there?" This woman looked like she could have been my sister.

"Stop that. It's not true. I've only been here a few weeks. Don't say those things." They had made me angry.

They ceased laughing and gazed at each other. "We're sorry. We didn't mean to upset you."

As a child, I would sit under our tables and listen to my aunts gossip as they read through a local paper or magazine they religiously bought every week from a newsstand. Much of the time they didn't mean any harm or believe half of what they were saying—it was only fun, a way to pass the time.

"It's okay." The image of my village lingered in my mind. "What was your name again? I'm Shula."

"Minrada. I'm about ten houses down. We're at the end of the street." She swiped her index finger in the direction. "You can come by the house sometime if you like. Bring the little one. During the day it's me and the kids. They have a housecleaner too, a lovely woman, but she doesn't speak very much, so it's lonely."

"Thank you. That would be lovely. I'd better get back. I'm not sure the Mrs. would want Maryam out in the heat for too long."

The other ladies waved and smiled. I felt I'd overreacted as I replayed the scene in my mind, following the sidewalk back to the house. The car was still gone. I heard myself exhale in relief. Ousha hadn't come out from hiding since our conversation yesterday, and then she was gone before I got up this morning. I imagine she went shopping and eating at the fancy stores and cafés I had passed on the bus ride here. She always returned home with bags full of new clothes and accessories.

I gave Maryam a bottle and let her drift off to sleep. I stood in my bathroom and washed the sweat from my face and neck. Thinking of the notes I had found, I looked at the small space behind the mirror where the bottom shelf and the back of the unit pried slightly apart. Enough to fit a piece of folded paper through.

Tomorrow I'll ask Minrada what she thinks. She's older; she lived as an adult before the tsunami and dire poverty. Maybe she'll know what the notes mean and can give me a reason for what's happening here.

I ran my fingernail in the space; I knew what I was doing: looking for more. My finger touched a piece of paper, folded over many times like the others, but it was too far to reach from this side. I closed the door to my room tightly and made the seven-step journey to the laundry room door, stepped inside, and moved the storage crates out of the way. It was routine now, where I stacked them to block the room to the hallway and make enough space so I could move around. After the hidden door clicked open, I turned on the flashlight I had stored in the cabinet above the washing machine and turned myself to the side, leading with my left shoulder into the darkness. I got to the point where I saw the spikes of light from my bathroom. This was where I had stopped before, taken by the knowledge that I was or could have been spied on. I ran my finger under the back of medicine cabinet and found the paper. It was a photograph, hanging from the white border of the picture, scratched from passing through the metal opening. It was of a boy from my country. He looked frightened and gaunt, with a forced smile. Written in dull marker were shaky words. I held on to the picture and swung my light deeper into the darkness, where I knew there were stacks of magazines. Then I bent down and picked one up: a handsome American on the cover with two letters on the top left, *GQ*. There was a full stack of them, different issues. I stepped over them. There were other bits in this space. The types of pieces that a person who lived here would leave in their wake. Small tears of paper, a patch of cloth, a bone from an eaten piece of meat. The copper pipe that led to my shower had deep scratches in it, as if someone had intentionally scraped metal against it.

I left the passageway and stepped outside the laundry room. Beyond my bedroom door, the hallway ended in a circular shape and the ceiling bowed up into a lit dome. The air here smelled of dried flowers, and it was unusually cold. There was a flat handle painted the same color as the wall on the curve. I looked back, the light coming in from the laundry room had faded. It felt distant down the hall, in the way my children and home did. This piece of the house had a strange dilution to it. A space between worlds. I pulled on the handle; there was a click and then a loud whoosh. I jumped and my back bumped into the wall. On the other side of the door was the formal dining room. Mohamed showed me this the first day but I hadn't been in here, only looked at it through the doors off the main entryway. The table was set for sixteen people. Thick oil paintings with modern strokes were framed on the walls, and hanging lights were surrounded by gems of glass and textured wallpaper. It was the showpiece room of the house, with sculptures of winged creatures, fantastical buildings, and dancing glass spaced behind each seat. The spotlights from the ceiling illuminated them. The world reset; the darkness fled.

The hallway outside the two glass doors leading to the main entryway of the house was quiet. I hadn't spent any time inspecting the individual sculptures and I wondered if each of them had a stand-alone story or a collective one which was told as one moved from pedestal to pedestal. My feet sunk into the carpet as I walked, and I heard the door click shut. I glanced to where I'd come through; the break in the wall had completely disappeared. I couldn't see where it was. My mind flashed to the open door in the laundry room leading into the passageway. What if Mohamed decided to use his secret door and saw it was open? He would know it was me.

I ran my hands over the wall, looking for a nook to grasp or a hidden space my fingers could get traction in. Not sure I was standing in the correct place, I brought my face closer. What magic had allowed this to happen?

"Shula?" My heart dropped, I felt lightheaded. I hadn't heard Ousha open the dining room doors.

"Yes?" I turned around, looking guilty and clasped my hands in front of me.

"What are you doing?"

"Looking for something."

"On the wall?" She wasn't mad; it was more bewilderment in her voice. "And what is that in your hand?" She pointed to the picture I'd forgotten I was holding.

She came to me and took it. As soon as she saw it, a heave of air came from her and she grabbed at her mouth. With tears in her eyes, she glared at me. "Where did you get this?"

"It was in my bathroom."

"Where?" Her voice was louder now; she was upset. But her attention was being pulled into remembrance.

"In the medicine cabinet."

"You're lying." Her face was red now, and she stepped into my space with biting force. "I checked in there before you arrived."

I shrugged at her insistence.

"If you find anything else, please bring it to me." She turned halfway to leave, and then her face morphed away from the pain. She pushed me out of the way, pressed on the wall with both of her hands, and the door sprung open. "The light bludgeons the darkness into mystery for a reason, and unless you are looking to be annihilated, you should leave it alone."

WICKED RETURN

Minrada and the other nannies were at the park, laughing together at 8:00 a.m. before the sun bombarded the city. Maryam had been restless during the night, and I barely slept. She was still squirming when I changed her before taking her to the park. I walked with her cradled in my arms, trying to entice her with a bottle. She opted for a pacifier.

"Shula, we thought you weren't coming," the youngest of the nannies said. "We get worried with your bosses." She didn't look like she was from Sri Lanka; she was light like a British person, but she spoke perfect Sinhala.

"What does that mean?" I asked.

Minrada jabbed her and gave her a warning look.

I let it go. I knew Mohamed and Ousha were a strange couple; I'm sure it didn't go unrecognized by the neighbors and their workers. I dug into my pocket, pulled out one of the folded strips of paper, and handed it to Minrada. "What do you think of this?"

A man walked by and made eye contact with Minrada and they both smiled at each other but said nothing.

"Who is that?"

"My husband. Never mind him, he's always checking on me."

She unfolded it and read it out loud. "'I love you. When can we be together?' She looked over her glasses at me. "Did someone give this to you?"

"I found it in my room. I think it belonged to the last person who stayed there."

"You don't want to dig into that past. Bad things will happen."

"What bad things?" It made me nervous that she—and possibly the other nannies—knew something so terrible she might not speak of it.

Minrada pointed to a bench and yelled at her toddler, who was hitting another with a dead palm frond. She sat down and reached out to take Maryam from me. "I love them when they're this age," she said. "So full of hope and possibility, but they always turn out like their parents. Now, what I know is through a man, who one of my friends here was *involved* with. She told me about Inesh, casually at first and then some of the stories he'd recount. We all talk about our bosses."

I raised an eyebrow. "Inesh?"

"The young man who used to be at your place, the houseboy."

"Did you ever meet him?"

"A few times," Minrada said. "More like pleasantries than actually meeting him." I started to speak, but she cut me off. "Hold on. Let me tell you the rest. Inesh began with them, and for the first six months, everything was normal. They weren't good or bad to him; they ignored him as he kept their house. Inesh began to have feelings for the wife.

He said she would talk to him in our language, which I believed. Why would an Emirati ever learn Sinhala?"

"She's half-Sri Lankan."

Minrada's mouth was open, ready to continue her story, but she stopped in midbreath. Then the *O* of her mouth turned into a smile. "You see, this is why it's so interesting to tell stories. There's more discovered each time they're told. I had no idea. Was she an order bride?"

"No, I don't think so. She grew up in the US and moved here for her father's job."

The excitement from Minrada was palpable. She clearly had told this story many times, but now I imagined how she might drop this fact in at the last minute and the listener would give her a reaction.

"I heard the husband locked him in his room and wouldn't let him out because he didn't want him to go near his wife." She paused; I felt like she might want me to applaud. "We never saw him again."

"Did he go back to Sri Lanka?"

Minrada shrugged. "Don't know."

"I have a handful of notes." I pulled one more out and gave it to her.

She greedily took it from me and licked her lips. Then she unfolded it and looked around before she read it. "I can't stand this anymore. I want to make love to you." She shook the strip. "This is pure gold." She opened and closed her hand quickly. "Any more?"

"Not with me." I weighed telling her about the encounter in the dining room and the picture, but I didn't want it getting back to Ousha, and with Minrada's love of gossip, I could tell she wasn't capable of holding on to information for too long. "I'll bring more the next time we meet."

"On Fridays we all go into town." With her finger she made a rough circle around all the women at the park. "There are usually ten of us, all from this street. You're welcome to join."

"But I need to watch the baby." It was obvious Ousha wasn't going to help me with her.

"The law requires we get one day off per week."

"I don't …" I thought about Ousha, even bringing up the topic. Maybe when she was in a good mood.

"Come if you want or can," Minrada said. "Don't let them take advantage of you."

This was the first time since my family had been wiped away and since I'd come here that I felt like I belonged to something. Dubai tugged at me, and I had an image of Ruka and Mewan sleeping in my room on the floor, where they would be safe, where they could take a shower and maybe go to school and learn things.

...

When I returned to the house, Ousha was in the sitting area, staring out the back windows, mindlessly eating from a plastic tray of shortbread. She would take a bite, hold the biscuit near her mouth, then take one more and a third until it was gone; then she'd go for the next. Never looking at the tray. There was a glass of caramel-colored liquid beside her. The scent of alcohol floated through the room.

"Can I cook you something for lunch?"

She didn't turn, but I seemed to break her trance, because she took a gulp of the drink.

"Maryam and I were at the park, getting some fresh air before it got too hot." I gave a nervous chuckle at the end. I wanted her to say something.

She kept eating. I laid Maryam in her crib, then went to the kitchen and made a boiled egg with a piece of spiced chicken. I made one for myself and one for Ousha. I took a cloth napkin from the drawer and a silver fork and knife and brought it to her and set it down on the table. I noticed her glass was empty. The new shelves had an open cabinet; inside was a tall bottle with a blue label outlined in gold with English writing on it. The cap was off. I refilled her glass halfway, closed the cabinet, and returned to the kitchen. Ousha grabbed the drink out of my hand and disappeared. I ate my lunch and cleaned the surfaces in the kitchen. I moved around the counter from different angles to see if the light would catch any spots I'd missed.

The door swung open forcefully. I thought Mohamed was home, but it was Ousha. Her eyes were bloodshot, her movements uncoordinated. "I want to see my baby." Her words were thick as she staggered toward me. "She's mine. You know that, right? She's my baby, not yours." I stood frozen. She was drunk. I'd hoped the extra drink would have made her return to bed.

"Did you hear me?" she screeched. "She's my baby! Not yours." She poked my chest. "Not Mohamed's, mine." She pointed to herself.

"Yes, Ousha. Maryam is your baby."

"Who?"

This was odd; she didn't remember her daughter's name?

"Your baby, Maryam."

"Her name is …" She rubbed her head as she thought about it.

"Why don't you go to your bedroom and I'll bring her to you?"

"Where is she?"

When I gestured to the hallway that led to my room, she took off in that direction. I followed her as she stormed the room. Maryam was up and reaching for the mobile spinning over her head.

"Why don't you sit down on the bed and I'll get her for you? She might need a change." I pulled a sour face and hoped through her alcohol haze she'd find the thought of having to do any amount of work unappealing.

Ousha complied and sat down. I took off her slippers and put her feet on the bed, then propped two pillows behind her; her eyelids were heavy. I took Maryam into the bathroom and closed the door. When I emerged a few minutes later, Ousha was snoring. I tiptoed out, catching the light switch on the way and closing the door. I lay Maryam on the floor in the sitting room and cleaned up the mess Ousha had created. I knew Mohamed would be home today, and I didn't want him to enter anything but a perfect house.

...

The front doors opened and the security system chimed. I stiffened. It had been pleasant not having Mohamed home and setting us on edge, knowing he might explode at any time. He went upstairs, and I heard him call for Ousha. It was customary for her to greet him when he walked in. I debated whether I should say she was out or if I should tell him the truth—that she was in my room, dead asleep.

He yelled her name a few more times, and then his footsteps became heavy and he pounded down the stairs. I picked up Maryam and held her tightly, bracing for the winds of his storm. He caught sight of me. "Where is she?" Mohamed, when standing at ease, was a delicate, handsome man. His body was lean and muscular, his fingers long and perfectly manicured, his hair always styled nicely, his face bright and clear. The anger that welled from him now seemed to possess him more than belong to him. He defied his nature every time he entered this state.

"She's in my room." I told the truth; it was always better that way.

He ran into the kitchen. I heard thumping, then screaming, followed by Ousha's screams.

They got closer and I heard him. "You whore. What are you doing in that filthy room, you whore? You can't stay away from the filth of your people, can you? Disgusting."

The kitchen door swung into the sitting area. Mohamed had a handful of Ousha's hijab and hair in his hands and was dragging her across the floor like a worker might drag sandbags. She screamed and choked, her eyes bulging, the fabric tight around her throat. He pulled her all the way to the stairs. I heard skin against skin slapping. I didn't dare go look; it would only provoke an attack on myself. So I went into my room and closed the door. There was a small wedge, which I put under the door. I made my bed, sprayed air freshener, and erased what had happened in the only space that was mine. I had found, after shock and tragedy happen, that it's better to return your surroundings to the way they were, an instinct to get us sane again. It was why my village had rebuilt their homes in the exact place where the wave had destroyed them, knowing the risk of their location. But, for now, they needed that normalcy to maybe pretend nothing had happened or reduce the impact of the happening.

I sang Maryam a lullaby. I heard more thumping from the room above us, and then everything went quiet. There was shuffling, but it was moving closer. The next recognizable sound came to me, the crinkling of the paper on the floor in the passageway. I froze. Mohamed was there, behind the bathroom wall, watching me. Now I was the subject, the prey, and the predator was breathing heavily and waiting.

Dark Places

The next morning, I chose to rise above my fear. I moved through my routine, taking a shower, fixing my hair the way Ousha had showed me. I even had a stick of eyeliner, which I put on. The night had been harrowing, between periods of not sleeping and then, when I slid out of exhaustion and into unconsciousness, my mind took me to dark places: meeting Mohamed in the passageway, when I was sure he was gone. Mohamed stealing Maryam away, telling me she was his baby and I shouldn't think she was mine. His striking Ousha repeatedly until she couldn't move. The morning revealed one of those dreams to be true. I was up early at six, and Ousha was already seated, hunched over a counter; she had a drink in her hand, the same caramel-colored alcohol. The bottle was beside her, more than half empty. She didn't register my presence until I set down a ceramic bowl, making a sharp sound. Her head lifted, tortoiselike, until her eyes settled on me. The skin around both of them was deep purple, her lip split open and oozing, and there were five angry red depressions the size of fingertips on her throat.

"Oh, dear." I ran to the linen closet, pulled out a clean towel, wrapped ice in it, and gingerly pressed it to her face. The alcohol likely was numbing the pain somewhat, both inside and out. Her only reaction to me pressing the ice against her eyes was to reach for her glass. I got her to hold the ice in place, then retrieved an identical glass and filled it with cold camel milk. She needed something nutritious to drink. Ever since I'd arrived here, I'd watched her live off alcohol, biscuits, and tea. I swapped the two glasses while her head had drooped down and her stringy hair covered her side view.

Mohamed's heavy footsteps. He yelled Ousha's name. Something shattered. He moved closer to us in the house. I remembered my dream: him coming for Maryam. I felt a strange tugging to help Ousha, a woman from my land, a woman who was now floating on an island with a lion lurking, but I had to protect Maryam. So I ran for my room, closed the door, and put the wedge in place. I picked up the baby and pushed myself under my bed. I knew if I held her closely, she would be content and silent. We were behind the boxes I had put under the bed. If Mohamed looked under here for us, he wouldn't see us. His yelling resounded; the bottle broke; a glass was hurled against the cabinetry. More thudding. This time Ousha didn't make a sound.

It took two hours for rage to leave the house. I pressed my ear to my door, waiting. Finally, when I heard nothing, I came out. Alcohol occupied my senses. I watched where I stepped, picking up pieces of the bottle. Then I retrieved the sponge mop and cleaned the kitchen within minutes. The real damage, though, was upstairs. I noiselessly moved through the house, looking out the front window. The car was gone, so I engaged the deadbolt on the front door. I climbed the stairs. At the top, my bare feet sank into the carpet, a feeling I'd relished the first time; now it felt like mud sucking me in. I walked the shallow hallway. The door to Mohamed and Ousha's bedroom was closed. My foot stepped in something sticky. I looked at it; it was warm blood, but it made me feel cold.

I didn't knock. I knew I'd find either terror or vacancy on the other side. In either scenario, the occupant wasn't going to offer me permission to enter. Turn, push, look. The room was torn apart. The curtains ripped from the window, the bedsheets swirled into the center, the nightstand overturned, the lamp broken, red on the white sheets. Maybe Mohamed had taken Ousha to the hospital after he'd rampaged. I stepped farther into the chaos—more stickiness on my feet, which I tried to ignore. I'd walked through animal blood before, on slaughter days. I had imagined it was the same, but it wasn't. Human blood was sacred.

I tipped the nightstand back into place and gathered the lamp pieces. Then I pulled the curtains down. I would mix them with the sheets and take them to the trash. I put a knee into the mattress to gather the stained sheets in my arms. On the other side of the bed, I noticed a black mass resting near the nightstand. Out of surprise, I jumped, but I was quickly back on my feet, the sheets left on the bed, my arms rigid at my side. I stepped, one foot in front of the other, until I saw Ousha's broken body. Her hands were clasped in her lap, her eyes closed, her mouth hanging open, her dress torn. She looked dead. I pressed my palms to the side of my head. Images flashed in front of me: my children after the wave; my father's dead body, emaciated and dehydrated from the cholera. My mother's last moments on earth, an image I thought I'd forgotten. Death always brought an extreme focus, a clearing of all the storms circling me on any given day. It was easy to see how ephemeral life was when death stood beside it.

I knelt beside her and touched her arm. Warmth and those micro movements living people have. I put my hand in front of her mouth and took in her weak, rancid breath. I hadn't realized I was holding my own breath until I relaxed and inhaled the fleeting life of hers.

Ousha pulled her head up and opened her eyes, tiny slits through swollen skin.

"You should go to a doctor." I had no idea how to make that happen, but I knew doctors were like laundries here, plentiful and available twenty-four hours.

She murmured, her words tangled.

I was directly in front of her. Ice wouldn't help this time, but alcohol might, at least for now.

"I really did love Inesh." She lay down against the carpet and passed out.

RESTORE

The room looked like nothing had happened. I'd even found a new set of curtains to hang. The only thing missing was a lamp. Ousha was in bed, propped up, sipping vegetable broth and drinking water. When she sobered up, she told me where her stash of bandages and medical tape was, and I did my best to clean her and dress her wounds. It would be at least a week before she would be able to go out.

"My mother is supposed to come here tomorrow," she said. "I have to cancel her visit. If she sees me like this, she'll protest and cause problems with my father's job."

I nodded, knowing better than to interject my thoughts.

"If she comes to the house, will you run her off?" Ousha asked.

"How?"

"Tell her I've come down with the flu. No, that won't work. Tell her …" She was searching for an excuse.

"Maybe I can say Maryam had you up all night?" I winced at the mention of Maryam, since I didn't know how it would be received. This time she looked at me lovingly.

"You're a sweet, sweet lady, and you have no idea what you've gotten yourself into coming here. But everyone, including my mother, believes the baby is yours."

Of course. I had suspected this, but this was the first time it was verbalized.

"Why?"

"Because that's what Mohamed and I told them. We said we didn't know you were pregnant when you arrived. Only a few days later you gave birth, but you were so good at your duties we decided to let you stay."

"But why?"

"It was an agreement I made with Mohamed, for reasons that are none of your business."

Her words had an apologetic patina. I wanted to ask her about Inesh: the picture of him and then the mumbling of his name when she was drunk, but I restrained myself.

"Is the broth hot enough for you?" I cupped my hands around the bowl and whisked it away before she could answer.

I thought through what it meant that Maryam was mine. What would they do when I left in a year? Would they send her with me? As I carried the soup to the stairwell, the doorbell chimed. When I opened it, a man in a fine suit said something to me in Mohamed's language. I told him I would be right back and went to Ousha.

"There is a man at the door, young, well dressed. I'm not sure what he wants."

"It's likely Jaseem. He works for Mohamed, his assistant. He probably needs to get something from the house. Let him in. If he needs anything from this room, tell him no."

I felt my heartbeat in my fingertips. Telling a powerful man no wasn't something I wanted to do; I was only the housekeeper here. I opened the door again, invited him in, and stood out of his way. He politely bowed his head and took to the stairs. He returned a few minutes later with clothes that were hanged and bagged, along with a toiletry case, and let himself out.

Ousha had two pills in her hand, ready to wash them down, when I entered her room. "What now?" she asked.

"He left."

"Fine." She swallowed her pills. Within minutes, her world collapsed into itself.

Before she was completely gone, I seized the opportunity.

"Ousha?" I said it louder than I might have if she'd been staring at me. "Is Maryam Mohamed's baby?"

She only breathed harder.

. . .

Today was Friday and it was important because I desperately wanted to go with Minrada on the shopping trip. After working for three solid weeks, I needed a day away from this house. I prepared breakfast for Ousha. Two boiled eggs, warm pita, a fresh sliced tomato, and a scoop of olive hummus. I'd found better tea in the back of the cabinet, and I made it for her with milk.

When I set the tray on her bed in front of her, she appeared delighted. The swelling had started to recede, and she could give a half smile without pain.

"Thank you. But I know when something like this comes, there is an ask that comes after it."

I wouldn't lie to her. "I'd like my Friday off, to go into the city."

"No problem. You've been free all along to take your day off."

Then why did she let me work every single day?

"Would you like me to show you where the formula and diapers are?" I asked.

She dipped her pita, bit into it, and launched the tray of food at me. The hot tea sailed past me, but the hummus landed as a lump on my leg, the oil soaking into the fabric of my pants. She pointed to me. "You want me to take care of your child? Do you know your place here to even suggest this?"

This had gone too far.

"I ... I ... Ousha, this is your baby. I saw her come from you. I was there; I caught her head and clipped your umbilical cord. Why are we playing this game when it's only the two of us here? Maryam is yours. You named her!"

I expected vitriol from her, for disobeying her and steeping her in dishonor and shame. Instead, she cried and reached for me. "He'll kill us both if he hears you say that."

It was the first time I really trusted what she said. Ousha took hold of my hand and squeezed it. "Yes, it was Inesh, and Mohamed hates me for it. This was our solution."

"I'll only be here for a year, though. And then what will you tell people?"

"A year? No one only stays for a year. Khalid promised us five years with you so the baby could go off to 'school.'"

Her words echoed in my head, bouncing around and stunning my brain.

"No. I'm only here for a year. That's what he told me. The commitment was for one year; if I wanted to stay longer, I could renew."

"It doesn't matter either way," she said. "I won't be here in a year."

"Are you leaving him?"

She realized her mistake when I repeated it back to her.

"It's better that you don't know these things. Leave the baby with me. Mohamed won't be back for a few days. Jaseem took his clothes, you said?"

I nodded.

"It's fine. Go have your Friday."

. . .

I prepared Maryam for her day with her mother: I delivered Ousha a fully fed, changed, and happy baby.

I looked at the clock and sped up my steps so I wouldn't miss the bus. As I approached the park, Minrada held up one hand to the bus driver and forcefully waved me on with the other. I ran, embarrassed that I was holding everyone up on my first trip.

"I thought for sure you wouldn't come." She patted me on the back as I boarded the bus.

Sucking wind, I looked up when I was in the aisle. I could have been in my own country. The bus was full of Sri Lankans, with a few Asian faces among them. I found an empty seat and sat next to a Sri Lankan who looked to be a teenager. Her hair was an unusual short cut, and she wore her house uniform with glaring white sneakers.

"Hi." She was giddy.

"Hello. I'm Shula."

"You work for Mohamed and Ousha?" She didn't offer her name.

I was comfortable with everyone in the town knowing everyone else's business; this was the way of my small village. But here we were in a city of great proportions and it was still happening.

"Yes, for almost a month now. Very nice to meet you." I bowed my head.

"My brother worked for them."

It felt like thunder cracked next to my head and all I could hear was loud ringing. The seat in front of me became a blurry canvas I couldn't make sense of.

The girl patted my leg in a reassuring way, letting me know it was okay. I didn't know what to say. Her hands were creased and swollen, aged a decade beyond her face.

"That's nice." They were the only words that would come out of my mouth. I looked out the window; we were crossing the bridge to the mainland. To try to bring myself back to reality, to clarity, I counted the yachts passing under us. "I didn't meet him."

She sucked in a laugh. "I should hope not. He's dead."

If the mention of Inesh had sent me fuzzy, the knowledge of his death rang me so clear I could see each and every pore on her face.

"How? While he was here?"

"Yes, the authorities found him behind the wall. They think he got trapped in there while doing maintenance. When no one could find him, he died of hunger."

I knew that was impossible. There were multiple exit points. I felt nauseous thinking about exploring those dark passages alone and then hearing Mohamed in there watching me.

"Did you see him? After?"

A group of women erupted in laughter behind us. I wished for a second I was having their conversation instead of mine.

The girl nodded. "Yes, I flew home with him. Mohamed paid for our trip back and my brother's funeral. It was beautiful; his favorite purple orchids were everywhere. It was bittersweet for my parents, though. They were happy their son had made such a life for himself abroad, but heartbroken that it had ended so soon. You know, life to us isn't expected the way it is here. The long arcs these rich people use to talk about their lives amuse me. As if they're sure the next thirty, forty, or fifty years are theirs to fashion how they like." Her hands were animated when she spoke.

"And for you? Did Mohamed and Ousha do anything for you?"

"No. They honored my brother. They owe me nothing." She turned her head to stare out the window.

The bus was passing tall buildings, then slowed. The air brakes engaged and the door opened. We made an orderly disembarking; the girl didn't say anything else to me. I found Minrada outside with three of her other friends. "This is Shula." She pointed to me so there would be no mistake for the other ladies. "She's never been out, so take good care of her." She came and put her arm around me.

We walked through the entrance to the shopping mall. The shimmering of glass, lights, high-gloss finishes, and pristine merchandise was overwhelming. I thought this was maybe what Nirvana looked like, a place where there was no suffering and a person might bathe in bright white lights, free to contemplate the mysteries of the universe. The rich aromas of food drifted up from the level below us. The center of the mall was open, with hanging plants and palms, which gave a clean natural scent as the backdrop to the finery laid atop it.

"I don't ever want to leave," I told Minrada.

"This is why we come, to spend only a few hours here. And the food below is from all over the world. You can travel with your mouth to places you might never go."

She threaded her arm in mine, and we shopped the windows with our eyes. I noticed how we were looked at when we entered a store. The shopkeepers spoke to us in Mohamed's language. I nodded and smiled, knowing I couldn't afford anything here. Touching the fabrics and imagining wearing them was enough; I didn't need to buy anything.

"What else do you know about Inesh?" I asked Minrada.

"I saw you were sitting next to his sister on the bus; I didn't realize it until we were going. She's an awkward girl. Young."

"She thinks highly of my employer." I didn't want to say his name right now.

"Where one comes from is very important to how they see where they are."

"Anyone can see there's something wrong." I stopped from divulging more, but my sense was Minrada would already have a whiff of whatever I told her.

"I know a place you might like." She led the way through the dizzying brightness of the mall. We took a lift to the fifth floor, then headed down a hallway. A door opened onto an outdoor space. Shoes were lined up, and I followed custom and took off mine, stepping onto the sand, leading to the artificial beach scene. It was deep enough for me to sink my toes in. Sounds of the ocean mingled with the air and coconut trees were precisely planted. A small boy ran between them; I imagined he was Mewan. He ran over to me and I picked him up and tickled him. He giggled. His nanny was close by, from Colombo, she said.

"He's attracted to you. He's usually afraid of strangers," she told me.

"And me to him. He reminds me of my son."

She had to know my son was back in Sri Lanka; she probably had children of her own she'd left behind. We all had a similar story. We all had left something, to strive for more.

"I'd better give him back to you before he gets too attached," I said.

Couples stood at the edge of the water, gazing out at the city. "Makes you wish you had someone, no?" Minrada said.

"I had someone. He was everything, but everything has an end too." The white piping over the seams of a black blazer caught my eye. It was the same one Mohamed had. Then I spotted the back of his head, with the same close crop that seemed popular with the men here. He turned with his arm around another man and immediately caught me staring. His face looked different. His jaw was relaxed and his forehead smooth, instead of the insatiable worry always plaguing him in the house as he moved from point to point of dissatisfaction. He ignored me, and when the other man wasn't paying attention, he gave me a look that dared me to go anywhere near him.

I turned and looked for Minrada; she was standing inside the glass doors, checking her phone. I met back up with her. "My boss is here."

"Where?" She craned her neck looking for him.

"No. Don't do that. He's with a friend."

She nudged me and smiled out of the side of her mouth. "I bet she's more attractive than his wife."

"It's a he."

She looked disappointed at the fact.

"Let's catch up with the other women," she said.

I didn't see Mohamed again, and I'm sure he was happier for it.

SEA CHANGE

My feet hurt. We'd walked the entire mall several times, then strolled along the water. I was looking forward to cuddling up with Maryam in bed and falling asleep. I unlocked the doors to the house and immediately heard her crying. After setting down my bag, I followed her cries upstairs. Maryam was lying on a blanket on the floor of Ousha's room.

"Ousha?" I called.

No response.

I picked up Maryam and gave her a pacifier. She appeared to have been crying for some time, and her diaper was full and leaking. The bedroom level was silent, the bathrooms empty. I went downstairs to look for her; the pool was vacant, the kitchen serene. I took one step into the hallway toward my room and saw the storage crates stacked on the threshold of the laundry room.

"Ousha?"

Noises this time. Someone was in the laundry room. A door closed, followed by a weak "I'm in here."

I stood in front of the door and looked over the crates at her. She had her back to the passageway door.

"Are you looking for something?" I asked.

"I … it seems I lost a piece of jewelry, a necklace. I thought maybe it was in—"

"The crates?"

She didn't move from the door; it was as if she didn't want me to see the door handle. I assumed she would know I would've seen it while I was working.

"No, in the wash." She pointed to the washer.

"Maryam was crying when I got in." I searched her face to see whether the gravity of it registered with her.

"Shula, can you go to your room now? I don't need you for anything."

Her legs were shaking, and her unwashed hair sprang from her head. She looked weak from her injuries.

I would appease her. "Sure."

She moved hastily, putting the crates in place, bumping into the walls, and then quiet.

I fell asleep quickly. I woke in the night and heard scraping and weeping behind the wall. Thin beams of light cast out from the holes in the wall Mohamed had watched me through. Who was there now? Mohamed was gone. I would have heard him enter the house because the chime of the front door opening always sounded in my room. I got up and walked into the hallway. The laundry room door was shut. I opened it to look in; it was dark, but the blue glow from the control panels of the washer and dryer let me see that the crates were back in front of the door. Looking for clues, I kept walking. The doors to the pool were open. I stepped into the desert night air; the light in the pool was on, and the water bubbled from the jet. The boat traffic in the canal had died down, and the lights of the homes and tall buildings beyond twinkled in the night sky.

There was a tote bag on the dock, close to where the stairs led to the boat tied below. I listened in that direction and heard someone below.

"Hello?"

The steps clanged. Ousha came into the cascade of the pool lights.

"Why are you up? Stop spying on me." She waved me away.

This time I decided to ignore her. "Are you taking the boat somewhere?"

She climbed the ladder and came close to me, an inch or two from my face. "I'm leaving. You can't say anything; he'll beat me, worse than last time. It gets worse each time."

"Go back to your parents."

"No, I won't risk my father's job and their life. It's easier for them—for everyone—if I'm suddenly gone."

"And what about Maryam?"

"Why do I have to save everyone? I lost one before, you know. A boy, to make it worse. Mohamed told me I should have saved him. How could I let his son die? It must have been something I gave him. My milk, my body. He called me a filthy piece of refuse. It's always me. I'm his problem. I'm everyone's problem."

I, maybe better than most, could understand leaving your young for something else, but this situation seemed full of alternatives. This choice was an extreme measure.

"What do you want me to say?" Ousha walked past me and into the side door that led into the narrow passage. She returned with a lifejacket and a lantern. Her motions were dulled, her eyes protruded; she appeared under the influence. I watched her load the boat, and when she was ready, she started the engine. "Wish me luck." The sentiment felt disingenuous, as if she hadn't thought this through. I looked in the boat; there was a bag stuffed with clothing, a sealed pack of crackers, and one small bottle of water. I didn't know how far she planned to go, but in this heat, she wouldn't last long.

I thought about the future, of my telling Maryam one day about this moment when her mother had sailed off in the night to escape the abuse. I didn't know if it was bravery or cowardice, but I probably would have made a different choice.

The engine revved, and Ousha pulled off the final rope that had moored the boat to the seawall. She parted the water and was gone. I watched her until the light at the front of the boat twinkled out.

When I returned to Maryam, she was still content. I realized it was just us in the house. I could go anywhere and do anything. I felt myself pulled toward Mohamed's office; there was more I wanted to know about him. He was frustrated and violent, but those emotions don't rise in a vacuum. What was driving him? If I was going to spend time here with him alone, I'd have to know how to navigate him. At the door, before I even recognized my feet were moving, I reached for the handle and turned. Locked. I went outside and in through the door that Ousha had left open, then felt my way until I could turn on the lights.

The passage was beginning to feel familiar; the chill of the air conditioner and the dark crevices had lost their creepy feeling. I climbed the ladder to the upper level, making sure I had a hand on the wall at all times. There was a smell I didn't recognize, a strong astringent, maybe a cleaner. At the juncture I turned left, then bumped into the magazines. Knowing the door was nearby, I lightly ran my hands over it to feel for the handle. It turned, I pushed, and I was standing in his den again. This time I felt bolder. I knew what he had done to his wife, and I saw him at the mall acting as though nothing had happened, a man with no remorse and a broken moral compass.

I got close to the bookshelves and looked over what Mohamed was reading. It was all in his language, symbols I didn't recognize. I pulled at the drawers, each one filled with more books and papers. Under the television, I pulled at the cabinets, which clinked as the doors opened. Thin chains, shined and greasy, partially fell out. I picked them up and then pulled. There were ankle shackles on the end, something brown speckled on them. Blood maybe? I'd seen plenty of that after the wave had come.

I found small plastic bottles inside, along with gauze and a collection of articles so strange I couldn't imagine what they were used for. I put them all back, fluffed up the carpet, and kept searching. Mohamed had a laptop computer on his chair, but I didn't know how to use it, although I'd seen people stare at them for hours. There were pictures on the window ledge. Mohamed with his parents, his brother and sister, a baby, pictures of other young men. I didn't know who they were; they hadn't been at the party a week ago.

The doorbell chimed. I looked out the window, unsure which direction of the house this faced. Then I saw the house beside us. I traced my steps back to the door, stepped into the passage, and closed it. I waited. Voices echoed through the ventilation, and I heard Mohamed's tinny masculine voice and another man. I hoped he wouldn't look for me or for Ousha. In the next second, I heard him call for her. Then again. Followed by him running up the stairs. "Ousha?"

Silence greeted him. He happily called out something in his language. A second running of feet, and I heard them enter the office. I saw the light flicker from under the door. I tried to find a peephole, to spy as I suspected he had done to me, but I couldn't find one, so I stood next to the door. If he opened it unexpectedly, he wouldn't see me. I was in a space beyond my past exploration.

They were in Mohamed's office now. A type of giggling. Not sounds I'd expect from two grown men. More movement. They were on the couch; I heard their bodies against the leather. Expressions I didn't understand left their lips, but I knew the emotion behind them. The hurried desperation of desire, followed by increasing movement. Moans of pleasure. I knew the feeling between my husband and me and had even once heard this between two of the village women, who burned with passion for each other after their husbands had died. I didn't know men could feel this way about each other, and beyond feeling surprised that Mohamed was more interested in men than in women I felt a fleeting affection for him—that he had found love somewhere else in the world.

Their final cries led to silence and heavy breathing. I considered leaving, getting back to Maryam. I could come at any time and listen in to his world. A cabinet opened, and then the chains came out, followed by a loud thump. Someone had fallen. Clinking and then footsteps near the door. My mind told me to run, but my legs locked up as if someone had fused my bones together. The door opened, and light flooded the space, but not where I was; he wouldn't see me here. Mohamed grunted; he was in his underwear. His sinewy body, his chest and belly covered in whorls of hair, strained to carry the young man, the one I had seen at the mall, in his arms. His feet were shackled together, the chain extending up to close around his wrists and then a neck collar. He was unconscious. Mohamed set him down gently, with the care I would set down Mewan or Ruka when they fell asleep somewhere outside our home. I spotted an extra chain extender, and there was a device on the wall with a keyhole. Mohamed inserted a key into it, turned it, took the end of the chain, and fit it inside; then he relocked the device. He kissed the boy on the lips, ran his thumb over his eyebrows, then left, closing the door and locking us in the dark together. When my eyes finally adjusted, I could see enough to step over him and get back to the ladder. I would check on him later.

CUSTODY

The doorbell chimed. I was beginning to realize only bad things came through the front door. I gave the stew, with bobbing pieces of lamb, another stir. Maryam was in a swing Mohamed had let me buy for her so she could sleep while I cooked and cleaned. It was light enough to move from room to room. Her lullaby was playing and she was content. A second chime. I walked quickly; I didn't want Mohamed to be agitated. Over the past three days, he had largely ignored us, and I wanted it to stay that way. When I opened the door, two police officers flanked Ousha. Her hair was stringy and wet, and she wore the clothes she had left in. Her bag was over her shoulder, and there was a life jacket stuffed in it, among wet clothes. She looked at me with defeated eyes.

The officers said something to me in Mohamed's language. Then they pushed Ousha forward. She tumbled in my direction and I caught her, hugging tightly. I knew what was coming next for her likely wasn't pleasant. The officers left, and I closed the door and led her into the kitchen. Mohamed almost never came back there.

"What happened?"

"A downpour flooded the boat. I had no choice but to call for help. When they came, they asked for my papers and wanted to know where my husband was."

"The world seems so big because we are so small."

She locked eyes with me. "Who told you that? It's a strange saying."

"A nun I grew up with."

"A Catholic nun?" she asked.

"Buddhist."

My father had taken us to a tea plantation in the mountains for a business venture he was considering. My mother had to stay with my brother, Sahan, at home. He was up for an important exam at school. Our local nun, Dwhelli, came along.

We wound through the mountain roads until we reached collections of tree trunks, which had been cut down and tied together over the roadway, with the name of the camp carved into the horizontal tree. I couldn't see the name in my memory, just the way the grooves filled with the sap from the tree in the bottoms of the letters.

The first building was colonial era, something the Brits had designed, with lots of stone; originally, it would have been someone's house. These buildings dotted the rural parts of the countryside, reminders of our oppressors. Father stopped the car and turned off the cranky engine. Dwhelli and I waited in the backseat.

After too many minutes had passed, I said, "Let's go look around while he's inside."

There was no expectation other than to keep out of the way.

The road followed the rough path of the brook, running down the mountain. Likely an old horse path. Two silos went up, doubling the height of the trees. The road led between them; when we stood in that space, we could see into each of them. The grassy smell of the tea leaves filtered out to us.

I pointed to one of the silos. "Let's go in."

Dwehlli was always a proponent of exploration.

Inside, we stood in the middle of an interior cylinder, rising to the dome. Circling it were splintering rattan shelves, filled as far as we could see with drying tealeaves. A ladder, as wide as my young body, went up the middle, and before Dwhelli could stop me, I was scaling the rungs. I kept my eye on her orange robes, which got smaller the farther I went.

"You're not coming?" I taunted.

"My feet belong firmly on the ground. You go ahead and soar."

I watched the tea shelves go by, their waning life insulating the space into quiet isolation. The heat expanded, and the dome cover felt more like the sun the closer I got. This time I glanced down, and the height spun my brain on a stick; I hugged the ladder tightly. Right now, all I wanted was to crawl into one of the shelves and fall asleep in the citrusy heat.

"Come down," Dwellhi said. "Your father is calling us."

I listened; I always listened to her.

When I stood next to her, I looked to the spot I had climbed to. "It looks so daunting from here."

"It only feels so big because we are so small," Dwellhi said. "Little specks of light in the darkness."

Ousha looked like she was absorbing the story; it was the first time she had listened to me for any length of time. It was hard to tell with her.

"Did you tell them you were escaping abuse?" I asked.

Ousha laughed with clarity, unlike the last few times I had interacted with her. "The police don't get involved in domestic issues. Here in Dubai, they're worried about keeping up appearances and peace. Whatever happens in a home is up to those who live there."

She went to the bathroom. When she returned, her hair was pulled back and she wore a dry cotton robe.

"He's not going to be happy." I pointed up.

"When is he ever happy?" she said sharply. "The man is a conflicted, miserable creature."

"There's something you should know." I treaded lightly, unsure how to break the news.

"Yes?" Ousha went to the stove and waved the smells of the stew into her face. It made her smile warmly.

"He has someone up there."

"A lover?"

I nodded.

"A man?"

I was shocked she would have guessed that. Had she known all along?

"Yes, but—"

"Shula, you don't have to explain for him. I've always known he was more interested in men than me. We talked about it before we were married, one night when he'd had too much to drink."

I was taken off guard by her casualness. "There's more," I said.

Ousha had started to ignore me once she understood my big revelations were mundane to her. She was looking for something in a drawer as I talked.

"He has someone chained in the passageway. He's unconscious."

Her hands stopped moving in the drawer, and she turned her head to me in slow motion, her mouth slightly open. "Is it Inesh? Is he there now?"

Why would she ask that? Didn't she know Inesh was dead? I wouldn't be the one to break the news to her. "No, it's not the man in the picture I showed you."

"Who then?"

"Someone I saw him at the mall with—"

"On Friday? Why didn't you tell me? Why are you hiding things?" She became defensive.

"I'm not hiding anything. It's just that when I returned, you were leaving on the boat, and you were"— afraid of calling her drunk, as it would insult her, I looked for another word—"not yourself."

Ousha slammed the drawer shut and stormed out of the kitchen. I saw embarrassment and sadness on her face when she understood I knew something about Mohamed that she didn't. I started to understand their marriage was a business contract; each wanted to know the full extent of their partner's existence, even if they shunned engaging with it.

...

Back in the darkness, I carried a flashlight, sweeping it until I saw the frightened eyes. He didn't make a sound as he stared into the light, maybe hoping for a savior. I pushed the beam toward the floor, and when I got to him, I whispered as softly as I could. Although he wouldn't understand my words, he'd understand my intention. I lifted the bowl of lamb and vegetable stew near his mouth. I had been careful on the short journey through the passage, and none had spilled. I set the flashlight on its end, illuminating the space, then took the spoon from my uniform and held the bowl in front of him. He inhaled. I found a meaty chunk of lamb and fed him his first bite. He chewed in ecstasy and finished the entire bowl.

We both heard it at the same time: footsteps; we looked at each other with a touch of fear and building anxiety. I wiped the young man's mouth to banish any trace that I was there. He understood. His actions were gentle. The door flew open with malice. I hid in the shadows, the light off, the bowl gripped tightly. Mohamed pulled the young man into his den, like a monster ready to devour his meal. I heard whimpers, weak protests, then grunts. I fled, unable to stomach the images my mind translated from the sounds.

...

Minrada would be in the park in thirty minutes. I wanted to go to escape the spiral of craziness I'd found myself in. Maryam gurgled at me, her eyes wide when I picked her up. Over the last few days, she'd held a pink rattle and wouldn't let it go. I let her keep it; she was happy. I swaddled her in a new turquoise cloth that was softer than rabbit fur. I didn't tell Ousha where I was going; I figured she'd fume about what I'd told her for days before she'd be able to bring herself to speak to me again.

The group of nannies I had come to expect had gathered in the park. Two of them looked shaken, as if someone had told them bad news before they'd arrived. Their babies were in strollers; I noticed a stuffed bag in each of the bins beneath them. The women jerked the strollers back and forth. I preferred to carry Maryam, who nuzzled into the closeness of my bosom even on the hottest of days.

Minrada pulled me aside as soon as my feet touched the artificial green park turf.

"What's happening?" I asked, concerned by her abruptness.

"It's a pickup day," she said.

I shook my head; I had no idea what she was saying.

"Pick. Up. To Kumzar," she whispered.

"Kumzar?" I repeated, sure I'd misheard her.

A few moments later, a white truck, with no windows and a sliding door on the side, pulled up to the park. There were hundreds of these same trucks shuttling around Dubai at any given time, delivering and transporting the city's commerce. Two of the nannies grabbed their bags and disappeared behind the sliding white door before the truck pulled away. This left the two strollers without anyone attending them. It was all over in less than a minute.

"Where are they going? What about the babies?" I hugged Maryam tightly. I couldn't imagine leaving her here with no plan in place for her survival.

"Eventually, everyone wants to go home. Sometimes their families won't allow them to. Where there is a need, there is someone to fill that need."

"But how?" I knew one of the women who had left was from the Philippines. I didn't know exactly where that was, but I knew it was even farther away than Sri Lanka.

"There's a place," Minrada said, "maybe a few hours' drive from here, in Oman, called Kumzar. A tiny village on the edge of the peninsula. I've never been, but I hear it's otherworldly. The people are remote and disconnected from most of civilization. They're very much outside the law of the country and seize opportunities when they come to make money. Many people want to leave here and Abu Dhabi, but their employers hold their passports, so they don't have a legal way to leave. They can't fly or cross the borders legally. So a route has developed to bring them to Kumzar."

"And where do they go from there?"

"Iran, usually, on the other side of the water. From there, it depends on where they're headed."

"Terrible."

"What is?"

"It's terrible that someone would hold them against their will." The image of Mohamed putting my passport in the safe came to me, but I quickly dismissed it.

Minrada looked at me as though she couldn't believe what I was saying. "Is this not the situation you yourself are in?"

"I'm here for one year and then I'll leave. That's our agreement."

"Pffft." She waved a hand at me. "Agreement with who?"

"Mohamed and Ousha."

"You're fooling yourself. Do you know what we are to them? Like a basket you buy at a market. They'll barter and tell the person selling it whatever they want to hear to get the price down. And when they get what they want, they won't give a second thought to what they said in the moment of trade. Don't think they'll live up to their promises. It's better you look after yourself and prepare."

"And you?" It seemed Minrada often thought she had the whole world figured out, but she was sitting right here next to me, so our paths weren't so different.

"I have no one to go back to. My husband will never leave here, he loves this city," she said. "It's better to stay here in the comfort of this city than to wallow in my poverty. My children are grown and have moved to Colombo. If I had little ones like you, I'd take what I needed from here and go."

"Even if they won't uphold their commitment, I'll uphold mine for one year. It's the right thing to do."

"In this city, doing the right thing can turn out unfortunate for you."

She was probably right, but to me, having respect for myself was more important than winning.

"It's getting hot. I'm going to bring Maryam home." I was tired of Minrada's negativity.

PARENTS

Three mobile phones in the house blared warning beacons, and sirens outside filled the air with their voices. Ousha looked at her phone, then turned on the TV. "A sandstorm is coming. We have to bring everything inside."

I left Maryam with her, pulled the cushions from the pool furniture, collapsed the umbrellas, and grabbed anything that appeared lightweight. I stacked everything in the hallway outside my room, because I knew Mohamed would be upset if he came in the house and the sitting room was a mess.

"My parents are coming tomorrow. Did I tell you?" Ousha called to me as I was shuttling cushions into the house.

I didn't answer because I wasn't sure why she was telling me this.

"You'll enjoy talking to them." She sounded hopeful.

I looked at her face where the cuts were healing.

"I can cover them now," she said touching the red marks.

I wanted to ask if her mother had enjoyed speaking with Inesh, but I knew that was toxic territory.

"Yes," I replied.

When I stepped outside, I saw the wall of sand engulfing the city. The nannies had talked about this once at the park, saying it was better on these islands because the water killed the momentum of the sand. The wind was pulsing hard, and I imagined it would roll over us. I had one umbrella to get down, which took muscle. When I came inside, Ousha was rolling kitchen towels and setting them where the windows and doors met the sills and floors.

"You'll have your work cut out for you when the storm is over. Mohamed loses his mind during these."

The mention of him made me think of the man in the passageway. Would he be scared at the hollowing wind or would he know what it was?

I changed the subject. "Why are your parents coming?"

"A reschedule from the last visit. We usually have dinner once a month. It's all Mohamed can stomach with them. He finds their presence unbearable."

A moment later, Mohamed appeared from the office on the first floor. Ousha jumped when he mumbled hello. I didn't think he was there either. She looked at Maryam, whom she had set on a blanket on the floor. I could tell she wanted to pick her up.

He breezed by the baby; I think he didn't see her. Then he kicked the towel away from the door and went to the pool area. He put his hands on his hips and surveyed the dust storm, which was closing in. He spat and wiped at his eyes, then came back into the house, shutting the door behind him. I put the towel back in place.

As I stood at the glass doors, I heard sand scratch against the glass. The sky darkened, and within minutes I couldn't see the canal or the pool. Mohamed and Ousha watched too, all of us spectators. Maryam was still lying on the floor. She began to cry when the sand pelted the glass. Mohamed covered his ears and headed upstairs.

"I'll prepare the food for your parents?" I picked Maryam up and comforted her.

"No, no. They'd be offended if I didn't cook for them. Please make sure the house is spotless, the dining room is ready, and Maryam is out of sight."

…

I was looking forward to Ousha's parents' visit. I wondered what type of parents had given rise to a woman like her. If nothing else, it would be an instruction regarding what I might or might not do with Ruka. I spent the day vacuuming and dusting, amazed at the places where the sand found its way to in the house.

The doorbell chimed. Ousha told me not to answer the door, but to stand beside it and wait. She ran from the kitchen, the smells of her meal woven into her clothing. Mohamed appeared, his face bright with a smile, his hair slicked, a gift in hand. I'd recently fed Maryam and put her down for a nap in her crib, with the door tightly shut and a towel below it to dampen any sound she might make. It felt as though we were getting ready to perform a show, and in fact, we were.

Ousha's mother entered first, in an orange suit, her black hair parted in the center and pulled into a braided knob at the back of her head. Her round sunglasses had gold rims. I thought she had told me her mother was Sri Lankan, but this woman's nose was thin and pointy, her forehead and cheeks high, smooth, and milky.

"*Oui, oui*, you look like you haven't slept for days." She put her thumbs on Ousha's face and swiped them from her chin to her ears.

Her father stood there, slightly stooped, in a suit and tie and a fedora with fabric around the brim matching his tie. He wore thick tortoiseshell glasses with gold hinges, and his hands and face were dense with freckles.

"My doll, my doll," he said.

He then switched to Mohamed's language and greeted him with a handshake. Her mother hugged them both. Mohamed was on his best behavior, his demeanor like the first day I had arrived. Now that I knew him, I could see what a struggle it was for him to hold himself this way.

"This is our new housekeeper, Shula," Ousha introduced me, then gave me a look that encouraged me to say something.

"Hello. It's very nice to meet you both," I said in Sinhala, then bowed. "Can I offer you a refreshing drink?"

I took her mother's purse and her father's hat. I had prepared a fruit spritzer. They both nodded. Her mother laced her arm into Shula's, and they set off for the sitting room. "How do you find such good help?" she asked. "Your house is spotless after the dust storm. Before we lived in the condominium, it used to take me weeks to clean up after those, and here we are, one day later, and it looks like nothing has happened."

"I must give the credit to Shula," I heard Ousha say as I went into the kitchen to fetch the drinks. I quickly checked on Maryam; she was up but occupying herself in her crib with a stuffed elephant. I brought the full glasses out on a tray and served them.

"I'm glad you're feeling better. Do you know it's been almost three months since we've been over here, between your vacations and sickness? At first I thought maybe you were pregnant." Her mother swiped her hand through the air, dismissing the thought.

I lowered the tray and placed it on the coffee table in front of them. Ousha's mother picked up a glass and gulped the bubbly red liquid.

Mohamed and her father were talking seriously; I couldn't understand them.

Ousha's mother turned to me. "Shula, what part of Sri Lanka are you from?"

"Balapitiya."

She raised her eyebrows. "They were hit hard by the tsunami, yes?"

"Yes. I lost my husband, but thank the gods my children survived."

"Children? And that's right! Ousha told me you have one here, but there are more? You look too young to have grown children." Her full attention was on me now.

"They're three and eight," I said. "My oldest daughter is taking care of the little one while I'm gone." I didn't acknowledge her comment about Maryam.

"And the newborn? Where is she?" She held up her hands.

"My mother loves babies. Go get her." Ousha pointed to the kitchen door.

I was shocked at the instruction. Was she really going to have me bring her baby out and pretend it was mine? Regardless, I did as told and went into my room and got

Maryam. Such a happy baby; she was babbling the entire way to the sitting room. I grabbed her pacifier in case she got fussy.

"Oh, just look at her." Ousha's mother put her arms out, and I handed her granddaughter to her. She looked at the baby, then at me several times. "She doesn't look like you at all. A shame ... you're so pretty," she said to me. Ousha stiffened at the comment. Her mother had just insulted her looks, and now to compliment me was harsh. She fiddled with Maryam, put her nose to hers, and murmured sweet things to her. I retrieved the light snacks Ousha and I had prepared earlier in the day and set them down. Meanwhile, Mohamed paged through a construction project document, explaining various pieces of the building to Ousha's father.

Her mother came up for air and looked squarely at Ousha. "You know who this baby looks like?"

Ousha shook her head.

"Your last housekeeper. What's his name?" She snapped her fingers a few times. "Inesh?"

The color drained from Ousha's face.

Her mother turned to me. "He isn't your husband, is he?"

"No, madam."

"Well, someday I'll have a grandchild of my own, gods willing." She handed Maryam back to me.

Mohamed's eyes shifted to the baby for a second when Ousha's father was busy studying the building documents. He tensed and I saw the red in his lower jaw spread.

The next time I returned, everyone was speaking in Mohamed's language and ignored me. I made sure drinks were full and stood by waiting for instructions, wiping the sweat droplets from beneath their glasses and offering help where I could. Then I made sure the dining room was prepared and went back and forth through the side door to the hallway behind the kitchen so I wouldn't disturb them. When Ousha gave me the signal, I brought all the food into the dining room and set it on the table, then appeared in the sitting room to announce, "Dinner is ready." I held my arm straight out in the direction of the meal.

When everyone settled, I backed out of the room and closed the doors. Missing my daily trip to the park, I looked out the front windows. Were Minrada and the other women talking about me, wondering where I was? I heard it in their voice sometimes, the fear for one another. Whenever someone didn't show, they'd speculate about the person's whereabouts, whispers of beatings and detainment. The next day, the missing women would appear with bruises or limps. Two weeks ago, Yeihma, the housekeeper a few doors down from us, showed up, unrecognizable as her face was beaten so brutally. When I asked if she'd seen a doctor, she said, "The doctors won't care for us. Don't you know that?" She was sharp in her response, her justified bitterness pointed at the world.

A loud thumping noise came from upstairs. If I could hear it, it meant they'd be able to hear it in the dining room too. My mind went to the young man in the passageway; I hadn't had time to check on him today, and I was too afraid to attempt anything while Mohamed was roaming the house like a lion. I stood where I was until fifteen minutes had passed, just as Ousha had instructed me.

The thumping continued. I slipped into the dining room from the side door with hot tea, offering refills. Mohamed tracked my movements as I made my way through the room. I made eye contact with him only once and smiled.

He glared in response, then said something clearly directed at me.

Ousha translated. "Why are you making so much noise in the kitchen?"

I knew what he was doing, making sure there was an explanation for the noise. "I'm sorry," I said. "I'll be quieter."

His face changed when I played his game; the displeasure he transmitted to me had abated.

I left hastily; if the young man made noise while I was in the room, our game would be up.

The final course was cheese, dates, and small plates of colorful macaroons Ousha had picked up in town. I arranged them on dessert plates printed with eraser-size red circles, then set them on one serving tray to deliver them in one trip to the dining room. The cheese was overpowering and pungent. I arrived to hushed conversation and set the tray in the middle of the table, distributed dessert plates to each person, and refreshed their napkins.

Looking disgusted, Ousha's mother pointed to the tray and said something I didn't understand.

"Can you open the doors to let some air in? My mother doesn't like the smell of the cheese," Ousha told me.

I obliged, opening the double glass doors and pressing the fan button on the thermostat to circulate the air.

When I turned back to them to reenter the dining room and ask Ousha if she needed anything else, the four of them were looking above me in disbelief. Ousha's mother screamed, pushing herself back from the table and running her hands along the wall, looking for the hidden service door. Mohamed stood up, pressing his hands, up and down, his palms toward the floor, in a gesture to tell everyone to calm down. Ousha's father was looking at Mohamed for an explanation, as was Ousha.

I didn't know what was behind me, and the feeling I'd had before the wave had taken me sat like a crouched feline ready to pounce. If there was a fright, was it better not to face it?

I looked at Mohamed, who now had a gun in his hand. He screamed in his language and pointed it in my direction. I ducked, hands on my head as if the roof were falling in. Then I turned and saw the young man, who had his hands up as far as he could pull them with the shackles.

"Is that Inesh?" her mother asked.

"No, Mother. Every Sri Lankan man you see isn't Inesh. Inesh is gone," Ousha said.

Ousha made pleading gestures to Mohamed to put the gun away. I remained motionless; I felt like a statue, cold and stiff. I wouldn't move until someone gave me the okay to do so.

Ousha's mother calmed; she kept her eyes on the man and inched toward her husband. When she was near him, she made a needy grab and held him tightly.

The shackles pinged together as the young man slowly walked down the stairs. I didn't know what Mohamed would do; I tried to read his face. Now confronted with his three very distinct worlds, he seemed to have no idea which one to choose. He spoke to Ousha's father and waved his hand as though the man descending the stairs were an anomaly of the house. No more serious than a broken lightbulb or rug that was beginning to fray. He would deal with it and all would be fine.

"He's lying to you," Ousha's mother said in Sinhala. "He's lying and there's something very serious happening here." She looked at Ousha for confirmation.

When the young man reached the bottom of the stairs, his eyes focused on the door. Despite his shaky legs, he moved with purpose and left the house. Lumpy waves of awkwardness vacillated through the home. Mohamed excused himself in a jerky, noncommittal way, checking the front windows and locking the door before scaling the steps two by two.

"What the hell just happened?" Ousha's father bored into Ousha.

She shrugged. "Mohamed is a strange man and keeps strange company."

"You think he knows him?" Her father pointed to the door.

Ousha spoke freely in her own language, confident Mohamed couldn't understand what they were saying. I moved in and began to clear the dishes. Dinner was clearly over.

"I don't know what Mohamed does. What about you, Shula? Do you know anything about that man?"

My hand was on a white saucer with ocean-blue swirls. I pressed the porcelain hard between my fingers, hoping it would give me grounding. I searched Ousha's eyes, wondering what she wanted me to say. I read it as the truth; she wanted me to speak the truth to her parents, which she was incapable of.

"The boy was chained in a small room for Mohamed to use." It was as eloquent as I could make it.

"To use?" her father asked.

I looked at Ousha again; she knew I had more information, perhaps more than I'd even told her. How far did she want me to go?

She nodded as though she were encouraging a small child.

"To use," I continued. "For pleasure. For sex."

Slightly stooped, her father unhitched his spine and stood up straight. His face looked as though he were ducking a ball thrown at him.

Ousha's mother diminished what I said. "Impossible. Who is this man?"

"It's true. I believe what Shula says," Ousha replied. "She has no reason to lie."

"Your father was coming to tell you and Mohamed the news that he's retiring after two decades of service to Mohamed's father, and you tarnish it. You say his father comes from a dishonorable family? You're a selfish woman. Never worked a day in your life, living in this world like it's yours." Ousha's mother pitched barb after barb at her until Ousha broke into tears and left.

I nodded at her parents and slipped out of the room. I found Ousha in my room, cradling Maryam. It was the first time she seemed genuinely interested in her. A comfort maybe.

"And what should I do now?" A tear fell from her eyes and landed on Maryam's nose.

I wouldn't answer her. This was her life, with no place for my intervention. Because intervening meant I cared, and if I were true to myself, I knew I cared only about one thing: the way home.

Abandoned

The next morning was strangely quiet. Maryam was still swaddled, purring in her crib. I had been up an hour ago giving her a bottle. I walked the house. Through the kitchen, into the sitting room and main hall. In the dining room were half-eaten plates of food, along with a clipped packet of papers Ousha's father had left, likely under duress by the bizarre atmosphere formed after Mohamed's captive had appeared. I listened at the foot of the stairs, heard nothing, then looked out the front window; Mohamed's car was gone.

Upstairs, Ousha's door was closed. Something told me she wasn't inside. I knocked before entering. Her bed was neatly made, the towels in her bathroom folded, her perfume bottles lined up with ruler precision, all of her makeup put away. Ousha wasn't messy, but these were things I did during the day.

I checked her closet. Her hard-case brown leather luggage was stacked against the far wall. I stood in the middle of her room, crossed my arms, and thought about what I was seeing. *The boat.* I ran out of the room, down the stairs to the wall of glass doors in the sitting room, and out to the pool, which I nearly fell into, before I arrived at the ladder where I had confronted Ousha a week ago, and then I remembered the boat had sunk. A minute later I was back in her room, on my hands and knees, looking for clues. My fingers were covered in the long, velvety fibers of the rug. Underneath the bed, I saw the slats that held the mattress in place, along with glints of the metal hanging from them. I lay on my back and pushed myself under the bed like a car mechanic. Underneath, I saw a cheap necklace, not real gold. I could spot real gold quickly; one of my jobs back home had been to assess the jewelry that came through the tourist market. Several rings hung from the chain. I pulled one toward me and flipped it around between my fingers. Written in Sinhala were short phrases Mohamed would never be able to read. *Come with me. My love is yours. Help me leave through Kumzar.* Had Ousha gone searching for Inesh?

I wondered if Mohamed would take out his frustration on me when he returned.

I went downstairs and locked the front doors. I set one foot in front of the other until I was at the safe that held my passport. I opened the cabinet and stared at the keypad with the red blinking dash on the screen above the numbers. I could never guess what numbers Mohamed had used to bind my life.

...

It was cloudy when I arrived at the park.

Minrada's dark eyes were fixed on me. "What happened?" She took my hand and led me to the bench. The other nannies gathered with her, their eyes on me.

"I don't know. You mean about Ousha?"

Minrada looked as though I had lit another match in her brain. "No, the shackled man. I saw him from the window; he was wandering down the street. He came from your house. Who is he?"

"Something that got out of hand," I told her.

One of the ladies I didn't recognize stepped forward; her uniform was black, with white writing above her breast. Her nails were painted white. "I heard he tried to kill him, like he did Inesh, but this one got away. Is that true?"

I shrugged. "I'm not sure."

"Minrada said you're trying to escape," another voice interjected from behind me.

I looked at Minrada. "Why would you say that? It's not true."

She deflected my glare and shot the woman a glance. "I said I think she might want to leave." Her tone was tense.

I stood up and tried to work my way out of the circle they had formed around me.

"We all know he likes other men. It's not really a secret," one of the other nannies, Partha, said.

I picked up Maryam from her carriage, adjusted her giraffe onesie, and popped a bottle into her mouth.

"If you want to leave, you probably can," Minrada said. "I hear Khalid has a new houseman for Mohamed. He's just waiting for the government's approval to let him into the country. You'll have company soon."

This was the first I had heard of a new employee. "Where do you hear these things?" I asked her.

"I keep my ears open." She gave me a sideways smirk.

Everyone laughed. It was a joke I didn't understand.

. . .

Half an hour later, I found myself back in the house, the silence amplifying everything I did. Eventually, via the passageway, I made my way to Mohamed's office. I wanted to know what he might do next. My ears were tuned to any movement outside the door and for Maryam. Wearing my white serving gloves, I opened the drawers in the media cabinet, careful to use my eyes to search instead of my hands. There were movies arranged neatly, a set of colorful headphones, coins and bills that looked like they'd accidentally fallen into the drawers. I closed them and looked over the coffee table, scanning for an awkwardly turned book or a corner of a paper displaying a clue as to what was happening here. I was good at finding things; Ruka would lose the trinkets tourists had given her or a used doll would wash up on the shore, and I could spot it many paces away. I was hoping to find out something about this man to explain the madness I'd found myself sinking into.

I lifted the couch cushions, which were stuffed with feathers and wrapped in the smoothed-out hide of a very tough animal. Flush into the leather on the base of the couch was a gold loop, large enough for an adult size finger to slip into and pull. I did just that, then stepped back so the light could shine into the compartment and reveal its contents. I took out a photo album; its green cover had a blank space for a title. The first page held a four-square display of rapid-developed photos. The same kind I had found of Inesh. A man from my country appeared in each of the pictures, staring deeply into the camera. In the photo in the top left, he was happy, his eyes playful and bright. Top right, he looked confused—his hair was messy, and his cheek had a deep bruise. Bottom left, his shirt was missing, his ribs showing, his lip fat and purple, eyes angry. Bottom right, his cheeks were sunken, his body caked with blood, his right ear gone, dark eyes pleading.

I turned the page: a different young man appeared, again Sri Lankan, with the same progression. I kept turning through the pages; each of the men I saw called out to me, and most of them I was sure hadn't walked out the front door like the man did yesterday. I wanted to take the book and show it to someone, give proof of what Mohamed was doing, hold him accountable, stop the abuse of these men from my country. But as I ran through the faces of people in my head, I knew all of us were powerless against this beast. The front doors' cold security chime immobilized my brain and held me captive as I tried to work through the merits of taking the photos versus not. I dropped them into the compartment, deciding that without Ousha here I had no protection. I shut the lid, flopped the cushion into place, and darted through the secret door. As soon as the door was closed, I was crouched in the dark confines of the passage. I heard Mohamed's voice vibrate through the walls, calling for me. I knew he wouldn't dare go into the laundry room and see the open door to the passage. Mohamed despised any part of the house I spent considerable time in. Even so, he would expect me to come to him on command, like an obedient animal.

I climbed the ladder and, with my hands out, shuffled toward the light of the laundry room. Then I closed the door tightly and emerged into the kitchen, where Mohamed was yelling my name for the fourth time. He appeared deranged, as though he had rolled around in his bed for a week and then came directly to the kitchen looking for food to fuel his madness.

I hunched my shoulders and bowed my head. My body knew the ways of submission, even if my mind was a tiger poised for attack. He yelled something in his language, letting the words wash by me as the ocean might pass by a tightly anchored buoy. When he was done, I looked in his direction but not in his eyes; I believed you could see the real person in their eyes, and an evil as deep as his wasn't worth engaging, for even if you won the battle, you were left with an unshakable residue.

He chucked a glass at me; it sailed past my right shoulder and shattered against the dishwasher. I didn't flinch; his anger wouldn't touch me. His face ignited in rage. If it weren't for Maryam, I would have walked away, but I was the only thing that safeguarded her from this crazed man.

He had a spoon now and was acting out, shoveling food into his mouth, and then he held his hands up in question. I nodded, and began to prepare a chicken for him. My movement seemingly satisfying him, he stormed out of the room. As I cleaned the chicken and shoved herbs under its skin, my mind drifted back to the pictures, and I reviewed them again in my head. The young men, who could be my brothers, all had journeyed through the same stages: delight, confusion, anger, and despair. What had he promised each of them? The image of the man he was with at the mall came to mind. If he had taken a picture there, it would have shown happiness, almost a wide-eyed fascination with Mohamed. The oven beeped; it was ready for the chicken. I slid it in, then peeled the vegetables.

The smells from the cooking chicken would soon fill the house and settle Mohamed's unsteady soul. Cautiously I walked across the sitting room to the doors overlooking the pool. The sun was going down; its light filtered through the two date palms on the property line, casting feathery shapes onto the surface of the water. I looked out at the boats passing; the riders were lying back on the bows, eating and drinking, music pulsing through the air, with the crisp smell of the things only mountains of money could buy. The water was so smooth it looked like I could walk across it. I wished an escape would be that easy … which gave me an idea.

...

Minrada took my hand and pumped it. We filed off the bus; two of the other nannies had stayed behind to watch our kids. They said the cold from the ice-skating rink chilled them. Her eyebrows were high with excitement when she stopped at the door. There were four others with us today. They lined up behind me. She had asked us to come here for weeks.

"You've never seen anything like it."

"The man Khalid is here … you're sure?" I asked.

She said he could be seen here often at night, skating with his male friends. She patted my arm, then added, "I do what I say I'm going to do, no?"

We stepped through a door, followed by clear strips of plastic that hung above the threshold. The air turned biting cold, and our breaths swirled in front of us. The domed ceiling rose up, with banners I couldn't read hanging from the exposed trusses. The rink below had a smattering of people gliding along the inside perimeter of the ice. I followed Minrada to the edge and stood there, unsure what to do next.

"Touch it!" she said.

I didn't care about the ice. I was moving my eyes from face to face, looking for Khalid.

Khalid was there, just as I had remembered him in my village. Wide face, patting backs, tapping children on their heads and rubbing their cheeks. His white leather sandals poked out from his robe, displaying his manicured toes and soft feet.

It was an offense to see a man with such softness, unworked, simply trading words and favors for money. Even my father, who had ended his life with considerable wealth, had the rough hands and feet of a farmworker. Khalid ran through his act with the others at the ice rink; it seemed rehearsed and stiff. I'd seen this trick before.

I nudged Minrada. "There he is."

"And what do you think, lady? You can just go up to him and ask a question?"

"I need to talk to him. I want to make sure he knows I'm only staying for a year and my journey home is planned."

She threw her head back in laughter. "That's why you wanted to see him? I thought maybe you had a crush on him." She laughed harder, covering her mouth.

I left her side and walked toward him. He didn't look up from the man he was talking to until I stood a few feet away from him. He appeared friendly at first, eyes crinkled, mouth upturned, ears pitched back. He looked directly at me, his brain searching my face for who I was. Then the connection happened, and he shook the hand of the man he was talking to and let him know he needed to talk to me.

He stepped in close to me. "How is your placement going?"

"I want to make sure I've only signed up for one year. All the other maids tell me this isn't the case. They say I'm bound for as long as the family wants me."

"Of course, of course, one year." Khalid waved his hand, swatting away the idea as something frivolous.

"How will I get back to Sri Lanka? How will I get in touch with you?"

He looked over his shoulder, then over mine. His expression of happiness relaxed, and he pulled his mouth back in a straight line, showing his teeth. "You will find me just like you found me this time. Dubai isn't that big of a place for those of us who know it. The transportation will depend on the time. Change is always afoot here in Dubai."

His words held little meaning. I turned to get back to Minrada. When Khalid forcefully cleared his throat, I turned back to him.

"Will you tell Minrada something for me?" he asked.

I shrugged, not thinking of a reason otherwise.

"Tell her it's better to respect the snake that protects her than to agitate it."

WILLING FOR CHANGE

Five days passed. Ousha hadn't returned. Mohamed arrived home from work with a new man, who was slight and joking. They were dressed in hats, sunglasses, polo shirts, shorts, and high-top sneakers. The only thing familiar was Mohamed's gold watch with the blue face, but this was now on the other man's wrist.

Mohamed looked in my direction before they climbed the stairs. I went to the kitchen and fixed them tea, along with coin-size cookies, and set the tray outside the door to his office. I knocked lightly, then darted downstairs so I wouldn't have to encounter him.

...

Five more days passed. Ousha's mother stood at the front door when I opened it to water the plants in the morning. Her hair looked like black silk. Her gold-and-red eye makeup and formal sari made her look like she was going to a wedding.

"Where's my daughter?" She pushed past me and charged into the house. Her expensive shoes clacked against the stone floors.

"Ousha?" she yelled toward the ceiling. "Ousha? You need to answer me!" As she rounded the corner toward the kitchen, I lost sight of her.

She returned a minute later, then went upstairs. Mohamed hadn't come home last night, or if he did, he somehow had evaded the security system. I heard Ousha's mother slam her hand against the door to Mohamed's den and yell for him to open up.

"He's not there," I called up. I didn't want her damaging the door and then get blamed for it and have the cost of repairs taken out of my wages. She was at the top of the stairs now, gripping the railing and staring down at me.

"What did he do with her?" Her voice sounded like she was talking into a megaphone and shaking it.

"I don't know. She's been gone for ten days."

"Animal! That man is an animal."

The photos in the album flashed in my mind. The man on the third page stood out to me. Faraway amber eyes, bony forehead, wavy black hair. He seemed hopeful in that first picture, hopeful something wonderful would come out of his relationship with Mohamed.

She was in front of me when I stopped seeing those pictures. "What do you know?"

She wasn't angry with me; I could tell by the way she spun her ring on her finger. It was an agitated but friendly gesture.

"Nothing." The number-one rule we were warned about on the flight over was that we should never get involved in family drama. No matter how helpful we might feel we were being.

"My daughter doesn't tell me what's happening here, but I know things go on. Why else would she run away?"

She knows about the boat escape? Or what is she referring to this time?

I shrugged again, unsure what else I should do. Maryam started to fuss. "I'll be in my room," I said.

A few moments later, I was sitting on my bed, feeding Maryam a bottle.

Ousha's mother stood in my doorway. "Why don't you breastfeed her?"

"Because she's not mine," I said before I thought.

She tilted her head, and her sunglasses fell off the top of her head. "What do you mean?"

"Sorry. I'm not feeling well. Would you mind leaving us alone?" I waved at the door.

"You don't tell me when I should leave. Who do you think you are? My daughter owns you."

I crinkled my face at the word "own."

"In fact, my husband's company paid for you, so *we* own you. That's how it works here. You know that, right?"

"That wasn't my understanding, ma'am."

"Then your understanding is wrong." She pulled at the thin folds of brown fabric of her sari, then checked her arms to make sure it fell right.

I didn't want to alienate the only person here besides Ousha who spoke my language and had power to help me. But her frenetic energy was draining, and I couldn't meet her eyes. I could only imagine her moving away from me now. I looked into Maryam's eyes, focused there, and cooed to her. I heard Ousha's mother walk away, and it wasn't until the front door closed that I relaxed.

I don't know what it was in that moment that made me think of Ousha's blue passport with the gold eagle and the words *United States of America*. It was stuck in the side of her suitcase, behind the suede netting. It made me believe Ousha hadn't left on her own accord; rather her departure was sudden. I knew a passport, especially from the US, was a tool of freedom. I knew because the women from the park often spoke about different countries with longing, and the United States was spoken of as a magical destination where all things were possible.

I climbed the stairs to Ousha's room and nudged the door open. I set Maryam on the bed and put her pacifier in her mouth. In Ousha's closet was the suitcase containing the passport. I undid the shiny latches and pulled it open. The gold print on the front of the book caught the overhead light and beckoned me with a hallucinatory aura. I looked behind me, feeling wrong for thinking about taking it, or even being in here when I wasn't cleaning. Still, I slid it out from the netting and flipped through the pages of stamps. The second page showed Ousha's picture. I stared at it until the lines of her face were the lines of my face. The black hair under the head covering was my black hair. Her nose was turned ever so slightly to the left of her face, as mine was. She was me, or she could be. I walked my mind through the border control here and saw that I could walk through as Ousha. I felt the possibility.

I dropped the passbook into the netting, closed the suitcase, and stood up. I was on the ground floor before I could think my way into any more trouble.

The front door rattled. I was near the new shelves, and I looked around the corner, expecting to see Ousha's mother storming in. Someone was pressing the handle outside, then shoving the door. The lock held tightly. As I walked toward it, I was reminded of the people at home walking toward the wall of water before it had slammed our village into oblivion. Something in the danger drew me. Another thump of a body against the door and this time a crack. I stood next to the window and looked out. It was Mohamed. He looked out of sorts, his movements jerky and uncoordinated; perhaps he was drunk. I went to the door and unlocked it, then opened it. He stared at me with glassy eyes, mumbled something, and swayed. He had an erection, and there was a wet spot on his pants.

I moved out of his way. He entered the house, sat on the steps, and removed his shoes, which were covered in wet cut grass. Then he tipped over and began to snore, his face mashed against the carpet.

I left him there. The pool area of the house was beginning to appear sandy, with palm berries on the lounge chairs, and I needed to get it clean before he sobered up and became unhappy. Maryam had drifted off during the knocking charade, so I put her in my room, retrieved the broom from the laundry room, and headed outside to sweep. The heat felt good as a balance to the dry coldness of the air-conditioned house. My eyes closed as I swept, savoring the quiet with only the sound of the water slapping against the seawall. The door to the patio clicked shut; it wasn't locked, nothing to worry about. I picked each of the palm berries off, skimmed the pool, then stepped back to look over the area. I spotted one small stain on the white cushion of a lounger.

I walked toward the door. A figure moved behind the darkened glass. I waited, my eyes squinting. Was it a reflection or really someone inside? It was likely Mohamed, but he'd seemed so incapacitated not too long ago. Maybe a slog to the kitchen? I gripped the broom in one hand and pulled the door open, then pushed my head through the space, looking back and forth. I almost expected him to jump out of a dark corner like Mewan would do when I wasn't expecting it. Mewan's face was in front of me now— it was his look the night before I'd left him, when I'd held my lips on his forehead and inhaled his sweetness as he slept. The image cleared and I entered, pacing my steps to the kitchen. My bare feet against the floor made no sounds at all. I pushed on the swinging door to the kitchen, but no one was there. A glass teacup was on the countertop, near the sink, haphazard drops of water next to it. I placed the broom in the laundry room, then listened for Maryam. Usually I could hear her noises even when she was sleeping. Nothing. I stepped in front of my room and pushed my ear to the space where the door was cracked open. Silence. I held my breath and tried to ignore the heartbeat in my ears. Then I pushed the door open and reached into the shadows of her crib, where I knew she was sleeping. My hands touched the sheets and patted the mattress. Nothing. Could she have gotten out? Impossible.

I swiped my hands across the length of the crib, expecting to feel her swaddle, and didn't move my feet in case she'd somehow gotten to the floor. My mind raced for explanations; I told myself for a moment not to turn on the light and wake her up, but then my hand was on the switch, and when I flipped it, my eyes urgently searched the room. One of her socks was on the bed and a pillow was missing. I looked over the floor; pieces of wet grass were on the carpet and the edge of the pillowcase was lodged under her crib.

CHILLED MUD

The room temperature dropped, and cold sweat ran down my torso. I forced myself to the floor. As I did, each of the fibers of the carpet came into crystal-clear focus. I pulled on the pillow, which caught on something and then let loose. I inspected it: a wet spot on the end. I tossed it onto the bed and looked under the crib. I saw the red stripe from the blanket I had wrapped Maryam in. I reached for it; my fingers got a hold of it, and then I pulled and I felt the deadweight unroll from the blanket. Gold stars blocked my vision; when they cleared and allowed me to see, I was sitting on the bed with Maryam in my arms, cradling her and tapping her blue cheek. I held her up and gave her a shake, being careful with her head. Then my memory took me into the sediment again. The sinking cold sludge covered my legs; Mewan was in front of me, facedown, and I was hoping for him to take a breath. Ruka was in the unknown distance. A current meandered through my insides, scooping up the resident warmth and emotion and bringing it elsewhere. The imagery cleared and the cold held tightly. She was gone. I held her and kissed her forehead. "It's okay, little baby," I said, just in case within her there was a piece of consciousness that felt scared or alone in these last seconds she was in this place.

I wrapped her, put her back in her crib, and set her elephant next to her. I'd watched babies die before. I'd held their bodies as their mothers dug their nails into the dirt and convulsed with sadness. I'd placed them in tiny boxes when others couldn't. I'd witnessed this, but fortunately never with my own. Nothing is permanent and each time a final blink or breath was taken, I knew that for sure.

When death visited our village, a protocol went into action. There were certain words spoken, traditional dishes made, arrangements organized, and ceremonial traditions brought to life. Here, it was me, the small room, and the murderer somewhere in the house. I shut the door. *Think, Shula. Who can you call? Who can you trust so this man is caught? How can you get out to tell them?* Minrada came to mind first. Out of anyone, she would be able to get Maryam to the right person. I looked at the small clock on the wall; they wouldn't meet in the park for more than an hour. I tried not to think about being in this room all that time, with each minute feeling like an hour. I needed to stay out of the house—I didn't want to run into Mohamed. He might target me next since I knew what he had done. I went into my bathroom, stripped off my uniform, got into the shower, and let the hot water run over my head. I hummed with the beat of the water, trying to clear my mind of the sickening images taking up space there. A thumping outside the bathroom started. Then Mohamed's voice. It didn't sound like it was coming from my room. Was he watching me on the other side of the wall? Would there only be a picture of me to send home to my dear Ruka and Mewan when all this was over?

I turned off the water and let it chill on my skin. An irrational feeling of safety surrounded me as I stood wrapped in the tiles and tub. I was one foot out, my hand reached for a fluffy cotton towel, and I wrapped myself in it. Maryam's face, swaddled in this towel, was in front of me. I dried quickly. The thumping had stopped; he was quiet. I'm not sure what happened next because now I was standing in front of Minrada under the sunshades and misting fans at the park. She was snapping her fingers in my face.

"Where is the baby? Where? What did you do?" She clapped loudly next to my ear.

The other women were watching, waiting for something to happen. Minrada was in green today, with green earrings and a green streak in her hair. I thought I was staring at the grass when my eyes came into focus.

"I've seen this before," she told the other women. "She's snapped. The stress was too much. It takes a strong woman to do what we do year after year," she said knowingly.

"I haven't snapped. Stop saying that." Though I wasn't sure this was really the case.

Minrada took me seriously, because she shushed the rest of them and looked squarely at me.

"The baby is ..." I wasn't sure if I should tell her the whole truth. Minrada was a woman of favors and information, trading each one for the other. "I need to go to Kumzar."

She shook her head as soon as I said it, as if she were trying to avoid the information coming into her ears. "The baby? What have you done?"

"I haven't done anything." Why was Minrada accusing me?

"Look who's coming." She glanced behind me.

I turned; it was Mohamed's car, accelerating, until it zoomed by us, blasting us with hot air. He didn't look at us; I don't know if he even knew I was here.

"Kumzar. What do I have to do?"

"I need evidence of"—Minrada walked me to the edge of the artificial grass. She got close to me—"his friends."

"There is a book. I can get it to you." The reality of going back into his office made me clearheaded. "That's it?"

"More if you don't have your passport. To pay the Kumzar fee."

"How much?"

She looked around, "You'll see. Bring me something of value and I'll let you know if it will be enough."

There were plenty of small valuable things in the house, but I couldn't give them away until I left.

"I'm so worried they're going to arrest me, when the police find out about—"

Minrada waved a hand. "No one cares about that baby. Mohamed and Ousha told everyone it was yours. A baby of no one is no one. They'll be glad she's gone."

As I folded my arms together like thin paper, I realized I'd been sent here for an illusion. My dream of provisions for my family was tightly wrapped in the dream of honor for Mohamed—the illusion that I should be the sacrifice to restore his family. But there were two lives here, two very different tellings of the same story. In my story, a child had been lost, a great potential of life the world would never know. In Mohamed's telling, a stain had been erased, the failed result of the grinding vicissitudes that everyone, rich or poor, was dealing with and better without.

"I'll do that." When I put my foot in the road to cross, a horn blasted.

"At midnight, meet me under the small bridge to our island," Minrada said softly. "There's something more to see."

Normally I would have minded the intrusion into my sleep. Tonight, however, with Maryam silent and Mohamed in the house, I would be wide awake.

THE BRIDGE'S SECRETS

I wasn't sure if Mohamed had come home. At 11:30, I felt my way through the darkness, into the laundry room, and through the door into the passageways in the walls. The moment I stepped into the passage, I smelled something foul—whiffs of where death had passed through. It reminded me of the time of year hunting happened in our village, when the group of men returned and dragged their wild boars through the center street, leaving trails of blood in the dirt. I'd pulled a bath towel from the laundry to wedge the exterior door open. I felt for the wires near the top. They were still disconnected from the door sensor. This had been done long before I arrived. Presumably, Mohamed had brought in his men this way.

The night air in Dubai cooled down like at home, but here it picked up a tinge of wetness. It made the air less choking, though tonight it felt like even the stars were pressing down on me, threatening to flatten me against the earth and extinguish my breath. As I walked along the road, where no others were treading, it felt like the eyes of every house gazed at me. I arrived at the bridge, my only greeting was silence. Had Minrada played me this time? The breakwater rocks and boulder-size coral stacked from the side of the road to the water didn't reveal an obvious path to get underneath the bridge. I stepped a few paces off the road until I was at the water. The way the rocks were stacked had pushed me even farther from the bridge. I saw tiny lights tucked in the underbelly of steel girder supports. A moment later, a light flashed quickly in my direction and illuminated the water closest to me.

It had to be Minrada. I couldn't know at the time, but I would look back at this moment as the precipice before the long slide, when the pain of my situation became so great that it blossomed into an anesthetic that would numb me from the soul-piercing barbs that sliced me all the way down. Whatever crazy scheme she had concocted would play out. My fate pushed me to the lessons I needed to learn, complete with the pain and pleasure stored up for this incarnation. I left my shoes on the shore, rolled up my uniform pants, and waded into the water. Back at home, this was an invitation to be snatched by a constrictor or crocodile that waited for an unwise animal to wander in too closely. But I only felt a purpose about me, driving me. I knew the fears of nature were nothing compared to what people could bring about for us.

The water was still and warm, the silty smoothness sliding underfoot. I was up to my thighs, my pants soaked, until I stood directly under the bridge where the light had appeared. It flashed again, this time to show me a path, a human-size space where I could climb between the rocks. I followed dutifully until I smelled wisps of burning herbs.

A leg dropped down from the girders and touched the ground. Minrada's thick body followed; she wore an abaya I'd never seen.

She pressed her palms together. "Can you believe it?"

"Believe what?"

"That this exists right under the nose of the Emiratis?"

I wasn't clear what *this* she was referring to.

"Come. You'll see." She pointed up to where she had come from. A small opening in the boards created a floor or ceiling, depending on which side you were looking from. When I didn't move, she gave me a light push. I reached into the space and stuck my head inside. At first I wasn't sure what I was looking at. The strung lights, through the heavy sweet-tinged smoke, took the shape of colored butterflies. Then sets of hazy eyes looked back at me from the closed-in space. After a nudge from Minrada, I climbed into the roomy hideaway.

"Welcome." It was a deep voice from my country. I realized how much I had missed someone who might have been my father. The strong certainty in his tone.

Behind him, the others paid no attention. Some were in uniforms, while others had changed into the flowy traditional clothes of my home. They were reclined on woven pillows, the sweet and musky smell of opium drifting from their lips. My brother, Sahan, if he had come to Dubai to work, might have ended up here.

"Hello," I replied.

He handed me a pipe. I took it and puffed lightly. I didn't like the way smoke of any kind made my mouth feel, but he was generously offering me something of value to him, which made the smoke sweeter.

"This is Chamara," Minrada said. She held out her fingers, asking for the pipe.

His hair glowed white under the strung lights and against his dark creased skin. When he turned to talk to me, I saw his hair was pulled into a bun at the base of his neck.

"Where do you want to go?" he asked me in my language.

"Home. Balapitiya."

"That's a difficult journey. Some don't make it." He squinted at me.

"I won't make it if I stay here. My boss will kill me." I surprised myself by verbalizing this.

"In that case, can you be at the place Minrada tells you at eleven thirty tomorrow morning? There's no turning back once we start. She tells me you don't have your passport?"

"No. Mohamed, my boss, has locked it in a safe,"

He waved a hand at me. "No names, no names."

"But I have a US passport. It's not mine but close enough."

Minrada's eyebrows lifted, and she leaned in so her arm pressed against mine. "You never told me this."

I shook my head, not willing to offer any more information.

"Oh, I see how it is. You think now you're going to keep this train moving without me," she said, laughing.

Chamara ignored her. He seemed, at best, to tolerate her self-importance. "If you have that, life will be much easier. But you still need something of value. Jewelry, cash, a piece of gold. Things your boss hides from you."

"Yes. I'll bring something."

"Okay. Go now, and if for some reason eleven thirty doesn't happen tomorrow, be patient." He turned away from me and spoke to someone behind him.

Those last words were the most frightening, because I knew Mohamed wouldn't let me be patient.

As I approached the house, I saw a light on in Ousha's room upstairs and Mohamed's car in the driveway. I stopped on the sidewalk and couldn't look away. The shades were pulled down, but I spotted erratic shadows moving behind it. I went to the back door and let myself in; the towel was still in place. As soon as I entered the laundry room, yelling reverberated through the house. I closed the door and pushed the containers into place in front of it. The kitchen lights were on too, but it was quiet. I looked out and saw several alcohol bottles and a mess of food from a takeaway vendor.

I listened at the kitchen door. No Ousha, only men. And they weren't fighting; it was more of a raucous party, the way all men get when they drink too much and are together. The voices came closer now, down the stairs. I scurried out of view and into my room, closing the door tightly behind me before I turned on the light. My eyes immediately darted to the crib. I went to the side and looked down at the sweet girl. Tears welled in my eyes and rained down on her. I touched her shoulder. A moment later, I went to my bathroom to retrieve some scented oil from behind my bathroom mirror. I thought, like in my country, I might put some on her forehead. When I pulled open the mirror, leaning against my tube of toothpaste was a picture. Me holding Maryam, who was clearly dead.

TO KUMZAR

It was 4:00 a.m. before I found the courage to walk upstairs toward Ousha's bedroom. At the top of the staircase, a young man was passed out against the wall, a drink next to him. I stepped over his legs and kept moving slowly. The door to her room was open, but I felt the presence of someone else inside. I hoped it wasn't Mohamed, though I knew he was up here. I moved inside; a small lamp next to the bed was on, and I saw several lumps under the blankets on the bed. Heavy breaths. They were asleep.

I precisely remembered the placement of the suitcases inside the closet, and I quietly unlatched them, holding my hand over the shiny metal so it wouldn't click and wake the sleeping men. I slipped my hand inside and felt around until my fingers brushed the small book. I was rounding the corner of the sitting room before I realized the suitcase was still open, but it didn't matter now. I put the book in one of my interior pockets. In the kitchen, high in a glass cabinet, were three ornamental eggs. They were decorated with gold and gems and held in gold stands. I stood on a barstool and reached for them. There were more in the cabinet than I could see from standing on the floor, and I only took the eggs in the back so that at a casual glance nothing would appear missing.

When I had them, I placed them in a cloth bag and went back to my room to add the sari I had arrived in a few months ago. I felt I needed to return in the clothes I left in. Four thirty a.m. Seven hours. I wouldn't move. I pushed my bed in front of the door and went to Maryam.

"Sweet girl, I hope you're with someone who loves you very much."

I let her be; my time to leave was coming. The layers of sleep deprivation were piling on top of me, asking me to shut my eyes, but I resisted. I would sit for one minute on the bed then continue.

. . .

Footsteps and craggy talking. I had fallen asleep; the clock said 11:02 a.m. I jumped off my bed, my bag still on my arm. I ran to the bathroom and pushed the bed aside. I listened, but there was no time now. I went. Three shirtless men stood around the bar, drinking tea. They looked up at me when I was in the hallway, then returned to their conversation. I walked past them, thinking the blood in my head might explode. But I kept going until I was at the front door.

"Shula?" It was Mohamed; he was at the top of the stairs. He didn't sound mad, as I imagined he would be. Rather, his tone sounded surprised. I had my hand on the door handle. "Shula?" This time he was more insistent, but nothing approaching angry. I turned to face him, nodded, then fled. I walked as fast as I could, worried that if I ran, one of the other residents might stop me or call the police.

The entire time, I glanced over my shoulder but saw no one following me.

Minrada was at the park with the usual group of ladies. There was one I didn't recognize. She looked nervous and guilty, wearing a white turban and a sari with orange threads. She looked so thin the wind might blow her away. As I stood waiting to cross the street, the van I knew was there for us slowed its approach. I crossed in front of it. Minrada stood in front of the passenger-side door with her hand out.

"Don't forget who set this up for you," she said.

I reached into the bag and handed her an egg.

"What is this? Where is the album?" She scowled at me.

In my panic, I'd forgotten about my promise of delivering the album to her.

"Go get it." She pointed toward the house.

"I can't. He's home. I'll never be able to—"

The door behind her opened, and she allowed the woman in the white turban to board. I saw other women inside.

"Well, then you can go next time." She handed the egg back to me. The gems caught the sunlight. Behind her I saw the driver staring at the egg.

The driver said something to Minrada in Mohamed's language. Then they began to argue. He pointed to me and beckoned me into the van. Minrada tried to stop me, throwing an elbow at me. But the tiger rose within me, and I snarled, then forced her out of my way. I was inside the van now, and Minrada lunged for me, but the driver automatically closed the door and accelerated away from her. Through the window, I saw her shake her fist. We were on our way.

"Lady …" The driver looked in the rearview mirror at me and held his hand out. I knew he wanted the egg, and I was more than happy to give it to him. I wondered what the repercussions of angering Minrada would be. I hoped I'd never see her again.

I handed him the egg and he stashed it away under his seat. He raised his voice. "Get comfortable," he said. "We'll drive for two hours, and then you'll board a boat to Kumzar from Al Rams. I won't come with you."

We were on highway E-11 heading north. The woman next to me smiled. "Are you going back to India?"

"Sri Lanka," I answered.

"How long have you been here?"

"Two months."

She scoffed at me. "That was all you lasted? You must have made no money at all."

"You're right. A few dinars." I always felt money wasn't a good topic to discuss.

"It's all so horrible, isn't it?" she said. "What they do to us?"

When we pulled into the parking lot, I saw a dock with boats. I was heading home, or so I hoped.

SEA TIGHT

There were seven of us in the van. The driver opened the door and let us out. When I stepped off, he pulled me aside and made me stand behind him. He smelled like wood smoke. He pulled the egg from his pocket and spun it close to his face. His eyes darted between the gem-encrusted bauble and me.

"Where did you find such a piece?"

"I have many," I lied.

"You can have anything you desire if you pay with these. Call me if you ever find yourself in need. I owe you." He slipped me a piece of paper with a phone number on it and then pointed me to the line forming at the gangplank.

The ship had been painted red at one time, but was so rusty that it appeared brown. I stepped foot on the top deck. The ship held still in the calm blue water. In front of me there was an enclosed space where I could see the crew and helm. The line of people was disappearing into a hole in the deck down a white metal ladder.

Each rung I descended filled my mouth and nose with heavier and more stagnant wet air. My foot splashed into a puddle, and I followed the dimly lit path.

A man shouted behind me; it sounded like the driver, but he spoke Mohamed's language. And then a grab to my arm, pulling me deeper into the ship's belly. There were at least a hundred bodies tucked away in the sagging wooden shelves. When we were at a porthole that was open, letting some of the warm air come into the space, the man pointed to an empty shelf next to it and pushed me gently toward it. It was clearly the choice seat here, and he hung around for a few seconds. They thought I had many things to give; I would have to manage those expectations. There were only two eggs left. The ship moved, and I heard groaning among the passengers. I stared out the porthole and focused on the water, letting my mind wander.

I stood at the edge of the water in Arugam; my parents had brought my brother, Sahan, and me here for a few weeks. The wind currents picked up sand and swirled it into dunes against the hills. Dwehlli, the Buddhist nun, came with us to visit the local temple. My father encouraged our religious education, along with new experiences. Dwehlli walked beside me as I took in the unusual blue against the rolling wall of sand beside us.

"Shula," she said, "while Sahan is running up and down the dunes, do you think we should talk seriously?"

Dwehlli was no taller than me, even though I had just entered my teenage years and she was an adult. She had a squinty, freckled face with a brash glow and wore the same light-orange robes every day. She said her shaved head once had bushels of golden hair piled on top of it, and she liked fashion very much but had given it up to become a nun. I envied her simplicity.

"About what?"

"The elements of desire."

Was she bringing up sex? I already knew about this. I'd seen the neighbors once and mother had explained it to me.

"I know about sex, Dwehlli." I was proud to say this to her, a one-up of an all-powerful Buddhist nun.

She put her hand on her stomach and laughed. "That isn't desire. That's reproduction. A mechanical process you should rightly learn about from your parents. Desire is what is sprinkled down on you like a misty cloud moving through. It leaves you with a longing for all you can't have at the moment."

We were moving on the boat now and the spray came through the window.

"I know you wish for a boyfriend."

That wasn't what I was interested in. I wondered if she said that to all the girls she was supposed to be schooling.

"What you must do is restrain yourself from boys in their presence, and then the desire will grow not only in you but in them as well."

I shrugged. "I actually want to fish."

She looked at me dumbstruck. "A girl?"

"Boys are as interesting as snails crawling. I want to learn to fish. Can you help me with that?"

"What does a teenage girl want with fishing? You'll forever be single."

This round it was my turn to laugh, and I did. "I might be single, but I won't be hungry."

A splash of water brought me out of my trance.

The fetid smell of fear and human waste threaded into the moisture of the air. I looked around. I was unassumingly clutching my bag, and there were two women at least ten years older than me sitting on my bunk.

"Move." I shouldn't have been so grumpy. They could force me to the interior, and then I'd be sick for sure. The women scooted. They were working on weaving a sari.

"You see?" one of them said. "You can do this for your daughter too. Make a sari, and then you can give it to her when you return home. It will pass the time of the journey." She pushed the seam she was working on toward me. Her hands were swollen with arthritis, her nails broken by work. She was kind and, admittedly, the prospect of having a gift to bring home would prove to my daughter I wasn't a total failure. To think I might bring something home for Ruka was nothing but pure *desire*.

"Do you have extra fabric?" I asked.

She lifted up her skirt. Various-colored fabric was wrapped around her waist in bands. She unwrapped a piece and gave it to me. Then she pulled two needles from her hair and handed them to me as well.

"Follow me." She worked the fabric in front of her slowly until the thread became something more.

"Are you going to Kumzar too?" I asked.

"Ha. No one is going to Kumzar. You will see."

I went cold at the thought I might have been duped. "But this is what I paid for."

The woman shrugged. It wasn't her problem.

The day passed. My fingers were poked full of holes, and I had little to show for my pain.

"Keep going," the woman closest to me urged.

Calls from the men of the ship herded us to the top deck. A spotlight on the beach appeared to be the only industrial light in the town. The beach was rocky, and the light bounced over the water until it met us. There was a great blackness on the other side of ship from where we had we come.

Clustered locals on small fishing boats met us. A ladder was extended into the water. They took turns rowing to the ladder, then collecting three of us at a time. One of the woman fell into the water; there was frantic splashing and scrambling, but I never saw her reemerge. I detested witnessing death. But here was a poor person, losing her life, and the first uninvited thought that entered my mind was the opportunity created by having one less person to compete with. Dwehlli would have called these unhelpful thoughts.

The two women I'd been with during the voyage stood next to me.

"Whatever you do," one of them said, "don't fall in. They only care about you if they can see you."

"How do you know anything about these people?" I asked.

"This is my third try. Last time, I was swimming to the Pakistani shore, and there was a border guard. He pointed a gun at me and told me to go back. I had to hang on to a rope on the side of the boat until they stopped at their next port and I was allowed to climb back in. I was sure I would be shark food."

The image was ghastly, and then the man standing at the ladder pointed to me and hurried me toward him. I held the ladder like I did when I first held Ruka. Shaky, too firm, and full of anticipation. I wouldn't drop Ruka then, and I wouldn't fall now.

Count, I told myself. There couldn't have been more than twenty rungs. My foot felt around for the next one; they were thin and slippery from the seawater. I held so tightly that the chips of painted metal dug into my palms. The woman above me came down fast and stepped on my hands.

"Move," she bellowed.

I scowled up at her. Not seeing me, she stepped on my fingers again. I was only a few rungs down; she was going to make me fall. The large boat was turning, and the smaller boats waiting for us were having trouble staying aligned with the ladder.

I looked down at the man in the boat. He was young, with a bushy black hair and an unruly beard. He was dressed in a plain robe, smoking, only looking occasionally to make sure he was somewhere near the ladder.

No one cared in this moment. I guess they didn't care in any moment, but right now I was fighting with all my strength to make it to the next milestone. I was above the boat now, my left foot hovering in the air, toes stretching to feel the wooden edge. *Contact.* I kept connected to the ladder until my foot was firmly against a seat. When both feet were in, I crouched so my weight would carry me to safety. There were two other women in the boat, our fill, and our local began to row for the beach. A hand from the water appeared next to me and yanked on the boat, tilting us and letting a piece of the sea spill over the edge.

The Ways of Kumzar

Our local took a stick from under his knees and whacked the woman's fingers, but they held and pulled harder. The man was yelling and pointing us to the opposite side of the boat; the two other women fearfully let out screechy moans. I reached for the hand; I was sure we could bring her on board. She had to be the woman I'd seen go under the water. The man swung the stick, and it connected with my shoulder.

"No, no, no, no!" he yelled at me, shaking his finger, and then he made a motion: his flat hand flipping over.

I stopped moving. He turned away, satisfied he had made his point. I slunk my hand over the side of the boat and fluttered my hand in case the woman might see it. I felt a brush of fingers, and then the stick hit my arm and pain shot through my entire left side. This time, when I looked at him, he snarled. I sank into myself; I couldn't believe that I was going to let this go, that I would sacrifice helping the woman for my own well-being. I imagined my bad karma stacking up like poppadoms next to a baker.

When we reached the shore, I couldn't get away from the boat quickly enough. Our local pulled it in until he perched it between a set of rocks where it fit comfortably and wouldn't wash out to sea. There were flickering lights in each of the buildings, which sat in a ramshackle fashion on the beach. The flames cast dim glows out of the gaps in the walls and doors. The buildings were low slung and created a border on the beach. We stepped into one of them, following the man's lead. One of the women from my boat went before me. Inside, there was another man, much older, with a white beard and dressed exactly the same way, with a Polaroid camera in his lap. His hands held it loosely, and his head dipped back, mouth open, in the unnatural pose of sleep having come suddenly. Our local slapped the old man's shoulder, and he woke up and pointed to a space on the wall where a sheet of clean blue paper hung. The local nudged one of the women toward it. The old man tried to direct her from his chair, until he got frustrated, jumped up, and used his hands to adjust her position and expression. She kept wanting to smile for the picture; I didn't know what about. But the photographer—and I use the term loosely—tried to dissuade her from it. Finally, he was satisfied and took her picture. Then it was my turn, a flash and half-blinded snap, before I was shown into the next building. The first thing I noticed was the cacophony of languages. I heard things I understood, brief moments of sanity amid the static …

"How long will they hold us here?"

"They took my picture two days ago, and I haven't heard anything since."

"I'm hungry. Where's the food? I gave my whole savings for this and no food."

I took a seat on the floor next to a woman who spoke my language. The mention of food made the cramps in my stomach feel tighter.

"What is your journey?" I asked, trying to settle into the space.

"We were in Abu Dhabi." She swung her index finger back and forth between her and the next woman. "And we're going home to Colombo. Eight years I've been away. My smallest children won't even recognize me."

Ruka and Mewan would know me. For that I was grateful.

"Did anyone tell us how long until we leave for our next stop?"

She shrugged. "Just be careful when you're walking around this town. There are no police, but there are plenty of men looking for a young woman like you."

I could handle the men; it was the trip that worried me.

. . .

Light came to the village through the narrow opening of steep cliffs that formed the bay we had entered the previous night. The settlement stretched up from the rocky shore as far possible into the hills before they became so steep that not even mountain goats might traverse them. The walls surrounding us, the land we stood on, the buildings around us were awash in light sienna. It had a tranquilizing effect, the way darkness does.

I walked through the narrow lanes; the streets weren't wide enough for a car, and they were dug into the bedrock in a V formation so that when it rained the water would flow down them and into the bay. At all points I could see the bay, and now two ships were floating outside it. They were substantial sea vessels, not fishing boats. I saw down to the line of white houses on the water; the energy of the people moving around was increasing.

"Shula?" I had walked past a house with an open door and a toddler drawing with charcoal on a rock.

I spun around looking for who had called my name.

"Shula." This time more direct and familiar. Then it dawned on me. It sounded like Ousha. "I'm in the house."

I pushed my head in and saw a woman with her head covered, only her eyes showing. She lifted the veil off her face. "See? It's me." It was a familiar smile, as if we were sisters who had lived on opposite coasts and hadn't seen each other in a while.

"Your mother is looking for you," I warned her.

"Is she here with you?" Ousha got up quickly from her chair and looked around me. "Well?"

"No, no. She's still in Dubai."

"I don't get it. Why are you here?" Her posture slumped.

"To escape Mohamed. Did you think I came looking for you?"

"I thought maybe my mother—"

I didn't flinch. I realized how much she wanted her parents to save her.

"I'm looking for Inesh. You … you brought him back to me, the thought of him, all the things I loved about him. I thought I might find him here. Someone had told me he had come through Kumzar."

"Ousha, I don't know how to tell you this, but—"

I saw her eyes narrow. Her shoulders tensed and straightened.

I reached for her; I knew she'd need some steadying when she heard.

"Where did he go?" she insisted.

I spoke garbled gibberish. My kind mind was telling her I didn't know; my truthful one was telling her he'd moved on to the next life.

"What happened to him?"

I settled on "I don't think you'll find him here."

She must have come out of her body in that moment because her eyes became vacant. Her body stood there, a shell that housed no emotion or life. I'd said too much at once, as though I'd prepared her for a punch, then run her over with a dump truck.

I put my hand on her arm and rubbed; it was cold and stiff. She'd eventually thaw from the inside out. I knew the feeling from when Pramith had gone missing after the wave. At first you feel the prickles of life on your skin, and as the months and years pass, they seep into you until you can feel again. In many ways, I think, were it not for Ruka and Mewan, my deepest pieces might have stayed in a deep freeze forever. Who did Ousha have?

"Come with me," I told her. I wanted her to know someone cared.

There was no response. I thought of the ships and the buzzing of the people and wanted to get back to the beach. "There's a ship leaving soon, to take us away. Come." Ousha didn't respond, not even with the flutter of an eyelid.

Staying with her would have been surrendering to the spider that had nabbed you in its web. She would come or she wouldn't, and as sorry as I felt for her, I also held her responsible. She was a woman of extraordinary means and hadn't used them to help other people but rather wallowed in the elements of her life that had gone awry. Her suffering was smothering, so I charged out, through the streets, until I was with the other passengers who had queued up neatly. The ships had moved closer in. The fishing boats were painted in blues and yellows and ready to serve us once again. The booming whistles of the ships let us know they awaited us. It was the next step—onto a fishing boat. I saw something roughly body shaped floating farther out; it could have been a log, but there were no trees in Kumzar. I told myself it was a tree from elsewhere. I knew what I had to believe to keep myself sane—anything that got in the way of my children and me was a problem for someone else to solve.

The fishing boat rocked, but my mind was steady and we rowed.

We approached a commercial ship stacked tall with shipping containers. The two ladies and I climbed the ladder to middeck, then entered the door of one of the crates. It was stacked to the ceiling with toys, with only a small walking space, about a meter wide, through the center. There was another door, deep in the center with a thin reflective metal, and we were told to enter. Once we were inside, shoulder to shoulder, the door closed and locked. There was light, but it came from two pipes that led outside. My body started to panic. I moved in every direction but was met by the push of other shoulders. I imagined that I couldn't breathe, that the air was getting hot and thin, like when you put your head under a blanket for too long.

"Push against the door," a woman yelled. There was a surge forward, our collective weight trying to break through the locks on the other side. But we only ended up trampling a small woman who whimpered on the floor, crawling between our legs. Our bodies were too close to one another to even bend down to help her.

I always thought I might die from coming upon an unsuspecting wild animal or crashing during the few times I'd ridden on a moped. Or maybe a terrible disease would beat me into submission until I gave in. There was, of course, the possibility of growing old, but that seemed unlikely. Those who made it that far were celebrated; the gods clearly favored them. But now what was slowly becoming apparent was that I would suffocate and some unlucky official would open this door and find all of us dead. It would reach the news for one minute, and then the collective watchers would be assaulted by the next tragedy.

The crying started after about an hour. Then grunts of frustration and anger, until eventually the entire room was crying for relief. I shut my eyes and tried to block out the sounds as shoulders and hips bounced into me. I thought it would never end. Then I passed out.

Pakistan

I woke up hanging upside down, the bodies next to me holding me in place. We were moving, more like swinging, all of us, the entire crate. I felt the rush of the air through the pipes, bringing daylight with it. The other women began to wake up. Someone squeezed my arm. And then we hit the ground, which sent a shock through my spine that made me dizzy. A few voices cried out. Then nothing. Time passed, the daylight faded. I was positioned under one of the pipes and saw the stars come into view.

...

The door opened and we spilled out. I'd lost all concept of time; it might have been hours or days. Pain and grief turn time into a rubber band. It was the same person who had locked us in here. He didn't direct us, but we could see we were on a pier. The world smelled of salty air and diesel fuel. We were all disoriented and wandered like shell-shocked dogs.

The man who let us out told us to keep quiet and follow him. The space around me was slowly coming into focus. Shipping crates, dark water, and cranes. I imagined a great wall of water coming over the fortress of concrete and steel. Did the civilization here have the power to keep the water out or at least keep everything from crumbling beneath it? It was a question I asked myself whenever I came close to water.

The main entrance to the port was ahead. The razor-wire-topped fence, bright lights, and three guards gave it away. We ducked behind a building and followed it until we reached a small gate in the fence that was closed but not locked. We filed through it; on the other side, we were on an unused side road that ended with a white cinder-block wall. We stopped in a circle.

"What do we do now?" I looked at the woman who had been on this journey before.

"I'm not sure. I've never made it this far." She looked around at the circle of women who were forming.

The man closed the gate, then walked back toward the ship. Two feral dogs snarled at us from the corner of the street, but they didn't dare approach such a large group. A man emerged from the door of a building with two kicked-out windows and shushed the dogs with a snap.

I felt an urge to run. We must have been much closer to my home than Dubai. The man talked in Urdu, a language that I'd heard from visitors and that one of my great uncles spoke for reasons I can't remember. He was waving his hands like he was conducting an orchestra, and his shirt was half tucked in with grease stains on it. One of the women in our group could speak to him; she looked to be pleading with him. Her face was sunken; the trip had taken its toll on her.

The man pulled a pad from under his arm and flipped through the pages until he found what I guessed was her name. He told her to stand near the middle of the road. He subsequently looked us all up and divided us into three groups. The two weaving ladies and I separated.

I thanked them, and they blew kisses to me and looked as though they were wishing me well on my journey forward.

When we had all separated, the man gave each group directions. To us, he gave a crinkled hand-drawn map with the word "Karachi" spelled out on the top and an X at one end and then arrows leading to a crudely drawn airplane. I led the group because no one else seemed to have the instinct to do so. There were eight of us, six women who could have been me, a man about my age, and an older woman who had trouble keeping up with us. The slack wires that crisscrossed over the road had streetlights attached that bathed the dirt roads in a mustard haze. I knew this road because Colombo had similar elements. The dust, the weaving human traffic, the buzz of poorly maintained rickshaws, the crackling oil of open food stalls, the guttural bargaining of shoppers, the congestive beeping of motorists oppressed by gridlock.

We walked for hours, moving into a multilane road. The sun rose, reflecting off the buildings, urging the city to wake up. Cars and busses took to the road. A determined but tired populace rose. The old woman in our group signaled she needed to use the bathroom. We were next to an empty stretch of land. Having been in Dubai, I realized how quickly I became accustomed to the organization and purpose with which the city operated. In contrast, Karachi was a city in convulsion, a new building with luxurious finishes, next to an abandoned sagging wreck of concrete, a stretch of modern cabling attached to a telephone pole of questionable integrity. It appeared to have two different minds racing in separate directions: one toward the future and one toward the past. The old woman finished her business but looked beleaguered.

A city bus, belching black smoke, pulled to the side of the road. The door opened, and the driver looked at our group expectantly. A damaged pole had bent so that its sign was facing the ground. I realized this was a bus stop. Nature had called us to stop in the place we needed to be. We charged for the bus like agitated schoolchildren; the first step was missing and it was more of a leap than a climb to get to the till next to the driver. I breathed deeply, expecting the refreshment of cool air. Instead, I encountered the dank residue of an unshowered humanity mixed with a lukewarm atmosphere, which left me regretting my decision of such deep inhalation. I passed the driver, pushed by the women behind me. He yelled in Urdu and flapped his hand in the air, then banged on the coin collector.

I took my seat. He realized his error of letting us on, muttered exasperated words to himself, then moved the bus on. I watched him, touched by his kindness or pragmatism, whichever he was displaying, each an honorable quality. I felt a tingle looking at him. His eyebrows connected, his slightly unshaven beard framing his tight angular jaw. But it was his nose, perfectly formed, with a dimple or scar at the bridge that drew me to him. I had a strange vision of Mewan sitting on his lap, delighted to be in control of a vehicle of size. He looked similar to Pramith, my husband, and my entire being cried out to be close to him again.

We stopped again, and then he floored the gas and we took off down the main road.

I stood up and filed past the few riders still finding a seat. I got to him and bent down to his ear level. "Is this the way to the airport?" I lingered to feel the heat of his body radiate.

He looked at me with something I couldn't place. It was somewhere between annoyance and intrigue. He said something to me in English, and I shook my head. Then he smiled, exposing a gap in the whiteness, reached over, and stroked my chin. He spoke again, then went back to driving. My head felt like someone had opened all the windows and a stiff breeze had blown through. Then he pointed hard at a sign. It was an airplane and he gave me a thumbs-up.

Eventually we arrived, and we stepped off the bus and looked up at the terminal entrance. The airport had decided to go toward the future. The front of it had shaded sheets of glass between sand-colored, fortress-type end towers. I pulled out the piece of paper the man at the pier had given us and flipped it back and forth. On the back side of the paper was a long number. When we were together we went inside. Jets roared overhead, and the smell of fuel and disinfectant permeated the building. I walked to one of the counters.

"*Peace be on you.*" That was one of the few Urdu phrases I knew.

I must have said it wrong, because the woman directed me to the other end of the airport. I saw my flag hanging above two ladies who were helping customers.

I led our group, waited in line, and when it was my turn, I approached. "We are trying to get back to Sri Lanka," I said.

They looked at each other, then typed a few things into their keyboard. "Do you have a ticket?"

"I don't know." I was relieved they understood me. I pushed the long number toward them; one of them input it into her computer, then looked back up at me.

"Nine of you?" She looked behind me at the group of women.

"Eight."

"Are you sure? Because this is a group ticket purchased for nine. Once I redeem it, you'll lose the ninth space."

Who had been left behind? Who was supposed to make it out of Dubai? It wasn't something I could consider now that I had to look out for those of us here.

"Just eight." I handed her Ousha's passport. The others followed suit and stacked them in front of the ticket agent.

The printer next to her hummed, and she slid the ticket into each of the corresponding passports. She handed them back to me in an organized pile.

"Have a wonderful flight." Her smile wasn't genuine. I didn't care, because these tickets were and I was going home.

MISSING PIECES

Two days later, I set foot on the sandy port shore of my village. It had been almost three months since my feet had touched this holy ground, but it felt like a year or that I had imagined the horrors in one unpunctuated stream. Except I knew my mind wasn't capable of producing such dreams. Minrada had done right by me, and I hoped she had received some of the bounty from the two priceless eggs I had used to pay along the way. If not, she surely had erased a touch of bad karma. I walked over the main road. More buildings had gone up, and bodies swirled through the natural landscape. There was a tree constructed of fashioned branches with monkeys in it. I almost didn't notice the leashes around their necks and the teenage boy standing beneath it, enticing them with treats to greet tourists and picture takers.

"Welcome home," he said, waving.

The anonymous rejection of Dubai and Pakistan gone, I was a person again, to be acknowledged and spoken to.

"Thank you. I'm happy to be here." I touched his shoulder as I passed him. His monkeys squawked at me.

The walk to my house flooded me with memories. My parents with Ruka in their arms; her toddling through the sand; my wedding to Pramith, which had taken place in the clearing away from the tourist area with the green-and-white variegated circle of low-cut hedges; and always the great wave. I was standing in front of my house. The door was open; someone was inside, a body lying down, a leg I didn't recognize. I grabbed the broom, which was leaning against outside of the house, and poked the leg. Definitely a woman's.

"Hey, you," I called. "What are you doing in my house?"

She rose, slowly, like a zombie.

"What are you waking me up for? Ain't no time to go to work."

"This is my house." I forced the end of the broom into the dirt, staking out my space.

"No one has been here for weeks." When I finally saw her whole self, I recognized her. Her name was Keldi. She was temperamental, and no one wanted to work with her, which was why she was often homeless.

"I've been away, but my daughter is here with my son."

"Haven't seen them."

She likely didn't know who they were, but still, where was Ruka?

"I'll be back. Get your stuff and get out." I went to Kiyoma's house, where I thought she might be. When I arrived, Kiyoma's mother was in front of the house playing a game with Mewan. In the short time I'd been gone, he had grown and was walking more steadily and talking.

"Sweetie!" I yelled, which made Kiyoma's mother turn to me. I got to Mewan and scooped him off the ground, kissing his face and mouth endlessly. At first, he squirmed against me, pushing back what I assume he might have found to be a relentless force before giving into the love. I bounced him around, then looked at Kiyoma's' mother. "Have you seen Ruka?"

She looked puzzled at the question.

"No?"

Her mouth moved to say something, but she was still working through my question.

"My daughter, Ruka?"

"You don't know?" she finally said. She stood up and dusted herself off.

"Know what?"

She spread her feet apart as though she were going to be buffeted by a strong wind. "That …"

My mind made a journey to terrible places. Places where Ruka was no longer, where Mewan was my last remaining tether to an existence my soul would flee if given the opportunity.

She gave a scratchy cough, then put her head into the wind. "That she went with Khalid? She said you knew, that you were okay with it. That life was good there and it was the best thing …"

I'm not sure if the sky opened at that point, or if my senses had turned on and absorbed every piece of external pricking to shield myself from the internal fire that had erupted inside me, searing away at my emotions as though they were fragile tendons.

"When?" The word itself felt like a jagged knife scraping down my spine, because it made real the truth that she really was gone.

"A week ago maybe? Not long. Khalid said life was great there. He said you were enjoying it and wished your daughter would join you."

I churned through the households I knew had openings in Dubai. The place, so far away when I first set foot on my village shore, rushed back to me with vigor.

"You're sure she went to Dubai?"

She shook her head, then held out her arms in front of her to hug me. I wasn't mad at her, but I needed action, not solace from a concerned mother.

"Anything else?" I wanted to get back to my house. To ground myself before figuring out what I could do. She still had her arms out to me, but I turned and walked away. When I had passed four trees, she called out, "You know he's still here."

Those words ignited an anger in me so fierce that I frightened myself. Mewan felt it too and began to bellow.

"Where?" I demanded.

"He's staying in the tourist tents near the river."

Mewan and I walked until we were at the tourist settlement. I knew locals weren't allowed in here. We were an attraction to be looked at, but they didn't want us coming too close or encroaching on their luxury.

A guard stepped into my path. He was from our village. "You can't go in there. This is the line."

The line, as he said, was a ridiculous thin piece of red string held up by plastic reflectors shoved into the sand.

"Fine enough." I'd sit where I could see the main path connecting the front of the tents into a makeshift hotel. I rubbed my fingers together, digging my nail into my thumb. At stressful times like this, I felt the lingering effects of the polio. One half of my body felt tense and weak in unison. I would watch for Khalid; Mewan would have to control his hunger for a few hours. The guard ignored me. From the beginning, he realized I wasn't a threat, and whatever I was up to did little to arouse his interest. Most of the people who entered and exited the tents were Westerners, with thin white skin and flimsy constitutions. Mewan was pulling at my hair. I looked down at him to see what he wanted; he was contemplating me, and I wondered if he knew I might have to leave again. I rubbed his nose in tight circles, then returned to my surveillance.

I heard Khalid before I saw him. The guffawing, wide laughs, the open syllables of his speech drawing everyone in. It didn't make much sense that he was with tourists, except that these were the nicest accommodations, and Khalid was a man accustomed to nice things.

When he came into sight, every muscle in my body constricted and my scalp pulled the hair toward the back of my head. The guard was looking at his phone, ignoring me. I gravely wanted to stand and run at Khalid, demand answers. This was my emotion, though, and it wouldn't give answers, however satisfying the confrontation would be. Khalid finished his conversation with someone I couldn't see and ducked into his tent. In the last row, against the trees. Three from the end. Easy to remember.

My heart ached for Ruka, her sassy obstinacy challenging me. It was a trait I couldn't imagined having displayed with my mother, but these times were different, and it showed me that women were gaining power, millimeter by millimeter. When Khalid was no longer visible, I left. My return wouldn't be so peaceful.

MACHETE

A panel of woven palm fronds was coming loose from the front of the house. I pulled it off, set it inside, unwrapped my spare sari, and laid it on top so Mewan could lie down and then I could wrap him. Although the air was warm, a chilled dampness was creeping in. I felt nostalgia and pride for my home, inflated by the furious energy sparking from my body. I fed Mewan coconut paste, then went to the common area where the fronds were stacked up and pulled a bundle loose. This was one of the few things our unstructured village shared. Probably because they were in such abundance and almost everyone used a part of the coconut trees in one part of their life or another.

The shadows of the forest canopy looked like delirious insects dancing on the sandy ground. I knew night would be here soon, and I had to look for the calm light inside me to ground my head until I made my move.

...

Mewan was asleep; Kiyoma's mother said she would listen for his cries. I walked to where the fronds and coconuts were piled. There was a tree where the machetes hung. I ran my finger along the blades until I found the sharpest one and it drew a line of blood. I pulled it from the nail it hung on and hid it in my sari. The last slivers of light disappeared in the sky. The land was moonless, with the continuous night shadow interrupted only by the burning torches.

A different guard was there now. It didn't matter, because he wasn't going to see me. I veered into the thick trees. There wasn't a path, and the fear of stepping on an unsuspecting snake normally would have kept me out of such dense plants. I reached the back of Khalid's tent. When my fingers touched the rough fabric, I let them slide against it. I wanted to make sure I had a feeling to ground myself against, when the fury I knew was coming clouded all I could see.

My hand slipped into the fold of the tent, and I unfastened the ties. I knew Khalid's headboard would be against this area. When they were undone, I lay on my stomach, pushed the machete ahead of me under his bed, then pulled my body against the floor of the tent until I smelled the tea he was brewing. He was whispering to himself, quiet musings of his day. I peered out from behind the headboard; he was sitting in a chair, legs crossed, pawing through the booklet he had shown me the first day I'd met him. Next to that was a journal where he was ticking off items I couldn't see. I crawled out on the other side of the bed, where one of the two lamps hung. When I had my feet placed firmly on the ground, I lunged and extinguished the lamp. I knew it would have the effect of only letting him see what was next to him.

"Who's there?"

I was against the wall; I knew I had seconds until his eyes adjusted and he'd be able to see me move. He reached for something in his pocket. I wondered if he had a knife or, worse, a gun. I tightened my fingers around the handle of the machete. Khalid turned for a moment to look toward the bed. I was behind him and pulled back to avoid him feeling my breath. I reached for his shoulder, and my hand hovered, the machete raised at the level of his neck. A slight move and the blade would make contact with his throat.

"Wait ..." I only wanted him to hear my voice and know my commands would come when I was ready. I trusted the unfamiliar steady confidence coursing through my body.

"Wait for what?" He reached back and his hand brushed my sari.

I pulled the blade but didn't slice his neck. He let out an involuntary squeak.

"Where is my daughter?"

"I don't know who you are."

His tone told me he was being honest.

"Shula. I'm Shula and my daughter is—"

"Ruka." Her name confirmed his understanding. "What are you doing here? You should be attending to my good friend Mohamed."

"Your good friend Mohamed is a murderer."

"That's an accusation, which in his country would get you hanged. How did you get away? It seems improbable. You were paid so little."

"How would you know that?"

"Because I receive my share at a certain threshold," he said, "and I've received nothing."

"I want my daughter back."

"It's out of my hands."

I knew if he turned around now, I might lose my fortitude.

"Where is she?" I demanded.

"Had you stayed put, you might have run into her. I heard you were getting around town with some regularity."

"Where is she?"

"Dubai."

I let the blade slide. I knew as it cut across his neck that I was cutting mine too. A man with this much power could crush me like a mosquito.

He shrieked.

I heard stirring outside.

"I'll get her for you, for whatever … Just don't …"

I kept pulling the blade, and then it was away from his neck.

He fell to the ground.

A voice came from outside. "Is everything okay in there?"

Split

Khalid kept his promise and never breathed a word of what I had done to him. He blamed the thin red line on his neck on an accident involving a fishing line he didn't see. Two days later, I was sitting on a plane again; it wasn't lost on me that I'd gone from never leaving the bottom half of my small island nation to my third flight in the last two months.

It was a repeat from the last time I'd left Sri Lanka. A cadre of women, with hopes and dreams, glossy images of their destinations in their heads. They tried to include me in the lighthearted banter, the epic delight of what they thought was their future. Khalid was with us; I caught him stealing nervous glances in my direction. He had nothing to worry about since I always upheld my end of the deal. But it was okay that he didn't know that. Three hours into the flight, I got up from my seat, holding the backs of the others as we crisscrossed a turbulent section of sky, and walked four rows until I was next to him. He was reclined in his seat, fingers laced on his lap, a drowsy smirk on his face, the line on his neck scabbed over.

"Khalid, I'd like to talk to you." My sudden proximity startled him.

"You're going, no? This is what you wanted."

"I can't leave the airport. You'll have to retrieve my daughter for me."

He pushed the button on his armrest and the back of the seat to bring himself upright.

"What are you saying?"

"Bring her back to the airport so she can come home with me."

He shook his head, then looked around. "I can't do that, Ms. Shula. She's under contract and so are you. But I would guess Mohamed might be more amenable to letting you out of yours."

I fixated on the line across his neck.

"You're no danger to me here," he said.

"Then what? I go back and have to stay?"

"You go back and stay, but you'll know where your daughter is. You don't think you're the first one, do you? The first woman to work alongside her children? There is work to be done in Dubai, and your country is content to send its citizens in a river of supply to meet that demand."

I was going full circle but in the wrong direction. I was ending in the place I never wanted to see again. I'd brought the third egg with me. I wasn't sure if it was a good idea, but it was the only thing of value I owned, and getting out the second time would likely be even more difficult.

"Have you spoken to Mohamed?"

He seemed caught off guard by the question. "I don't remember. I speak to a lot of people. You don't have to go back to him, but you'll be homeless. I can put you to work with your daughter, if you wish."

There was a twinkle in that statement that told me he would stand to make even more money if he could place me there.

"And where is that?" I hadn't even thought to ask what she was doing when I had interrogated him.

"She picks rocks for an area where a building will go. Clearing the land. We save the most demanding work for the young."

Did he have no idea what my life was like at home?

"Then put me where she is."

He acknowledged me.

The plane landed a few hours later, and the flight attendant asked me to keep seated while the other passengers disembarked. She put her arm across the seats while she stood. It might have been a casual stance, except her painted pink fingernails dug into the seat. When the last passenger stood in the aisle, waiting to get off, she moved and forced a smile for me to exit. I didn't pay her much attention as I passed her. As I continued through the airplane door and into the long connector bridge, everything was how I remembered. One more door and I was in the airport. The carpet changed its pattern there. Four pairs of patent leather boots were lined up. As my orange flip-flops crossed the threshold, a strong hand slipped under my arm.

It was the police, and they had surrounded me. All I could see were their black vests with red stripes as they led me away. The anger that burned in me for Khalid intensified. He had to have set this up. No one else would have known I was coming, and I was traveling with a different name. The police didn't ask any questions; it was all prearranged.

"What have I done?" I knew Mohamed would charge me with many crimes. The evidence would be his word against mine, which was all the evidence the court would need.

This time I had walked into Dubai's mouth knowing I could be devoured.

COURT

After three days in a holding cell, I stood facing the judge. The black glass behind his elevated bench showed the Emirati flag, centered and garishly illuminated. The walls of the courtroom were glossy wood, inlaid with small print in Mohamed's language. Mohamed himself was on the other side of the courtroom, glaring at me. I wasn't sure if he was trying to silence me or figure out what I actually knew about his life.

The judge looked sternly at me, through gold glasses with colored lenses that made him look more like a performer than a judge. He spoke at me, but I didn't understand what he was saying. They were harsh words, and I felt as though their intention was to strip me bare.

A lawyer named Breva had been assigned to me at the last minute. She spoke my language and told me I was being charged when I met her before entering the courtroom. She was beside me now. "The judge said you have been accused of theft, abandonment of contract, and illegally leaving the country." Her breath was sweet, as if she'd eaten pineapples before she'd spoken to me. She wore a rose suit with a matching head covering and a brooch of a gold cat. "I've asked to see the contract and evidence of any theft."

"Do you know the truth?" I asked quietly.

"That's not important. You can tell it to me later."

Maybe I shouldn't trust her, I thought. She could have been another element of the system distancing me from Ruka. But if I couldn't trust her, all hope was lost.

An attendant of the court retrieved papers from the judge and handed them to Breva. There was a picture of the eggs I had taken, along with the one they had recovered from me in the airport when they'd frisked me. I also saw a photo of my fake passport from Kumzar, which I had entered the country with this time, but it clearly lacked an exit stamp and the dates didn't match my story. What they didn't have was Ousha's US passport, which was tucked away in my sari. And though it was uncomfortable, it was my solace that this might all turn out okay.

The judge said something, and Breva leaned over to me. "He's asking if there's anything you would like to say." The look on her face was discouraging me from opening my mouth.

What could I say? "I'm innocent"? They didn't ask why I had come back or why I'd done any of this.

"Tell them Mohamed killed his baby, and that's why I had to leave."

Breva froze in place, blinking repeatedly, as if she were trying to clear the information from her brain.

"There is a dead baby in his house," I said. "He killed it while I was out one day. It was why I had to leave."

She put her palm up to me. "Stop, Shula. You'll get us both in trouble. You can't accuse him of these things."

The clerk came to us and handed Breva another folder.

The judge barked and rapped his gavel.

Breva shook her head and said something to him; I knew she wasn't communicating what I had said.

He slammed the gavel again, then got up from his seat and left the room. The tension broke in the courtroom, and Mohamed and his team left through the main doors.

Breva pointed to the seat behind me, sat down, and read through the folder. I looked up at the ceiling, where I saw a depiction of a holy book, with numbers and words next to it. My mind wandered to Ruka, working in the hot sun outside. I knew they would like her, because she never complained about hard work.

The courtroom began to fill up again.

"They're offering you a deal," Breva said.

"For what?"

"They'll find you guilty of theft and illegal departure of the country and sentence you to five years of labor. But you must relinquish all your wages to Mohamed." Without missing a beat she said, "You should take it."

"But—"

"No, it's not fair. No one said our justice system is fair; it just is what it is."

The main door opened, and everyone turned. It was Ousha. It was a surprise to see her. She wore a black suit with sequined embroidery that snaked up her head covering, forming a spiral over her forehead. She looked like a sorceress. She strutted up the center aisle of the courtroom as though she were on a runway. She was a different person than the broken woman I had witnessed in Kumzar. She stood in front of the judge and waited for him to acknowledge her.

He was polite and casual with her, as though they were old friends. Mohamed watched with a pale expression, his body tilting back. I thought he might fall over. His team steadied him. Ousha's mother was behind him, and she exploded into emotion when she caught sight of her. I heard Ousha say the name "Inesh" several times. Ousha had seized control of the moment, and I felt as though we were seconds away from the courtroom exploding.

She spun around, turning her back to the judge, and pointed at Mohamed, shouting. Even Breva gasped, then turned to me. "This could be very good for you," she said. This was news I wasn't expecting.

"She has accused him of murdering her friend. She clearly knows the judge. This won't be good for him."

The judge rapped the gavel and said something.

"He's suspending the trial. You'll go into custody, and I'll come and meet with you as soon as I can." Breva picked up her bag and hightailed it out of the courtroom, with no time for me to ask questions. The police waved me toward the door, while a separate force of police stormed the courtroom and detained Mohamed.

...

They brought me to a beige room with three chairs, a table, and a coffee machine. It looked like a break room more than a holding cell. The last officer who left tipped his hat and gently closed the door. I fixed myself some coffee and waited. The lights outside the door went out, and the sounds of the courthouse dulled.

Several hours later, Breva knocked at the door. She had changed into a different suit and waved through the skinny vertical window over the doorknob. Her excited demeanor gave me pause.

Now she was inside with me. "The judge said you can go."

"Where?"

"You're done. No more charges."

"Can you help me find my daughter?"

She ignored my question, opened her folder, and set it in front of me. I couldn't read the documents inside. But there was my fake passport from Kumzar and I put it in my pocket.

"You need to sign these and then you can go."

"What about my things, the ones I had on the plane?"

She tapped the blank lines of the documents. "Shula, just be happy you're leaving."

"Do you want to know what really happened?"

She put up a hand. "No. The truth won't help anyone, because everyone here manufactures their own."

...

I exited the building. On the other side of the door was a conditional freedom. I walked along the sidewalk, thankful the sun was still blocked by the tall buildings. A void engulfed me now. My only option was to search the city on foot, looking for Ruka, and when I found her, then what? Would I work beside her, both of us enslaved, until we could save enough money to buy our way home? Minrada would never help me this time.

The door of a new white SUV opened, and Khalid stepped out. "You got lucky. Mohamed's insane wife had impeccable timing. If I didn't know better, I would've thought you two ladies were in cahoots."

What did he want from me now?

"Would you like to see your daughter?" He nervously touched his neck.

"You know where she is?" I didn't want to trust him; I didn't want anything to do with him. But what choice did I have?

"Of course." He reached inside the car, pulled out two papers with pictures stapled onto them, and thrust them at me.

They were pictures of an empty lot surrounded by orange plastic roll fencing. Ten children carted rocks and debris to an open truck bed parked on the road. Ruka was in the dress I'd made her. It was torn, though; that fabric should have lasted years, because I'd bought it with a month's worth of wages. Her skin was the color of oil; the dress was discolored by dirt; her hair, which she had grown since she was a baby, with nights of combing coconut oil through, was broken and dry, tied in a ponytail by a piece of her dress that had been sheared away. I couldn't look away from her. My baby was alive, and though she had looked better, her young body would recover.

"Take me to her."

"Of course ..." Khalid moved out of the way so I could get into the passenger seat.

We pulled away from the curb and merged with the city traffic.

"You're a very creative woman. Different from the others I've placed. Driven."

I listened; compliments didn't come from Khalid without his asking for something.

"Could I interest you in helping me with a project?"

"We only want to go home." I stressed the word "home."

"But there's so much opportunity in Dubai, a city of intense desire for everything the world has to offer."

His words meant little to me. He always talked in grand ambitions and sweeping phrases. It had dazzled me the first time we met, but I had since learned better.

"Let someone else have it. We need to get home to my son."

He reached across the console and put his hand on my thigh. "So you can spend the rest of your life in poverty? That's what you're aiming for? Look around, Shula. There's so much more for you here." His smile was crooked, just like his morals.

I didn't know how to navigate this man. He was eternally selling gold paper as the precious metal itself. I thought it might make sense to be quiet.

We arrived at the place in the pictures he had shown me. I scanned for Ruka, and then her lavender dress caught my eye. I pulled at the door handle before we stopped.

"Patience."

I ignored him and fumbled with the lock.

"Shula, you're only going to have this offer once. Leaving Dubai will be impossible without me."

He didn't know about Ousha's US passport, which I'd been able to hide. But I still had the problem of how to get Ruka back. I decided not to play it safe. "Khalid, can I please see my daughter? I'll work too, for you."

"I can get anyone to pick rocks. I need someone like Minrada."

Was that the truth? Did she work for him?

"Minrada can go back whenever she likes," Khalid said, "but she knows a good thing when it's fallen in her lap."

He moved his hand farther up my thigh. I put my hand on top of his and pressed it to stop. I kept my eyes on my daughter. My anticipation was a ball of elastics, snapping within me at each second. After Khalid unlocked the door, his head gave an urging thrust toward Ruka.

I bound out of the car minus grace. My feet dug into the firmament, kicking up the rocks that were complicit in my daughter's predicament. She didn't see me coming, because she was carrying a heavy load toward a conveyor belt that was ingesting the rocks and busting them into smaller pieces before they clanged into a metal bin.

"Ruka!" I yelled when she was within earshot. Seeing she was alive and close enough that I could soon touch her made my heart strain with affection. "Ruka, Ruka, Ruka?"

She never looked up; she kept working. When I reached her, I threw my arms around her hunched back as she heaved the rocks forward. She pulled away from me in the way an animal, intent on a destination, ignores the touch of the people who wish to show it love.

"Baby girl, put down your work for one minute. It's your mama." I pulled at the basket, and it fell, tipping over. She bent to gather the rocks, but I forced myself in front of her so her eyes met mine. I smiled and searched her eyes for an iota of recognition.

She smiled back, but in the way you smile at someone you don't know when crossing paths at night.

I looked back at Khalid. He was still in the car, the window down, watching me intently; he held his hands up as if to say, "Now what?" But my *why* was bigger than his *what*, and it always would be.

I quickly gathered the stones, put them in the basket, and walked to where the other ladies hauled their work. I caught the eye of their watcher. He was in the shadow of a building with a vacillating fan blowing over him. His sluggardly body found purpose, and he turned to Khalid and then to me. I was too far away to see his face; it was enough that he saw me and let me continue back to Ruka and help her with her labor. That day, we outworked everyone in the field. When I looked for Khalid again, he was gone; in his place was something I could not have imagined, Mohamed's car. Why was he not in custody?

NEEDLING

The sun left the sky, making it impossible to discern the chunks of earth the workers were here to clear. The man who had been sitting on the edge of the parcel, smoking as we worked, barked words into the sky and then rose. He took a wooden baton and beat a metal bell repeatedly until everyone shuffled into a ragged line and followed him to the street. Ruka mumbled something to me. Somewhere deep in my brain I knew what she was saying, like when she had toddled and babbled and my maternal translator knew the words she used. We were going "home" for the night—to rest, for food, for a shot. We might have walked a block; this part of town wasn't delineated in the neat streets of the most developed sections.

Eventually a skinny light-blue door with three locks on it rose against the dilapidated sand-color stone of the building walls. The man who led us here had the key for each of the locks. I suspected they existed more to keep what was on the other side of the door in, rather than keep the nothingness outside from entering.

He opened the door and stepped out of the way to let us file in. As we got close, the ladies in front of us were engulfed by the darkness. We followed them and were greeted by a burned tang that filled my nostrils. The smell of boiling cleaning solution. Dim light came from a line of sconces on the wall; I could see the particulates in the air swirling above them. Everywhere was the sensation of close bodies on a packed bus. Radiant heat rose from sweaty bodies and gave the air a musty remainder of the tired permutations they had worked through until exhaustion. Ruka reached back, found my hand, and squeezed it. She was scared, and though I never would tell her, so was I.

The door closed behind us; the bodies bumped and shuffled, while muffled cries and serial weeping came from another room or floor. The rank smell grew stronger, and as we inched toward the back of the house, I saw fluorescent lights blasting a dirty food preparation area with soggy vegetables and dry falafel. The man who had led us was there now, banging through a small box until he pulled out a needle and held it to the light. A murky brown solution filled the vial, and he gave the plunger a jerky press, sparking an arc of liquid from the tip and sending it to the floor. A woman stood next to him with a plate of food. The girl at the front of the line sluggishly reached for the plate, but the woman holding it pulled it back and pointed to the syringe.

The man pushed up her sleeve and plunged the needle into her arm. Her tense neck muscles slackened and her face became flaccid. The meal was given to her, and the next woman approached. I didn't want Ruka getting this shot, whatever it was. I pushed her out of the line and told her to stand in the darkness and wait for me. When I approached the man, he looked me up and down and shrugged before sending the needle into my arm. I wanted to tell him that he shouldn't do this. That the girls would work for food alone. But my mouth grew heavy and thick, and the plate of food she placed in my hands felt as though I were carrying an entire cord of wood.

The next moment, my mind and body separated. I knew what I wanted to do, but I couldn't will my body forward. I felt a hand push in the middle of my back. I picked up momentum and was able to advance into the blurry darkness. Ruka found me, her words peppering me in rapid succession.

I only processed. "Food … okay … .tired … tomorrow." They all sounded like distant lands I'd never heard of.

I felt the food in my mouth, but it was tasteless, a vague substance that landed in my stomach with an adequate thud. Ruka brushed my hair and stayed close; I felt her breath on me. I drifted while she was constant. Her voice in my ear woke me. I strained to open my eyes, and when I finally did, Ruka was there. I had found her; the perilous dreams that bounced inside my head were only half true, and I was fully grateful.

"Mama, I've come up with a way to leave."

Her eyes looked like mine felt: swollen, red, and irritated. She tapped her fingers on the wall next to where I lay. She helped me up to a sitting position and gave me sips of warm water. Floating bits that tasted like rust made it into my mouth. My body felt as though I'd been asleep for years.

"Do you see this?" Ruka took a rock from beside her and circled a point where three of the lines came together. "This is where the bus leaves from. I've heard if we pay, they'll take us out of here."

Minrada appeared in my mind, the look she had given me when the doors closed on the bus as I left without giving her payment.

"I know." The words croaked from my throat. "I know because this is how I came home."

"Then we can do it again." She looked hopeful, the way children look when all the turmoil that surrounds their idea isn't visible to them.

"It's possible, maybe." I was too lethargic to explain what I'd been through.

"They said a new bus goes in two months."

"They?" Who were these people who had told her?

"One of the other ladies who works in the fields with me. She knows things the others don't. Secrets about how it all works."

"It?"

"Here. This place. Dubai."

Two months seemed excessive. "Let's go. Time to work," a voice commanded us.

Ruka stood up and pulled my arm. When we stepped outside, the sunlight burned the remaining fog from my brain. "Have they paid you yet?"

"No. They said they would pay us at the end of the month."

"And what about a passport?"

"The book they gave us when we came?" I noticed a twitch in the corner of her mouth, where she used to half smile. The injections.

"Yes."

"I don't remember. I don't remember much."

We followed the line, but it wasn't going back to the place where we were yesterday.

About five people ahead of us in the line, a woman, darker than me, with a yellow dress and a headband holding back her wiry black hair, bolted. She lost her shoes a few steps into her escape. It didn't slow her velocity as she slipped between condensing walls of stone. The man didn't look back; if he had, I wasn't convinced he would have made a chase of her. Physical force wasn't what was holding anyone in this line.

We arrived at the ground level of a partially constructed tower. I couldn't get perspective of the height other than the open top, where steel rods shot out of the concrete toward the sky and disappeared into clouds. The line moved into an open elevator with flimsy rope railings that delivered us onto a gusty platform. The views expanded over the city. A few of us tottered and pulled at our clothes to steady ourselves. From the platform, girders crisscrossed to form the base of a floor. The man handed us each a mop and pointed to the sand and bird droppings on the beams.

He took out his phone and immersed himself in it.

We all exchanged looks. I knew with the drugs still floating in my blood that I shouldn't step out over open spaces; one misstep would mean death. Ruka put one of her bare feet in front of her. There were harnesses hanging on the wall next to the man who had brought us here. I whizzed past him and retrieved one; it was connected to a cable above. A gust of hot wind surged between the open spaces and pushed me back on my heels. Ruka was off the platform, her arms out, turning her into a human letter T to balance against the wind. I didn't want to call her and have her turn around. In my brain, I was proud she was pushing forward through this terrible situation of dangerous and frightening events. My heart pumped gallons of anxiety throughout me, thinking of where this might lead her.

I stepped to the edge of the platform, which I didn't dare leave; I still felt my body swaying.

"Ruka, honey, turn around slowly. I have something you should put on."

She kept her balance and took a step toward me, I pulled some slack in the metal rope, which wove through the back of the vest and disappeared into a bank of reels on the other end of the rack of vests.

Ruka slipped one arm through and then the second. One of girls behind her reached for something that wasn't there. The girl's foot hovered in the air. I imagined, somewhere under layers of manufactured brain chemistry, her brain knew something wasn't right. But when she retrieved the something, then fell out of sight, she did it with a show of contentment.

"What is it, Mama?" Ruka asked.

She turned toward the air, where the innocent girl, who could have been her, was, seconds before. Ruka, however, had missed that horror and was better for it.

One of the other women gave her a mop; a few followed her and put on the safety vests. They looked like a pack of impoverished marionettes.

With the long eye of the horizon and pieces of the building to hide behind, I eventually lost sight of Ruka.

A cloud of smoke surrounded me, and the man pushed my shoulder. "You. There." He cast his hand lazily in the direction of a beam caked with bird feces.

"I'm not feeling balanced from my shot last night. I can't go. I might fall, like …" I didn't even know the girl's name.

"Doesn't matter. You fall, your fault. Go now or else." His Sinhala was broken; he knew just enough to direct us.

Or else what? I wondered. He didn't seem enthused enough to even smoke his cigarettes; I couldn't imagine him having to deal with a defiant woman. As I suspected, he returned to his chair and didn't bother me further.

Only a few minutes had passed, and then there was fearful yelling, resting on top of the constant noise of the wind. I stood up and looked out. Some of the girls were pointing; a few were moving in that direction, while the rest had a hypnotized glaze about them. When I saw the source of the commotion, my heart fell through the stories below. Ruka was hanging over an expanse facing down, her body straining against the orange vest that was tethering her to this life. She had frozen, the look on her face vacant. I'd seen her do this once when she unexpectedly had come face-to-face with a mother elephant while we were walking in the forest. She didn't move, and she couldn't move then, as I calmly had called for her to back away from the elephant. There was no backing away this time. I followed the rope up to the bank of pulleys and looked for a way to get to it. Maybe I could reel her in. The elevator, which had left the platform, looked as though it went higher than where I stood. I pressed the button in the metal box to call it and heard it churning its way to me. I kept looking at Ruka. Tears were coming from her eyes now, her face contorted. The elevator arrived. I was on it and ascending to the next level of beams. When I pressed the red button to stop the elevator, the adrenaline running through me had flushed away the fogginess, and I was at the spools of thick wires, trying to determine which one was attached to Ruka. Three wooden planks were laid out in front of them, and I felt myself lower as the wood bent under my soles. The wind turned Ruka into a pendulum. I followed the line up until I was looking at the reel. I pressed the button on the side of it, and it let her down. She screamed as she dropped to the next level. I pulled my finger away, then pushed the other button. The swing and the movement got her close enough to the platform so someone could grab her.

"Please, someone." The other women looked at me, then turned back to cleaning. "Can someone get my daughter? Pull her to the platform?"

The man stood up and shushed me. He grabbed Ruka when she got close to him, then yanked her down to the platform. He went back to his seat and picked up his cigarette from the ground.

When I got to Ruka, I put my arms around her and kissed her head. Then I looked up; in the distance over the low-rise buildings, I saw the formation of the Palm Jumeriah, where Mohamed lived.

The man gestured for us to get back to work. Ruka looked up at me and I shook my head. "You're not going back out there." I pulled her to face me and unzipped her vest, and then we casually walked to the elevator. Ruka was still young enough that she thought I had more influence on the world than I actually did.

"You can't." The man's tone was mellow, and he was half out of his chair as we passed out of sight.

"Where will we go?" Ruka asked.

"I know someone." I was thinking of Minrada. What kind of groveling would I have to do to get her to help me again? She was a woman of connections and profit. So I would have to make it worth it for her to trust me again.

From up above, the walk looked doable, but as we trudged on, trying to stay in the shade of the buildings, I realized how far we might have to go. I had some Sri

Lankan money with me, which I knew was worthless here, but I offered it to a vendor on the street who was selling screw-cap bubbly water for ten dinars. He looked at Ruka and me, took my money, and waved me on. I let Ruka have the first sip. "Don't spill any. We won't likely have someone so generous at the next stop."

It was night before we reached the first bridge into the complex. I had Ousha's passport which showed this as my residence. They stopped us at the entrance, looked for less than a second at it, then let us pass. I hoped Minrada would be under the bridge. And if I could be brave again to get her what she wanted, she might help us.

THE BOOK OF MOHAMED

Ruka coughed as we walked along the red path in the center of the island. At first I thought it was the salty air from the water blowing through that was catching in her lungs. Light in Dubai was ever present; the glass buildings, water, and bulbs turned the city into a crater of mirrors. I missed the quiet darkness of my home, where I could look up and be peppered by the intensity of the starlight. I pulled Ruka closer to me and rubbed her arm.

She looked up at me. "I'm thirsty."

On either side of us, restaurants were filled with well-dressed patrons enjoying meals, smoking hookahs, and laughing. Some of their jewels looked like lights themselves. My stomach cried out for the plates of succulent meats and sugary delights. I caught the eye of one man; his face was full of all that was good. He was handsome, scrubbed clean, and he was chewing. He held a light-green glass with olives bobbing in it. He watched us; at first I thought he might be able to help me, but then he scoffed and used his eyes to direct the woman sitting across from him. She turned and looked, made a face, then laid her hand on top of his.

Ruka didn't see it; it was enough to be poor in a land of wealth, but to suffer the embarrassments of that poverty could tear a tender soul apart quicker than the pain of hunger.

There was a water fountain ahead, and Ruka ran to it and drank, filling her empty stomach. Water dribbled from her chin and made a butterfly shape on her dress. I rubbed circles on her back as she gulped.

"Where are we going? It's so far." She wiped her mouth. "We're very close."

She let me have a few sips, then spent the next few minutes lapping up the water. The injection made me feel as though moisture wicked away from me; I tried to distance myself from how she might have felt.

Ruka held her belly the way a pregnant woman might, and we walked away. There was something about being full, even if it was only with water, that made the stares sting less. A grand hotel with a wall of lights and screens flashed the time as 10:13, and the coolness of the desert night had set in. For a moment, I wished to be back in Mohamed's house in my cozy room. I pulled Ruka in closer. The water had lightened her mood; she'd skip and hum some of the songs that were common in our village.

"Do you remember your brother's favorite song? '*Hinchi Pinchi Hawa*'?"

She giggled, then hummed it, winding through the high notes, then faking sadness with the low notes. When she was done, she asked, "Do you think Mewan misses me as much as I miss him?"

"I'm sure of it." I tapped her shoulder. "Look there." The next street was only a hundred paces ahead of us. "That's where we're going. You must be very quiet and follow me. No complaints, okay?"

Nodding, Ruka picked up the pace. The bottoms of my sandals had worn thin, and the bones in my feet hurt from walking, but I matched her. There was no traffic on the bridge, and the streetlights made the water underneath complete darkness. We crossed and went down the slope, as I had the first time I'd met Minrada here and waded into the water. The tide was higher this time, and the water came above Ruka's waist, but she said nothing and only gripped my hand tightly. She had avoided the shore since the great wave, treating it like a vicious dog.

"Hello?" I called into the darkness when we emerged from the water.

I could see some light now as we got close. Two bats darted in ragged lines in front of us.

"They …" Ruka took cover.

"Fruit bats. They aren't interested in you." It was a voice I recognized. "I'd heard you showed up in one of the work houses downtown. Did it make you appreciate where you were before?" Minrada's words were caustic as she emerged from the shadows, adjusting her clothes. A figure scurried deeper into the night behind her. "I think you owe me something." Her hand was outstretched, palm open.

"I'm sorry … It was a situation … I didn't …" The words I had planned so carefully had abandoned me.

"No, no. I know you will make amends. Find a way into the house to retrieve the book."

She couldn't be serious. "But I don't work there anymore. I don't have access. He'll never let me in."

"Ousha took care of all that, no? When she dropped into your hearing?" She cackled, then couldn't catch her breath. She doubled over and ended her fit with a huge cough. "Oh, what I would have done to trade places with you. He must have wet himself when he saw the woman who knew all his secrets tear open his privacy. She wrecked him with that, you know. Split him wide. I wouldn't be surprised if he jumped off one of those towers." She looked toward the mainland.

I covered Ruka's ears.

"There isn't a—"

Minrada cut me off and held up a finger. "There is always a way. And I'm not done with him, because behind Mohamed is a string of gems I intend to collect. He's one little piece of shit propped up by his father. But the men he's been with … Ooooouuuee, it's like someone took me to the racetrack and gave me all the winners to bet on in advance." She leaned into me and clenched her fist. "But I need that book. And you're just the person who can get it."

Minrada pulled a pack of cigarettes from her dress, lit one, and examined the fiery orange tip. "I always knew you would be an asset. And if you want, your daughter can stay with me. I'll keep her busy." The smoke curled around her smile, and I knew I was deeper into this than I ever wanted to be.

…

When I reached Mohamed's house, only the lights in the driveway were on and his car was in the driveway. I crept between the two houses until I stood before the door that led to the utility hallway. What I'd remembered from being on the other side of it was that any time it was opened it would catch and have to be pulled hard or it wouldn't fully latch closed. I tapped the bottom of the door to scare off any scorpions, then slid my fingers into the space between the bottom of the door and the concrete slab. Bits of stone jabbed under my nails, but I forced my fingers forward to get a grip on the door. When the first joints of my fingers bent at the other side, I pulled. The door moved. I pulled harder; it let loose, and I tumbled backward, the door flying open and hitting the bushes behind it. Inside, the hallway was dark, with a lingering smell of rot and bleach mixed together. The light from the outside went only a meter in. My footsteps were relying on memory. I reached the ladder and heard susurrant words. The darkness and closed quarters made it difficult to figure out where the man was who spoke them.

Ever so quietly, I climbed the ladder. Ruka was with Minrada, and I had something to find. I couldn't spend time righting the misdeeds of Mohamed. He would always operate at a level above the law and morality, and his punishment wouldn't be from the authorities but from the gods themselves. Once I reached the top of the ladder, I crawled until I reached the door to Mohamed's room. There was no light from the other side. He could have been sleeping; I had no way to know what was over there. I was sure if I opened the door and he woke up, he would kill me. I began to sweat and feel closed in; my hand was on the knob to open the door, but my hand wouldn't obey. I clenched my teeth to keep them from chattering, then turned the knob and pulled the door open. The house smelled like a mixture of thick dust and unwashed clothes. I listened for anything. Breathing, clothing against leather, even the tick of a watch. Nothing. I stepped in; a sliver of light came through the curtains from the streetlights. I knew where the couch was, and under the middle cushion was the compartment that held the book. My leg struck a table, creating an echoing bang. I froze. If anyone was in the room, they would be awake now. I held my breath, trying to detect motion. The light flickered from the outside, the wind moving the trees between the house and the streetlights. My legs moved again, and then my hand was in the compartment until I felt the texture of the cover I had remembered. I opened the book and felt the sticky clear plastic that covered each of the photos.

A thud outside the door in the hallway. The sound of a heavy load of cloth being dropped. Quickly I was back in the utility space and closed the door behind me. I put the book under my arm and descended the ladder with my left arm. When my foot touched the floor, I thought of Maryam on the other side of the wall. I knew Mohamed would never go into my room to retrieve her, if he had even come back. Her sweet face tugged at my heart, the way her lips cooed at me. I hope she had taken all the love I had poured into her during her brief stay with me.

I felt my way back to the utility door and pushed it open. I thought words were coming from behind me. Maybe instead it was the creak of the door or the wind blowing the neighbors' yacht into the mooring posts. My mind was jumbled with fear, and I knew not to trust all the things it told me.

"Help." The word was distinct, crisp. It was him, the man I'd heard earlier.

I could run away from this house forever, leaving the nightmare of it behind, back to my Ruka and then my home. Or I could stay and delay the Nirvana I was on the precipice of achieving and help whoever was behind this voice.

"Please, it's me." His voice reminded me of the way the people in my village sounded when they'd coughed for months from tuberculosis.

I set the album against the doorframe and let the darkness envelop me. The decision to walk into the darkness this time wasn't frightening. I met the junction where the hallway narrowed and went behind my room. I paused. I could see nothing with my eyes, but everything with my mind. When I reached him, there was the smell of human excrement and filth, but I held my mind above it. His hand touched me first. The rough, dry fingertips. I met him with my hands, and he led me to his restraint: a single shackle around his ankle. My fingers felt the keyhole.

"I don't have the key," I said.

He didn't respond. I patted his greasy hair and climbed the ladder to Mohamed's room. The booming in my head from my heartbeat made it hard to listen for other noises. I went through the hidden door and flicked lamps on. Somewhere in the base of my skull rose a power from knowing what Mohamed had done, that whatever weapons he wielded now would slice back at him. The room looked ransacked. His expensive books were pulled off the walls; all the cabinets were open; and the table I had run into was oddly out of place. I pressed my ear to the door to the hallway before I opened it. Mohamed was lying on the floor and was breathing, a syringe next to him. The hallway had dirty dishes piled up in it with rotting food. I passed them, zooming from room to room, searching for keys. The formal dining room was the only room that had kept its composure. Full place settings, a vase of fake flowers in the middle of the table, dim lights. When I stood and looked into that room, I could imagine dinner guests were five minutes away, I was behind the wall preparing Maryam to be quiet and ferrying trays of succulent dishes from the kitchen. I let those thoughts go; they were from a past that never would manifest again. I rounded the corner to the kitchen and clenched my teeth as I pushed the door open. My vision zoomed into the cabinet where the safe was hidden. It was open, as was the safe door. Inside was my passport. I thanked the gods; I'd received my reward for coming back to help the shackled man. I took my passport and the few dinar bills next to it. I could use these to get Ruka out of the country. Then I opened drawers, looking for keys. Where would Mohamed keep them?

I went to the laundry room. My body wanted to open the door to my old room, but I knew that was a door to a piece of my life that should always stay closed. The storage crates in the laundry that normally neatly hid the door were tipped over, and my first step in crunched over their contents. The door was haphazardly boarded with strips of wood and random nails.

I didn't want to go past Mohamed again, even if he was passed out, but I had no choice.

I stood over him, looking at the man I was so impressed with upon first meeting. Now he was a collapsed soul under the weight of his excess. There was a bulge in his wrinkled blue pocket. I knelt, waved my hand over his face, and snapped. No response. I pushed my fingers in and found his leather wallet. I opened it and searched through the thick layer of dinars, credit cards, and his government identification. A glimmer at the bottom of the bills. A key. I pulled them all out, and they fell across his stomach. It was half the size of a normal key. I thought about the mini keyholes all around his room; I bet the key matched those and the shackle too. I took the key and the bills. Mohamed hadn't paid me in full, I rationalized.

I was in the darkness again, my mind filing in the blanks of what I couldn't see. Inesh walked with me the whole way, his eyes coveting the key that would have been his freedom if someone had found him earlier.

"I think I have the key," I told the young man.

I was right, and it unlocked the restraint. I helped him stand. He was weak and leaned heavily on me, limping to the door. When we were outside, the album under my arm, I closed the door to contain the evil in the house. He pressed his back against the house; it was the first time I could see him. He was very young, a teenager from my country; his face was sunken, his lips cracked.

"Here." I directed him to the hose spigot so he could drink fresh water. "I don't know what I can do for you. I'm escaping myself."

When he came up from drinking, he pushed his hand toward me. "It's my punishment for who I am. You shouldn't have saved me."

How could he think for a moment this was his fault?

"This ogre has beaten us both down," I said. "Our situation tells us only of him and nothing of ourselves."

"What do I owe you?"

I handed him the dinars I had taken from Mohamed. "Only that you get someplace safe." I touched his face, then fled. I walked quickly down the empty streets; it must have been early morning now. A golf cart appeared behind me, one of the community security staff. I wouldn't turn around, not now. The guard yelled something I didn't understand.

I pulled out Ousha's passport and held it up so he could see I was a US citizen. He sped past me and waved.

Under the bridge, I went to the board that Minrada had moved last time and knocked on it. She slid the board open and appeared. "Your daughter is sleeping." Her eyes were fixed on the album. "Let me see it."

I didn't give it to her; it was my only power, the way I would make Minrada arrange passage for us.

"Let me see Ruka," I said.

"It's your choice, but she needs her sleep. Come look."

I pulled myself into the space. Minrada cast a light in her direction. "You see?"

Ruka's dreams were animating her sleep, but she was as Minrada had said.

"You can sleep too." Her eyes returned to the album. "I won't mislead you—I do have one more thing I need from you."

No reaction was always the best stance with Minrada. She would seize on the smallest expression and use it to her advantage.

"I need you to identify the men who went to Mohamed's house to do the unspeakable acts."

I dug my nails into my hand; the pain kept the rest of my body still.

"The time you were there, the men coming and going, the violence. There is a case against these men and the judge will want to hear your testimony. He'll especially want to hear it from two unrelated people."

"They won't believe me, and those poor men, why? Plus, it will implicate your husband."

It was the first time I'd seen Minrada's jovial sarcasm vanish. The tight noose she always used to wrangle conversations lay shredded at her feet.

I opened the book to the page of her husband and handed it to her. She looked over it. It was a solitary picture of him, smirking and playful. He was the color of lightly toasted coconut; his long fingers held his drink. The starched collar of his white cotton shirt paralleled the strong line of his jaw. Nothing in the picture gave away his location or intentions.

"This doesn't mean anything." Her tone was defensive.

I knew different, but didn't care enough to argue the point. She had what she'd asked for.

She slammed the book shut; a few bodies around us rustled in response. The look on her face was the look of my mother when my father had died. Heartbreak.

"The feeling will pass. You will go on," I offered.

"But his feelings won't pass. He always said he loved me."

"You deal in secrets all the time. Didn't you think others do the same? There are secrets, and there is love and sometimes they occupy two parallel places."

Minrada set the album down, opened a blanket, and invited me to lie next to her.

. . .

Water was everywhere. Soaking my clothes and invading my mouth. The wave would come next. An ominous specter behind me that I couldn't see. The cries of worry rose. My shoulders shook. "Mama, wake up."

I opened my eyes and sat up. Adjusting to the darkness, I pulled my hand to wipe water off my face. My hand was wet; my clothes were wet.

"Mama, the water." Ruka's voice was panicked, and she clung to me.

"Minrada?"

There was splashing but no answer. I knew the opening we had come through was only a meter from where we slept. I tried to keep calm and orient myself. I crawled over the space, my fingers went down into the water until I felt the board. I strained to move it, but it wouldn't budge. Maybe I had the wrong board. I went beyond it, I was sure I was too far now, and then my hand touched the wet stone of the connection where the bridge met the land.

Where was everyone?

"Mama, the water is getting higher."

I felt the water at my chest.

The bridge arched over the canal. We were at the bottom; if we could get out of here, maybe we could move to higher ground. I touched the stone once more, pointed my head in the opposite direction, took Ruka's hand, and crawled. As we moved higher, we saw waving lights and finally reached the top. A few people were huddled around an opening that looked through to the water below.

"Can you swim?" one of the men asked us.

I nodded.

"It's still rising," he said. "You might want to go. But the police are waiting for us at the shore. They flooded the canals to get us out. Someone must have complained."

"Let's go." Ruka was pulling at me.

"No, we'll be arrested."

"But if the water reaches any higher, the current will make it hard to swim out. It's a wager," the man said.

I appreciated his experienced voice. My mind flipped through our options. In the few seconds I had to make this decision for our lives, I tried to grasp what the outcomes of those decisions might look like. Water had taken everything from us in the past. I saw Pramith standing in front of our neat home, with a vegetable garden in front of it and a goat. In the next thought I saw the broken power line that lay across a washed-away piece of earth. I decided I could work through anything if I was alive. The space was only big enough for one person at a time to jump through, and the water wasn't far away now.

"I'll jump first," I told Ruka. "Then you come right away."

"Yes, Mama."

I fit my legs through and let my body fall. When I submerged into the water, I remembered the passports I had in my pockets. I kicked my legs and felt around for them. They stuck with me, a good omen. There was a spotlight on me, the light making it impossible to see up to the bottom of the dark bridge. When Ruka splashed down next to me, she quickly came to the surface. She was a strong swimmer; I knew she would have no problem making it to shore. We swam toward the light because we didn't have a choice. Our feet touched the sand, and before we were even clear of the canal, strong hands grasped our arms, forcing us into submission with a group of others who must have spent the night with us under the bridge.

Minrada wasn't there. Had she escaped some other way?

The spotlight was fixed on where we had come from. Three more bodies dropped into the water, and the police retrieved them.

Ruka huddled into me, shivering, half from fear and half from being soaked. "What will they do with us?" she asked.

"I don't know, but ..." I put my hand to her ear so only she could hear me. "You will take my name, and I'll take the name Ousha. Those are the documents I have."

The police came to us and tapped all the men on the head to stand up. Then they led them up the shore and away, beyond where I could see. Once they were gone, they had us stand and led us to the roadway. The homeowners stood like an audience waiting for the first act to arrive. The police roughly directed us to stand in a line.

One by one, the homeowners pointed at us. The police nudged the first few forward, and the women and young girls walked with them.

A woman, whose face was covered, pointed to me, then moved her finger back and forth to signal Ruka too. I took Ruka's hand and stepped forward. We followed her to the back of the crowd. The woman opened her purse and pulled out what would have been two years of wages for me and put it in another woman's hand, whose head also was covered. When I passed her, I kept my face on the back of my new master's head.

"Don't forget what you owe me." I turned to see Minrada smiling at me.

ENSLAVED?

I realized Dubai was a city where people like me were in a circle they could never really leave.

There was one apartment building at the end of Al Hilali. We approached the main doors to the lobby, and the woman we'd been following turned to us and pointed to a small pathway. There was a sign written in Sinhala and a language I didn't recognize that read, SERVICE ENTRANCE.

"I am Fata. You go to floor ten."

We stepped off the elevator, and Fata stood in front of open double doors flanked by two lion statues. Inside, the brown-quartz streaks through the floor tile looked like a crooked path. Fata didn't stay within them; instead, she gestured broadly and her presence owned the house.

"The main reception," she said. The round room we were in had a round brown leather couch and glass threads of bubbled amber glass, lit from the inside, flowing up and connecting into the light fixture in the ceiling.

Fata walked through an archway deeper into the apartment. The hallway widened, its walls covered with pictures of a family: a husband and wife and two children. We hadn't seen Fata's face yet, but I assumed it was her in the photo. There were several doors farther down the hall, and I spotted a bright open living space with couches, chairs, and thick rugs. The coloring in the quartz was deeper here, and it gleamed from the sun through the windows, coming up from behind the skyline. The views over the water made me want to take a seat and watch.

"I need someone to keep the house. Cleaning mostly. As you can see, we like everything to be perfect."

Ruka elbowed me. "How does she speak our language?"

"Nothing more than study." Fata came to Ruka and bent down to her. "My oldest is your age. You two will get along." It sounded more like a command than the sweet musing it was supposed to be. "What is your name?"

"Ruka."

Fata rubbed her head. I imagined her smiling behind her covering.

I was having flashbacks to my first day with Mohamed. He had seemed so kind, their family so together. What horrors would this woman bring upon us?

"I'm Shula, her mother."

Fata nodded. "There will be other jobs, like watching my daughters. They're five and eight. They'll be back in a few hours. Your room is at the end of the hall through the laundry. I was only expecting one of you, so I'll need to order a uniform for Ruka." She sent us off with a wave.

The last door was actually the entrance to the master bedroom. The door to the left, however, led to a laundry room. Unwashed clothes were everywhere in piles, and at the other end of the room was a door. I pushed the switch. The room felt like a leftover piece of the building. We took three steps into the room before we were confronted with a support column wider than the two of us standing side by side. To the right of it was a cutout where a mattress squeezed between the two walls. The sheets were half on. Ruka and I moved around the column; there was a second mattress on the floor, more piles of clothes, and then another cutout in the wall closed off by a glass door. I saw a toilet, along with a hose for a shower. The floor and walls had been tiled. A fan was running overhead. It was more than we had back home.

"There's a lot for us to do," I told Ruka. "Let's get these sheets washed and our beds put together so at the end of the day we'll have a nice place to sleep."

"How long are we staying here?" I wasn't sure if Ruka was asking because she wanted to stay or because she was anxious to move on.

"I don't know. I still have these." I pulled the wet passports from my dress.

In the pile were uniforms that fit me. Ruka found a pajama set with yellow and purple fairies on it. We washed and ironed until the clothes were in neatly folded stacks on the shelves above the washer and dryers and laid out over the first mattress, which was now neatly made up with pink floral sheets.

The clock in the laundry room read 8:30 p.m. We had worked for more than twelve hours in the windowless rooms, with only water to drink from the laundry sink.

"We have to be careful when we go out there. Make sure we don't disrupt their lives."

Ruka's left eye twitched. Although she hadn't received a shot in over two days, there was still a residual effect. I opened the door slowly; a young girl raced by, then slammed the door to her room. Smells of their dinner clawed at my stomach. We each carried a completed set of laundry; I wore an ill-fitting uniform. Fata was sitting in the living room watching television next to her husband, who turned when he heard us. I recognized him from Mohamed's house; he was his assistant, Jaseem. I didn't want to see him as an extension of Mohamed and what he represented, but my mind made disassociation impossible and made me feel like running away.

He said something to Fata, who raised her voice slightly. "The house is yours to find your way. No place is off limits."

Ruka and I held the children's clothes. I knocked on the doors and we entered the rooms. The older of the two girls looked at us for a moment, then returned to reading her book. I searched through her closet and drawers until I found the correct place to put the clothes.

When we lay in bed that night, before sleep could claim us, I wondered about the young man I helped out of Mohamed's house, and then if where we were right now was the life Khalid had shown us in the shiny laminated brochure.

...

Ferial was smaller than most five-year-olds I knew, but she was bright with energy. Her sister Raneen's eyes had deep circles, her hair was brittle, and her skin had a sickly pallor. She plodded through her day. I asked them what they wanted to eat as they sat at the kitchen table facing us. They looked at each other and shrugged.

Ruka took this as an invitation to entertain. She mimed out the options as I named them, making the girls break into laughter. They settled on poached eggs over toast.

When Fata appeared in the kitchen, Ruka quickly set a cup of tea in front of her with a sugar bowl as we had discussed the night before.

"Thank you, Ruka. Can I have the same breakfast as my girls, please?"

I cracked two more eggs into the boiling water.

"When the girls come home from school today, please take them to the park."

In my mind, Minrada was the first thing I saw, trying to get all the women to work her agenda.

"Yes." I knew that was the response all employers wanted to hear.

"Is there anything else you would like us to do today?" I pulled an egg from the water, put it atop a piece of toast on the pat of butter, then sprinkled some sugar over it.

"You're off to a wonderful start."

...

The girls arrived home from school at four and dropped their bags. I fed them a small bowl of rice each. When they were done, they stood at the door and waited with their trainers on.

As we walked down the street, I knew it would be hard for Ruka not to play on the swings at the park. I decided to see what would happen if I just let her go. In her fairy pajamas, she stuck out from the other kids in their school uniforms.

We were two houses away from the park when I heard tires slow and music from inside a car. "Shula."

It seemed I was under constant surveillance in this neighborhood. It was Khalid in the vehicle that picked me up from the courthouse.

"You landed in a good place." He raised his eyebrows and stuck his head out the window a bit to feign looking around.

I acknowledged him and kept my pace.

"It's too bad Minrada is still around, though. You know she'll hound you until you pay her back for her last favor."

What did he know of Minrada? He said nothing I was interested in replying to.

Slowly he rolled alongside me in his car. "You know, Dubai is like a big family. Everyone is tied into each other's business. Try not to make too many people angry while you're here and you'll be fine."

The three girls were at the park now; I saw a cluster of other children as well.

I faced him. "What do you want from me?"

Khalid grinned. "Ah, there's my feisty Shula. I want to know what's in that book you gave Minrada. She's holding it tightly. I know she always likes to have a few more secrets than the next person. But she snapped at me when I asked to look. There must be something very valuable in there."

I knew precisely why she wouldn't want anyone to see that book; a picture of her husband was in there.

"It's a bunch of faces. Everyone knows"—I looked up and down the street to make sure no one was nearby—"Mohamed had many men."

Khalid seemed somewhat satisfied by my response. "He's unpredictable, among many undesirable traits," he said. "I know you went back into his house. If I were you, I would steer very clear of him." He put his window up, then back down again. "If there's anything you think would be helpful to me, you know I'm the one who'll be able to get you and your daughter home eventually."

He dangled the word "eventually" in front of me. I was in front of the park now; the other nannies were looking at me as if I'd risen from the dead. I headed toward them.

"I thought you'd gone home?" one of them said.

"No, it didn't work out. I just switched families. Have you seen Minrada?"

They all shook their heads. The same young Indian woman responded, "No one has seen her for a few days. It's been quiet."

They all chuckled at the dig.

"You now have these three girls? That one looks more like you." The Indian woman tapped her arm. I knew she was referring to her skin color. Ruka and I were exactly the same tone. She also had my wide and perfectly set teeth, which our village doctor had marveled over.

"Yes, three girls." I broke from the group and went to push Ferial in the swing. Ruka and Raneen had made an immediate connection and were sitting on a bench using their hands to talk to each other. As soon as the other nannies heard Ruka speaking Sinhala, they'd know for sure she was my daughter. Even so, I felt it was better to tell them nothing. Each piece of news to them was like a tasty morsel they gobbled, and then they'd beg for more.

NEIGHBORLY FRIENDS

A week passed, and it was beginning to feel like I had moved to a new neighborhood. Khalid and Minrada hadn't resurfaced. If Mohamed came out of his house, it wasn't when I was on the street, and Fata was kind and happy to let me run her household the best way I knew how. She was insistent on cooking dinner each night for the family, and she always made enough for Ruka and me, which we took to our rooms and enjoyed after we had cleaned the dinner dishes and set up for the next morning.

When we opened the door from our daily trip to the park, the girls kicked off their shoes and burst into the apartment. Female voices came from the kitchen. I walked through the main reception and living room and turned left into the kitchen. A woman's back was facing me, and I could see Fata's face. They were drinking tea and eating sweets.

"Did the girls have fun at the park?" Fata asked.

"Yes. Can I get you anything?"

"Would you mind chopping those vegetables?" Fata never asked me to help with dinner, but I was happy to.

The woman sitting with her twisted toward me. "Shula?"

My first instinct was to run, but there was nowhere to go. It was Ousha.

"I didn't know you worked here. I thought you …"

Fata's eyes bounced between Ousha and me.

"Left? No."

Apparently, Fata didn't know I had worked for her, and I didn't want her to think I was a problem.

"I had to come back," I said matter-of-factly.

"What a coincidence. Do you know Mohamed too?" Fata asked.

I didn't know what to say; I wanted Ousha to answer that question.

Ousha blinked in rapid succession, tightened her lips, and barely moved her head.

"Why don't you come sit down?" Fata asked.

…

Time stood still as I relived the journey home and then back again. Fata knew about the court date where Ousha had come; it sounded as though it was a bit of epic lore already. They told me that Mohamed's father had gone straight to the sheikh, who had ordered Mohamed's release.

"There is no justice for a man like Mohamed," Ousha added.

I left out the terror Mohamed had sewn into my life, as well as the bit about entering his house and finding him drugged up on the floor.

Fata glided through the kitchen and refreshed our tea. Ousha didn't seem to notice the glaring breach of protocol when Fata served me.

"And what has your father done about all this?" Fata asked.

"He retired from Mohamed's father's company as this all came to light," Ousha said. "But with the marriage, there's a whole ball of twine to unwind. It helps that I'm not Muslim; I get a bit of a pass for being estranged from him."

She seemed like a different person, the weight of the onerous marriage taken from her. I was delighted to hear that Ousha, through the traditional mores of Dubai, hadn't been forced to return to him and she could escape the deep rut that centuries of tradition had dug.

Dwehlli was walking in circles in the walled-off empty adjacent lot to our house. She dragged a stick through the sand next to her and was repeating a phrase in a language I didn't understand. There was a cut-through in the walls between the lot our house sat on and the next. I stood in it and watched her. When she noticed me, she called me over.

"Shula, find your own stick and walk with me," she said.

I was no more than ten. The earth where she walked looked like chickens had pecked it. Dwehlli's stick had drawn spirals, and she expertly stepped between them, careful not to disturb the steady lines.

"What are you drawing?" I was looking for a picture in it.

"It's a meditation. But come draw your own circle. Only one's mind can understand what it creates."

I mimicked Dwehlli, because to me she was a divine incantation brought up by this place, with the breath of the spirit animating her. My stick dropped into the soft ground and trailed my path, marking where I wandered. My initial steps were an aimless journey through the lot. I kept my eyes open to make sure I didn't trip over an upturned stone or the stem of a barky green plant. Dwehlli's eyes were closed, yet the path she blazed was perfectly symmetrical.

I closed my eyes and concentrated. My parents' words bounced in my head; the delights I chased ran before me in sparks, each one encouraging me to follow. Then toys covering my room and bed. The pitcher of water that sat next to my bed emitting a fresh scent. I felt my body lose its center and list, wandering in a jerky path. I listened for Dwehlli, but her path was silent to me, and then I caught the breeze, just over my ear, the high vibratory hum. It lulled me into a trance, and the spiral I was trying to imagine unwound and became a straight path with two white chalk lines on either side, outlining it in soft suggestion. Darkness was on both sides, not frightening, like when one walks into the forest at night, where things unknown are watching. Instead, it was the light which came from the known, inside of me, emanating from my chest, illuminating the path ahead. My feet stayed in the lines with no effort. I was lost in there for days or years or maybe a few lifetimes; it was forever in the moment of each second.

"Shula, open your eyes. See what you have done." Dwellhi's voice called to me, and I had the strangest feeling she was acting as a vicar of the place I was immersed in, trying to urge me forward into a particular form.

When I was ready and the chalk lines ended, I stood before the widest expanse. It was like looking out into the ocean on a windless day with a the horizon that goes on forever.

"Put down your stick." Dwellhi had laid her stick against the wall, near the entrance. She always used her whole hand to direct my attention to things. "Look at your spiral."

There was a line that looked like a small child had tried to write her name, and then it crossed over one of Dwehlli's lines. From there it arced until symmetry took hold and my own spiral emerged.

"You see where you made that transition? I'm sure you know when that was. You felt it."

"Yes. Why did I cross your line?"

"Because we have the power to nudge each other into helpful or unhelpful thoughts. The trail of what we have left behind us continues to do the good work of the intention it was formed with. Your past is as powerful as your present."

There was a cadence to the conversation, which felt like sisterhood. Fata and Ousha looked at me like they wanted more.

"How did you both meet?" I asked. They seemed more interested in what I knew than telling me their history, but they capitulated.

"In the US … Washington, DC, to be exact," Fata said, looking at Ousha. "There aren't that many Sri Lankans in Washington. It's easy to spot one another. Our mothers became friends while our fathers worked."

"What a coincidence that you ended up living on the same street."

"Not really," Fata said. "When these islands were being built, Mohamed's father, whose company developed five of the streets, was looking for buyers and having trouble finding them. So he made everyone at a certain level who worked for his company purchase something as a condition of their continued employment. The quicker they sold, the more chance of convincing the emir to give him more to develop. This street is filled with Mohamed's father's acquaintances and family."

"My parents live two floors up from here," Ousha said.

Fata nodded. "And mine two floors down. My father and Ousha's were hired at the same time. We decided we wanted to be close to my parents, so we bought too. Mohamed was so pleased when he heard we were moving in. Dubai is a small place."

"Mohamed's father is on the next island up," said Ousha. "He needed an end lot for his boat, which wouldn't fit in one of the standard lots."

"His father must be livid about Mohamed. He's a disgrace to the family." I watched Ousha as I said this, in case I had pushed too far. She was still married to him, after all.

Ousha shrugged. "Hardly. Rich men in Dubai face little consequences for their bad behavior. Plus, he's one of five boys. There's someone else to take over the company. His father was just happy when Mohamed found a woman who would marry him."

"So you knew about me?" I asked.

Fata and Ousha looked confused.

"That I was here finding my daughter?"

"No," Fata said. "It was a real coincidence that you ended up here."

The front door opened. Jaseem called out something. Fata looked at me and shooed me from the table. I knew she wasn't trying to be rude, but Jaseem was an Emirati through and through, and he would have been appalled to see the three of us seated together. It was our secret, and I was happier because of it.

Meetings of Unintended Consequence

I watched the girls head to school in the back of Fata's car. Ruka and I both waved. We stepped into the service elevator and rode to the tenth floor. When we stepped out, Ousha's mother was knocking on the door to Fata's apartment. It was too late for us to close the elevator door and go somewhere else. When she looked at us, her face turned sour.

"I heard you were back. Don't go stirring up trouble here; you'll start a war." She moved closer to us. Ruka backed away, but I stood my ground. "You're going to give us a bad name. We've made a life here, and now you want to come and break it apart."

The accusation was extraordinary. That a house servant could take down their exquisite life. But from the few interactions I'd had with Ousha's mother, I knew blame was always outside of her own clan. If Ousha hadn't been so gracious to me yesterday, I might have barbed her mother with a reminder that we were the same blood from the same island.

"Yes, ma'am," was all that left my mouth.

When we stepped inside, Jaseem was fixing his ghutra on his head in front of the mirror in the entryway. His briefcase was beside him. I quickly handed him his agal to place over his white head covering. He smiled, then left.

"What did that woman mean?" Ruka asked.

"She's the mother of the woman I originally worked for. She likes to poke her nose into everyone's business. Don't worry about it. We have a lot of cleaning to do to make the house perfect for Fata and her family."

"I had a dream about Mewan last night," Ruka said as she picked up the teacup Jaseem had left on the table under the mirror.

"Me too. It must be a sign. I considered asking Fata about bringing Mewan here. We could all fit in our room."

"Really?" Ruka squealed and ran off into another room.

...

Later that morning, I was in the kitchen making the glass table spotless when Fata walked in. She set her bag down and was strangely quiet. I placed her breakfast of two eggs in front of her.

She took a bite, then looked up at me. "Did you see Ousha's mother today?"

I assumed she already knew the answer. "Yes, she was knocking at the door when we came back up from seeing you off."

"Did you say something offensive to her?"

Had I? My mind backpedaled through the moment. I was certain my mouth hadn't let out the words I'd been thinking. "No."

"She flagged me down in the parking garage to tell me she knows what I'm doing."

"What are you doing?" I wasn't following what she was trying to tell me.

"Exactly. Nothing." She paused for a beat, then added, "Do me a favor. Try to avoid her if possible. She can stir things up a bit, and that's the last thing we need."

I acknowledged Fata's wish and rounded the corner from the kitchen to the hallway, then headed to the laundry room. One of the pictures, in a black frame, caught my eye. It was a big group of people smiling at Disney World: Fata's family and Ousha's family, minus her father. I could tell Ousha was pregnant in the picture by the puffy glow of her face. She was wearing her abaya.

Ruka had finished folding all the laundry and was moving from room to room to put it away. I signaled for her to meet me in our room. She returned when she finished her last delivery.

"If you see that older woman we saw earlier today, stay away from her and don't answer her questions, okay? She's trouble."

"Did you ask Fata about bringing Mewan here?"

I shook my head. "It wasn't the right time."

"What will you do if she says no? I like this place."

I placed my hands firmly on her shoulders. "Don't get too settled, Ruka. I'm not sure this place is what it seems. It never has been in the past."

She pushed her lip out and went to sit on her bed.

...

Word must have traveled fast, because while I was standing in the kitchen feeding the girls their breakfast the next day, someone began hammering away at the front door.

Fata looked at Jaseem and shrugged. My guess was Ousha's mother, in a new fit of hysteria. He motioned for us to stay in the kitchen. The door clicked open and I heard the voice I'd hoped to avoid forever: Mohamed. He was yelling, which I was used to. Fata waved her girls over to her and brought them into the pantry. She waved me in as well, then closed the door and latched it from the inside. Ruka was in our room, folding sheets; I knew she was smart enough to stay put. The yelling continued; something smashed, and I imagined the glass bubble structure crashing down. The door slammed and then everything was quiet.

"Fata?" Jaseem called out. He said something else.

"It's okay to go," Fata told us as she opened the door.

We stepped out. Jaseem's eye was swelling up, and he was pulling ice out of the freezer. He spoke to Fata and kept looking over at me. He held the ice to his eye and Fata ushered him into their bedroom. The girls looked at me for assurance, so I filled their cups with juice and smiled.

Ruka appeared at the kitchen door.

"Did something happen?" she asked.

I shushed her.

Fata emerged from the hallway. "Shula, I need you to go back to your room and don't come out until I tell you. We need to have a conversation when Jaseem is gone and the girls are at school."

The brightening thought of an opportunity to ask about bringing Mewan to Dubai had overshadowed what I should have been worried about: Mohamed.

...

My hands were covered in soap bubbles as I scrubbed the kitchen floor. I heard Fata's footsteps in the hall.

"Shula?"

"I'm in the kitchen."

She appeared above me, tilting her head when she saw the bubbles foaming up past the cabinets. "Can you come to the table?"

I rinsed my hands and wiped my bare feet with a towel, then came to sit next to her. Her hands were clasped in front of her. She had taken her head covering off at the door; her hair was wound up in braids, a string of turquoise stones holding them up. "You know who was here this morning, right?"

"Yes."

"He was here because he found out you're working for us. He thinks Jaseem is disrespecting him because he hired an employee who stole from him."

"I only stole from him because I needed to escape."

"So you did steal from him? Shula ..." Her voice dipped down, and she pulled her hands back.

"He killed Ousha's baby."

When I said this Fata's eyes went in separate directions. It was as if her brain were trying to understand two contradicting thoughts. I'd said far too much, and I felt like I was hanging in the air by a string, waiting for it to snap.

"Are you lying because you're trying to get something? I picked you out of the lineup because Khalid told me you were the best worker he had seen in some time. But I'm beginning to think you're not what he sold me."

"Sold?" I was baffled by what she was saying. We might as well be speaking other languages.

"Khalid controls the flow of workers into the palm. He decides who goes where to make sure we get the best. As a result, he takes a percentage of your wages for placing you with us."

I didn't realize I was still under his control; his strings were invisible.

"I think there's a misunderstanding here on multiple fronts," Fata continued. "Tell me about the baby."

"Ousha's?"

"If you say so." She stood up and pulled a banana from a bunch.

I told her about Ousha and Mohamed's house as I encountered it upon arrival. I let her know the details of the birth and the abuse Ousha endured.

"You know more, don't you?"

"I don't think I should …"

"You don't work for them anymore; you have no allegiance."

I continued and Fata listened until all of the secrets of Mohamed's house were laid bare.

. . .

Ruka and I were cleaning the living area. She had the vacuum hose sucking up popcorn under the couch cushions, and I was wiping down each slat of the window blinds. Jaseem was at work; the girls were at school; and Fata had gone out. I thought I heard rumbling—a low, rolling drumbeat. I kept running my cleaning rag over the blinds.

Ruka turned off the vacuum and was replacing the cushions on to the couch when the knock came hard and heavy. I stepped lightly until I saw the door. The bolt was in place. I went to the kitchen and looked at the monitor; Mohamed's angry face filled the screen. He turned around and pushed the button to call the elevator. Who kept letting him up here?

I noticed he was going up. Maybe to terrorize Ousha's parents next.

I turned the lock to make sure it was fully engaged; it clicked and Mohamed must have heard it because he started pounding again. I stepped back from the vibrating door. Ruka stood in the hallway, twisting the fabric of her dress into her balled-up fist.

I led her into our room and locked both doors.

"Is that the man you used to work for?"

"Yes, baby."

"Did you do something bad? Is that why he's angry at you?"

I shook my head. "No. He did something bad, and I know about it. That's why he's angry. I have his secrets and he wants them back." I watched the clock on the wall, not wanting to fall too far behind in what I had planned to accomplish today. Fata had been very happy with what we had done so far, and I wanted to make sure Ruka and I stayed on that path.

I rubbed my daughter's neck until I heard her breaths increase in length. The vibration came through the floor, even in here. I would know when he was gone, and only then would we go out.

"Will you tell me a story about Dwehlli?" Ruka asked.

Ruka loved stories about Dwehlli; she thought of her as the older sister she'd always wanted.

I pulled the rubber band out of her hair and ran my fingers through it.

I woke up to a low vibration humming through my room. Dwehlli was sitting on the floor of my bedroom, her feet tucked under the carpet, hands on her thighs, eyes closed. Her orange hair had sprouted, a contrast to her normally skin-close shave.

"Get ready. We're going out," she said, not opening her eyes.

It wasn't a school day. I was sure my parents had enlisted her to keep me out of their way on my days off.

"I want breakfast first."

She opened her eyes and stood over me. "No food today."

I wasn't in a position to argue. I changed out of my pajamas into a plain sari. Dwehlli always objected to anything but plain clothes.

We walked down the dirt road. I didn't question where to. Our town was far enough away to keep strangers from wandering to us. There was a section just outside the town buildings where the outcasts lived and congregated, speaking strange words and smelling foul.

"Weren't you scared to walk near them?" Ruka asked.

"Just listen."

Dwehlli put her hands together and bowed to each of them. Her acknowledgement lit them up. A few paces out, there was a cripple, a man whose legs looked like they'd been attached the wrong way to his body then chopped off at the knees. He was dragging himself through the dirt with his arms. When he'd come across something he thought was edible on the ground, he'd pick it up with his mouth and chew on it to decide.

The other outcasts jeered him. Some of them put feces in his path so he'd eat it, and then laughed uncontrollably.

Your grandfather always told me to move quickly through these parts. But Dwhelli encouraged me, a moment before we made the transition into the village, to turn and soak in what was happening there.

"Shula, what is it you're seeing?" she asked me.

I was maybe twelve at the time. "It looks painful. He looks like he's suffering."

"Perhaps. But we're all suffering in our own way."

A monk sat with his back against a building and a wooden bowl of rice in front of him. He had his prayer beads strung around his wrist, with a single strand extending between his fingers.

"What do you think that monk is praying for?" Dwhelli asked.

I knew Dwhelli was connected to the spiritual world in some way, but was she really able to hear prayers? I shrugged; I had no such ability.

"For them?" I said. "That they might have food? Or comfort?"

"That would be a helpful prayer, wouldn't it?"

I shrugged again. I had no idea what answer she was looking for.

She put her hand on my back and urged me forward into the buzz of the town. The smells of noodles boiling and the salty tang of newly caught fish made my mind forget about those at its perimeter. I shuffled through the storefronts, waiting until I came to the fruit vendor. He took coconuts and stuffed them full of lychee and mango. The coconut water inside picked up their syrupy sweetness; it was a treat that would satisfy my mouth for a whole week.

I bought one for me and one for Dwhelli. At first she refused it, but then she gave in.

"Is there something you need here?" I asked her.

"There is something you need here," she said.

I took the first sip of the sweet nectar.

"No more until we get where we're going." She tapped the side of my coconut.

This was the first food I'd had in my mouth since I'd awoken, and my stomach lunged forcefully at the overflowing, colorful deliciousness. I also knew when a nun told you to do something it was important to follow her instructions.

Once again we reached the place where the outcasts dwelled. They moved in closer to us, their eyes fixed on what we were holding. Dwehlli went to the monk, plucked two pieces of mango from her coconut, and placed it on top of his rice.

"You must first nourish the guides," she told me. "Without them we are all lost. And what do you think we should do now?"

It pained me to say this. "Give the rest to them?"

"I won't suggest that; you look too distraught to part with your treat. And giving should always be done willingly. Instead, think of a way that you might give a piece of your happiness to alleviate these people's suffering."

The pounding on the door had stopped. I stroked Ruka's hair once more and pulled it into a ponytail. "I think we can go out now."

Ruka spun to face me. "So what did you do?"

"I went back the next day armed with a bag full of cooked coconut rice and a cauldron of tea and fed the man dragging himself on the ground. I kept going, day after day, feeding him and the others who lived in that place. My arms were tired from the lugging and I would arrive at school exhausted after spending the daybreak hours with them. But they taught me almost as much as Dwehlli."

"Do you think that's why you were placed here? Because you did something thoughtful and now it's paying you back?" Ruka stood up, ready to leave the room.

"I don't know, the gods have a tricky way of showing us their plans. What Dwhelli was trying to teach me is that serving someone had many lessons to teach. I had heard that before, we were well schooled in Buddhist thought. What was revelatory to me, though, on those days when I would eat with them, was they considered their poverty a temporary state. Something they had come into and might as easily come out of. I'd never considered this. Your grandfather always had more than enough. After the wave, though, I thought back to the people I had fed and knew then that we were no different from them. And by nothing more than the timing of our lives had we all arrived where we now stood."

We were back in the hallway, moving to the front of the apartment. The lock on the front door was turning. I pulled Ruka's shoulders against the wall, taking her out of direct sight of whoever was going to walk through that door.

"Shula?" Fata called out. "What happened to the front door?"

We peeled ourselves from the wall to become visible to her.

"Mohamed was here."

She swallowed hard but kept her composure. "Did you open the door?"

"No, we hid in our room." I wasn't sure if that was the answer she wanted, but it was the truth.

"I'm glad you're okay. He used one of the statues in the hallway to dent the door. Jaseem will have a fit when he sees it." She paused, then said, "I had lunch with Ousha today. Her parents told her if she divorces Mohamed, they'll leave Dubai. It will be too much shame for them. She said she tried to talk with Mohamed, but he said it was you who was causing his problems. He said you have something of his. Is that true?"

"Ruka, go to our room." I didn't want her head filled with Mohamed's misdeeds.

"I took a photo album from his house," I whispered. "You can't tell Ousha."

"This story is endless. I thought you told me everything yesterday. Why not?"

"Because Ousha has a fantasy about someone in the album, and it can never come true." Damn it, I'd said too much.

"Ousha?" Fata stopped what she was doing and put her hands flat on the table.

I explained the album, Inesh, and how I thought Maryam was Inesh and Ousha's child.

"You can never tell anyone what you told me," Fata said. "Where is the album? Can you give it to me?"

"I gave it to Minrada."

"Who?"

"She was the one who originally helped me escape from Mohamed. She was under the bridge with me when it flooded."

Fata picked up her phone and did a few things with it. "You know, this is all a bit much. I'm not sure it's good for my family."

I wasn't sure what she was getting at, but I felt like she was making decisions in her head and not telling me.

"I needed to ask you something else," I said.

She looked up from her phone.

"I'd like to bring my son here. He could stay in my room with Ruka and me. I promise he won't be a bother. It's just that I miss him and I would like us to all be together."

She shook her head before she responded. "How old is he?"

My spirits lifted. Was she considering this?

"Three."

"Shula, I don't run a charity here. How will you and Ruka get any housework done if you're chasing after a little one? I'm sorry he isn't here, but his father must be taking good care of him."

"His father died during the tsunami." I looked hard at her; it was the first time I had weaponized Pramith's death.

Fata was a very nice woman, but I also could tell she hadn't lived outside the comforts of wealth. It likely never occurred to her what my family had been through. My stories of Mohamed were gossipy musings she fretted over and thought about, but they didn't move her life in one direction or the other.

"I'm sorry—but no." It was final.

"Thank you for listening." Emotion bubbled in me. Finding a way home felt impossible. Minrada hadn't resurfaced, and even if she had, I had nothing to offer her. I went back to cleaning.

"When are you sending Ruka back?" It was a flippant question that struck me with epic force.

"I'm not. She has work to do here with me."

"But I can't pay you both."

"One salary is fine." I didn't have an expectation of payment any longer.

"It's not just that. Khalid gets a cut for each of you. I'll have to give him more of your wages to cover Ruka." She looked at me like this might change my mind, but it didn't.

SPITE

A week passed. Things felt as though they were settling, which gave me an uneasy feeling that trouble was close. Each day, I had looked for Minrada at the park at the usual time the nannies gathered.

This morning, as I approached, I saw her looming figure. She was taller than the other women, and her clothes were always a step above what the rest of us wore. When I got closer, I noticed her appearance had changed. She lacked the coy sarcasm she normally steeped in.

"Nice to see you," I offered.

"You still owe me."

"I gave you everything I had." I'd wrongly expected polite decorum from her.

"The album got lost in the flood. I need another form of payment." Her voice carried an air of despondency.

I didn't have anything else. The clothes she wore today were worth more than all my possessions combined.

"Do you ever want to get back to Balapitiya?" she asked.

Of course I wanted to see my home again. The mention of it alone made me long for it. But Minrada's threats felt empty now. It might have been because the house I worked in with Fata and Jaseem was actually what I had come to Dubai expecting.

"What does Fata have that would be valuable to me?" she asked.

"I took something from Mohamed because he was an awful man. Fata and her family are pure sunshine. I would never—"

"Ha. They have you. That's how they'll keep you here forever."

"It was a mistake to seek you out again," I said. "You're a miserable woman."

I was explicitly aware of the heads in the park turning toward me when I said that.

Minrada leaned into me; I could smell her acidic breath through her hiss. "You will die here."

Although her words shook me, I held a stern composure.

. . .

The walk back to the apartment felt heavy. The sun beat harder, and the road pushed back against me, striking though my sandals like a hammer against my heels. The muscles in my neck clawed at the back of my head.

That night Fata summoned me. "Shula, do you have any other clothes?"

I looked down at my uniform. "No."

"Come."

I followed her into her closet. There was a section of hanging dresses and abayas that were thick with beads and colorful waxed stitching. She pulled out a black dress. It had multiple layers of sheer fabric with gold-and-white teardrops dripping from the neck and over the arms.

"Try this on." She held it up to me.

She hung it in front of the dressing bust and left the closet.

I pulled off my uniform and let it fall at the feet of the abaya. When I slipped it on, it was soft and effortless, the fabric titillating my skin.

"How does it fit? Can I come in?"

"It's—"

She was behind me, adjusting the many layers. "I think we need to make it a little shorter. Otherwise, it looks wonderful." She stood back and looked me over once more, then walked out.

I changed back into my uniform and left it hanging perfectly. "Fata, what would I need something like that for?"

She was typing on her laptop. "Abdullah has invited us on his boat for a cruise. He specifically requested that you attend as well."

"Abdullah?"

"The owner of the company Jaseem works for."

"Mohamed's father?" The dress I had floated in a second ago was now repugnant.

"Yes. Adbullah called Jaseem to his office today. He said everything has become unmanageable, and he needs to reel this all back in before the news gets wind of it."

I didn't know what that meant, but I wanted nothing to do with this.

"Does Ruka have to come?"

"No, I was hoping she would stay here with the girls and my mother."

The mention of her mother watching my daughter gave me a clue as to the seriousness of this event.

THE BOAT

Fata, Jaseem, and I said nothing as the elevator descended to the lobby.

The car waiting for us at the curb of the building was Mohamed's. I looked at Fata for assurance that this was right.

"Just follow me," she said.

Jaseem walked around the car and got in behind Mohamed. Ousha was in the front seat. Fata sat in the middle and I sat behind Ousha. Light music was playing: an echoic, tinny Arabic melody. The doors closed by themselves, sealing us in. The mood inside the car felt like children being called by their parents after they'd done something wrong.

Abdullah's house was only minutes away and surrounded by gates taller than two grown men. Each gatepost was topped with a crystal that picked up the light of the sunset and fractionated it across the walls of the home. The gates opened, and we advanced into the circular driveway and under a portico. At each door, a man appeared to open and usher each of us out and position us so that we faced a short stack of stairs leading to an archway door we could have driven through. The glass above the doors was covered in fancy brushed metal crescents; the doors brandished handles the size of a small person and must have taken the entire day to polish. The four men led us up the stairs and into the first layer of the house. A corridor wrapped the outside of the home like a protective membrane. Our footsteps echoed and the servants made no attempt to engage us. They guided us through the house until we stepped outside on the half-moon tip of the island, which Abdullah had covered in palm trees, furniture, coves of light, winding hedges, and bubbling fountains.

At the end was the jewel of the property, his towering gray yacht. We stood at the white curving plank, with pinpoint lights illuminating from within, connecting the place where we were standing to the boat. Ousha took Mohamed's arm and boarded first. When they turned the corner and were out of sight, a booming voice greeted them.

Fata had made me practice a greeting in Mohamed's language for Abdullah. She said he wouldn't expect me to speak Arabic, but he would expect a greeting. From there, Fata would translate anything I needed to know.

Fata took Jaseem's arm and they stepped onto the path.

Two of the servants stepped closer to me, slightly ahead. When it was time, they both bent forward, arms straight out, inviting me to board the boat.

I rounded the corner, unsure what to expect.

Abdullah stood at the top of the boat as if he were heading up an official delegation with his contingent stationed neatly behind him. His white robe was lined with the matte-gray color of the boat. Each of the people standing behind him complemented the colors of his clothing and the boat. It was his portrait of power. He immediately made eye contact with me, and his fleshy face gave a welcoming smile. His arms opened. To his right, a woman shimmered in a gray sequenced abaya playing off of the yacht's hull.

"Shula. I've waited so long to meet you." Abdullah's Sinhala was precise, the way a professor in my country might speak.

"Hello, it's an honor to meet you," I said in Mohamed's language. My words were shaky. His personality pulled me close, but my body never touched his.

"This is my wife, Cynthia. We've been together fifty years. I plucked her out of London the day she was born," he said, again perfectly in my language.

She radiated hospitality and shook my hand.

I was the last guest to arrive, and when our introductions were over, one of the servants lightly touched my shoulders, turned me toward the back of the boat, then gestured to a photographer, who was set up and ready to take pictures. As soon as Abdullah moved deeper into the boat, a spin of activity swirled behind him. We followed him to four round pods of seats, each with a low table in the middle. The men who had shown us out of the car had multiplied and were now seating us and taking our drink orders.

There were several other couples I didn't recognize. Mohamed and Ousha were seated with Abdullah as well as a man I assumed was Mohamed's brother, who was understood to be the heir to his father's business. I sat next to Fata. She made conversation with the others in our pod, while I watched Ousha. I knew, from our conversations in the kitchen and when she was intoxicated, that she hated

Mohamed and his father. The way she interacted with polite deference, intense smiles, and affectionate touching of Mohamed was an act of betrayal against herself.

"Once Abdullah has his words with his sons, we'll all rotate until everyone has an audience with him," Fata said.

"How does he know how to speak Sinhala?" I asked.

"Abdullah is a smart man. One doesn't build a fortune this big without brains."

Jaseem seemed nervous; he'd sip his cocktail and then look at the ground. Fata did the talking for both of them.

It was time to move. We went to sit with Abdullah and Cynthia. Fata sat very close to me, and Abdullah began to talk.

"I'm so glad you've all come to join me for dinner on the boat," Fata translated. "We're here to discuss many important things. The most important is my appreciation for your loyalty and being my extended family. I value each and every one of you incredibly."

The way he looked at us couldn't have felt more sincere. His eye contact was long and interested, and his arms swept over our presence in generous arcs. Even though I understood the words through Fata's translation, it was the melody of his voice that made me swoon. I felt like he could entrance anyone.

"He's telling us about how successful his business is and we're all a part of that success."

Abdullah looked at me and spoke. Fata backed away so I could make a full connection with him. His words moved toward me. "You're the reason all of us can come to work, to have our beautiful children cared for. Shula, you're as much a part of all this as anyone. And when one of us is rewarded, we all will be."

Abdullah put his hand out. One of his employees handed him a box.

"Please come," he told me, and I stood up.

The guests at the other couches had been directed to look at what was happening between us. Abdullah had activated something inside me, and I bowed slightly to him. I wanted to please him. He pushed the box forward and opened it.

I was facing Cynthia so I heard her burst of breath, along with a word I didn't understand. Inside was a necklace: blue sapphires surrounded by diamonds; there were at least twenty of them. It looked like something our head of state might wear. "Whenever you look at this, you'll remember our journey together."

I started to raise my hand to reject the gift, but Fata cut in quickly. "Shula, you must accept it."

I heeded her warning, knowing this necklace was the price of my life.

Abdullah handed it to Cynthia, who stepped behind me and attached it. Then Abdullah put his hand forward and I kissed it. Everyone on the boat erupted in applause and words of praise for Abdullah. They looked at him as though he had saved the world from all its troubles, and he accepted it like a humble servant.

After a few minutes, we were ushered to the next deck up, which we entered through a set of spotless glass doors. The deck was encased in transparent walls. A glass dining table was set for all of us, the chairs a clear Lucite with subtle gray lines. There were name cards written in Mohamed's language, except for mine, which was written in my language. The details of the boat staggered me, and the weight of the necklace grounded me into the architecture of Abdullah's world.

I sat between Fata and Ousha. Fata squeezed my leg under the table. It made me feel as though she were trying to keep one of my feet in reality.

Deep-red wine was poured. Mohamed delivered a toast. Halfway through it, he looked at me.

"He's saying he's delighted you've come back to work as part of his family, especially after the tragedy you suffered of losing a child," Fata said.

I watched Ousha; the sting of putting us so close together was hers to bear, not mine. She and I both knew the truth. But Ousha had been inhabited with the spirit of this moment, which was joy, at any cost. As long as I was with Fata, I could shoulder the rest.

TRANSITORY GODITIONS

We were deep into the night when Cynthia announced that we would try to do this again. "After all, family should be together regularly."

"Thank you for translating. It must have been annoying," I told Fata when we entered the apartment.

She pulled off her vermeil scarf and spun it around the coat rack like a diligent spider. "We all had a job there. That was mine." In the safety of her apartment, she had returned to the person she was before the act we'd all been conscripted to. I reached for my neck to see if the necklace was there or if it had been a prop that would crumble with no more density than a painted brittle palm leaf.

"You understand what happened, yes?" She kicked off her shoes. A purple stain had taken hold under her eyes.

"Abdullah bought and sold us." It was a saying left over from our days when slave owners lived on our island and had bolted collars around our necks.

She blinked several times at me. "Yes, but there were things he said when it was just us sitting next to him. I didn't want to tell you while we were there. I was afraid you might get too emotional."

"What things?" I couldn't imagine what else he could have said.

"You must go back."

"Home?"

"No. To Mohamed's house. You're to go and work for him and Ousha. That's what he was saying. He's welcoming you back to his family. He wants to restore honor to everyone."

"No." I felt like someone had run away with all the air in my lungs. "Even if I could stomach it, I can't bring Ruka into that."

"There will be provisions for her. She'll stay with us. Jaseem and I have to do our part too, to right the wrongs."

"But we didn't do anything wrong." Abdullah's view of the world burrowed under my skin.

Fata put her arm around me. Over the weeks I'd been here, she hadn't been anything but gracious, but she'd never been this personal.

"I'm sorry." She patted my back, then went to her bedroom.

I went to our room; Ruka was asleep. I knelt next to her mattress and ran my hand over her hair and kissed her forehead. I'd deliver the news to her tomorrow morning. Someday this necklace would buy what Khalid had promised, when we returned home.

...

I felt Ruka nuzzle into me. It must have been morning. She always woke with the sunrise, whether or not she could see it. I didn't open my eyes, and I was back in our small room in Sri Lanka. It was still dark; the sun hadn't broken through the slits in the walls. Mewan was at my feet. I soaked in the moment of my whole family being together in a familiar place.

"Where did you go last night?" Ruka's voice shuffled through the darkness and into my ears.

"A very rich man had a party."

I felt her fingers on my neck. Before they were gone, the light clicked on. Ruka honed in on my neck. I'd forgotten; I'd slept with the necklace on.

Her eyes went wide. "What is that?"

"A bribe. To make sure I do what I'm supposed to." I knew she wouldn't respond, but I waited anyway. "Ruka, I have to go back and work for that man, Mohamed. You'll stay here with Fata and the girls. I won't be far, just down the street. I can see you every day." I was speeding up my words, hoping to explain what I didn't want to be true.

She just looked at me funny, as if I were lying to her, and then she went to the door. "But isn't he mad at you?"

"It doesn't matter. His father told him to do it."

She accepted the answer. Parents were all-powerful in her world. "As long as I can see you every day."

Ruka didn't know what Mohamed had done, and I'd never tell her. Those were things that should never be inside an eight-year-old mind.

Her eyes were still on the necklace. "Do you think I could wear it sometime? Just around our room?"

"I don't know. If Fata or Jaseem ever saw me without it, they might become angry."

"Well, okay. Whatever you say, Mama." She flitted out of the room, in her best mood.

...

It was decided that Ruka would go to school with Fata's daughters. A translator would be provided for her at Abdullah's expense. It was part of the grand bargain to reshape reality into what he desired. The reality where his son wasn't a drug-fueled murderer who slept with and tortured other men and where his daughter-in-law wasn't chasing the memory of another man. The world created was of orderly marriages and family bonds as strong as sapphires.

...

The next day, I approached Mohamed's house. The car was parked in the same place. I saw the window curtain pulled aside, as it had been the first day I arrived. Mohamed and Ousha opened the door for me with bright faces and clear eyes. Their looks made the acid in my stomach feel like it had leeched into my abdomen and burned through my organs. The air felt full of static. My mind rose above my body, because my body was screaming for me not to advance.

"Welcome back, Shula," Ousha said. "We missed you." Everything was wrong with that. There was no "we"; they hated each other. As the door opened wider it made sense. Abdullah and Cynthia were standing in the dining room. Their arms were open as if they were welcoming a long-lost relative home.

I did my best to pay them respect; I had no idea how I would leave this place, but I knew enough to keep myself fully in their good graces.

I quickly went to my room, which had been cleaned. The rug stood straight up, and the dresser had been moved back to where the crib had been at the end of the bed. Two new uniforms were pressed and folded on the bed. A picture of Maryam was framed on the dresser; I hadn't remembered it ever being taken. I was feeding her, my face a few centimeters above her bottle, watching her mouth suckle the milk. I looked under the bed, an ancient part of my brain expecting to see her. Then I went in the bathroom, which had fresh towels and pastel-colored, flower-shaped soaps. The walls had pictures of families roaming through the touristic sites of Dubai. They covered the holes through which Mohamed had watched me.

Ousha stood in the doorway, her hands crossed in front of her. The pleasant expression had vanished from her face. I noticed her nails were painted black, and the veins stood out on her hands.

"Ousha, are you okay?"

She looked over her shoulder. "We're getting out of here as quickly as I can think of a way to do it."

"Whatever you do, include Ruka."

"Who?"

"My daughter. She's working for Fata. You saw her last time you were there."

"I don't remember. Meet me in the kitchen tonight. Late, like two a.m."

I didn't think planning an escape from the house while Mohamed was here was wise, especially so soon after the whole charade on the boat.

"Shouldn't we wait a bit?"

"Mohamed is rabid. He'll only be able to hold this together for a little bit. And then … well, you've seen what can happen."

"Do you have—"

She waved her hand in front of her. "Later." And then she was gone.

I heard the clinking of bottles and glasses.

Mohamed appeared in the hallway a few minutes later. He didn't enter the room.

He handed me a paper, looked sincerely at me, and pressed his hands into a prayer pose. Someone had written this for him:

I know you saw some things before. I would appreciate it if we left all those thoughts in the past and that we could leave them just between us.

"Yes." I nodded my head with the force of a mother relieving her son of worry.

That was wishful thinking on his part.

PLAN B

Ousha stood at the island in the kitchen; I could smell the alcohol before I was next to her. She waved me over as though she were directing a ship into port.

"There's only one way out." She was looking at the door into the sitting room.

I wasn't following her.

"We've got to kill him."

"That's not something I can do." I reached for the bottle and tugged it closer to me; it smelled like pine. I took a sip. It didn't disagree with me, but I felt it stick to my throat and make me shiver. "There has to be another way."

"Let me tell you something about Abdullah. Everything is optics. And Abdullah never fails. Not in business, not in his personal life, not in his health. If I were to leave, he would hunt me down."

"Why? Why not just move on?"

"Because he *never* fails. I told you. Mohamed's younger brother had cancer and eventually died. The story is he decided to live his life in luxury in the Maldives. Abdullah bought an island there just to maintain the image. Every now and again, a story hits the news about a sighting of him. People claim to have had dinner with him. There are only a handful of us who know the truth."

I was being pulled into the darkness. "There is no way out."

"There *is* a way out. But it requires death. Abdullah will have no choice but to let me go if Mohamed is gone."

My mind toggled between the knowledge of sitting next to Inesh's sister on the bus and remembering that somehow the fact of Inesh's death by Mohamed's hand had been kept a secret.

"When was the last time you saw Inesh?" I asked.

Ousha's composure came into fresh focus. "We were at an underground party together. A place where all the domestic staff from the islands gathered. In one of the houses that hadn't been occupied yet. Looking back, it would have been a PR disaster if anyone had recognized me or found out I had gone. The customs there were different because all the staff was imported. The women and men ... they could touch and kiss. Inesh and I were in the main part of the house, but then we went up the unfinished staircase. The rooms upstairs had some other couples in them too. Inesh and I made love. When he was on top of me, I tilted my head back and saw the stars through one of the unfinished windows."

I imagined her for a moment until I realized what she was telling me. "Was that the night that Maryam was—?"

She cut me off. "Don't say that. You should never ever say that."

"But he was the father, right?"

"You still work for me." Ousha was tense; she poured herself another glass and glared at me.

"We have to work together if we're going to have any chance of success," I said. "Mohamed is powerful. The emir let him go even after you accused him of murder and the judge believed you."

We both knew I was right.

"How did you ever get this far with an attitude like that?" There was a smirk emerging from the gin.

"It's the reason I've gotten this far," I said.

For the first time, I'd seen Ousha amused by something, rather than the drudgery she usually displayed.

"This is never going to work," I told her.

"It will. I've thought about it for years. I've plotted every last detail, through nights when I could not sleep. Oh, I never thought it would come to this, but I do know it will work. And don't worry—the castor beans won't be detectable."

I shrank back from the insinuation. The idea that a person could ruminate for years on the murder of another human being. And now I was facing the force of it, its fruition brought to life before me.

"We'll poison him slowly," Ousha said. "No one will notice, not even him. I need you to go to the market near the central station. They sell castor beans there."

"You want me to buy the poison?"

"Shhh."

I knew Ousha was right. There wasn't another way out of here. And my whole being fought against it, which is why my voice likely had risen. Was I now no better than my brother?

Father's plantations were works of art. A blend of people, places, and things in the most exquisite combination. It was painful therefore as my brother, Sahan, tore it leaf by leaf, building by building, tea girl by tea girl.

"Stand back," Dwhelli whispered. She raised her arm in front of me and pushed back against my chest.

My eyes were on the back of Sahan's head. He sat at our father's dining table, where our father's body had lain just days before, accessible to the town to pay their respects. Two men in business attire stood next to Sahan, reading through the contents of my father's will.

"There is nothing to be done here. The law is the law. But he must take care of you. This is also clear," Dwhelli said softly.

I didn't want my brother in his opium haze taking care of me. I wanted my father with his confident and soft grace. He always knew the right way to care for our family.

"Sahan, show me what you are doing." I broke through Dwhelli's gaze and put my hands on the teak table next to him. The two men looked at each other, then said to my brother, "We need a break, sir."

Sahan pushed the papers in front of me. "What do you want to see, Shula? This, this, and this are mine." His finger went to each picture. The house we stood in now, the plantation on which I'd worked for five summers, and the last plantation, where I had climbed inside the silo with Dwehlli waiting below for me.

"You know I have a right to make decisions too. He was my father as much as yours."

"Yes. But I am the heir." Sahan turned his head slowly so that his eyes met mine and dared me to challenge him. "Don't worry. You'll be taken care of. You and your sidekick." He glared at Dwehlli.

She looked at me with eyes urging calm. Sahan had never liked her. Insulting a nun is much like fighting against a brick wall. You'll only hurt yourself, and the wall won't notice you one way or the other. He stood up, pushed the papers against me, and left the room to talk with the other men.

"Your father already had given you everything you need. Don't chase the things he left behind," Dwhelli said.

"But he worked so hard for them."

"And look at where he is now. Do they enrich him in any way? Do they carry his spirit or lift his mind? Do they help him on the journey he now takes? Shula, things you can possess are not permanent. Permanence lies in the love he gave you, the wisdom he imparted, the unconditional confidence he displayed in your work. Toil only for what is permanent, and you will always be moving in the direction of Nirvana."

Although it was the last time I saw her in the flesh, she would appear to me many times in my mind as the years went by. When I heard her speak, it was only about those things that were permanent.

No, I wasn't like Sahan, I decided. This was for Ruka and Mewan, and for them, I'd give everything I had.

Ousha held up her finger with inspiration. "We must go where everyone gossips and nobody listens. To the mall."

. . .

Ousha could handle her drink enough that she knew what she had committed to. The next day, she called a car service and left a full covering for me to slip into before we went out in public. There was a note on top in Sinhala: "Your invisibility cloak." She was silent during the entire ride. We arrived at the same mall where Minrada had taken me on an outing the first time.

"This is where I saw Mohamed with his friend." I don't know what I was expecting by divulging this information.

Ousha ignored the comment and whooshed through the spinning glass door into the mall. She locked arms with me, a common sight among the women shopping. I wondered how many of the women or men here were secret lovers, flaunting their closeness in the open.

"When will you get to the market?"

I knew she was talking about the castor beans. "I can go today, if it's open."

"This is what we'll do. You'll walk or find some other way to go."

"Some other way?" My understanding was the market was at least four kilometers from the house.

"Yes, yes. There are many people who will take you. Just pay them in dinars and use a different name. And of course I'll give you the money. No one can know your departure point. Go from here, and then go to someplace else on the way back. Talk to no one. You understand? This must be very secret."

I followed her into a store; she looked at a few hand-bags, then pointed to the one she would purchase. The bag was fifteen thousand dinars. A sum I couldn't imagine possessing. Ousha paid with a card, emptied the contents of her old bag into her new one, then handed me her old handbag, which couldn't have been more than a few months old.

"Take this with you. There's extra in the pocket."

We strolled to the bottom level, where fish ponds filled the center of the floor for the length of the mall, laden with lily pads and pink lotus flowers.

"When you have it, we'll do a bit each day. It will build over days until it does its job."

"Why not just leave now? Why do this? It's not right." How could I murder someone, no matter how terrible they were to me or others? How could I possibly possess the constitution for such an act?

"Of course it's right, after what he did to me." I could only see Ousha's eyes, and they radiated angry betrayal. "I'm working on how we'll leave," she continued. "I'll go to London with my parents and you can go back to your home. I need my passport back."

She slipped that in there without the slightest agitation or inflection.

"I knew you took it, but now that you have your own passport, there's no reason for you to have mine."

"But my daughter still needs one. I can't leave her here."

"Fata will take good care of her, and she will pay her. You have nothing to worry about."

"Jaseem works for Mohamed. She would be in danger if I left."

Ousha didn't say anything; she merely sat at the edge of the water and rubbed her fingers together so that the koi came to the surface and gulped the air. "You see how they're trained? How they react to stimuli they've encountered thousands of times throughout their lives? Mohamed's no different. I can lead him anywhere. I know his triggers."

"I think you underestimate them." I sat next to her and rubbed my fingers over the water. The fish ignored her and came to me. "You see? Distraction."

...

An hour later, we were at the entrance, where a sedan waited for Ousha. "I'll see you." She got into the car and didn't look at me.

I paced the steps until I saw the taxi sign a few meters away. I got into one of the cabs and told the driver to take me to the Dubai Spice Souk.

A few minutes later, he dropped me off at the market. There were five thousand dinars in the bag, more than enough to pay for taxis and many things at the market. I had the necklace around my neck, under the abaya. I wondered if I would be able to get a price for it. I walked the stalls until I came to a food stand.

"Castor?" I found someone I thought was Sri Lankan. He shook his head and replied in Hindi. There was beautiful pottery, which I knew I could afford with the money Ousha had given me. I imagined serving guests in our house in Batapitya on these bright orange and blue ceramics. I ran my fingers over their surfaces, the glazed ridges igniting my mind. I was in our kitchen, my mother cutting tea leaves, my brother filling the pot and adjusting the flame under it, where we would boil the leaves into tea. A crisp, earthy scent filled the room. I had the cups in my hand.

The merchant was asking me something. I ignored him and kept searching. The castor beans were in a burlap sack, hidden under a table of dates. I found them because one had fallen and had been trampled.

I reached for them. The merchant stopped me, put on some gloves, then took two handfuls and put them in a paper bag for me. It was more than I needed, but I didn't want to be memorable in any way. I handed him two hundred dinars, then left. He seemed satisfied with the price I'd paid. Three taxis later, I ended up at the bridge where Ruka and I had been flooded out and discovered.

Inside the house, Ousha had left an open jar in the kitchen. I crumpled the brown bag tightly around the beans and fit them inside it.

No one could blame me for buying beans. Women all over the world bought these same beans for a million reasons, but in my heart I knew intention was the only thing that mattered.

Ousha appeared. She had changed; her eyes were ringed in black makeup, her hair askew. She went directly to the jar and peered in, then looked at me maniacally. "You got them. Each day, in his breakfast you'll add the smallest amount. And the effect will build. He won't notice at first. But then it will come." She spoke with certainty, as if it were a family recipe.

I backed away from the jar. "I'm not going to do that. I got them for you. That's enough."

She drove her knuckles into her palm. "You will or you won't leave here."

You can only ask "why" so many times before you realize there are answers that aren't accessible.

"Understand?" She waited until I made eye contact with her.

I pulled the beans toward me, closed the top of the jar, and held it. I would do it; when I saw them in the market under the table, I knew I would.

Ousha pulled open a cabinet and fiddled with something inside. Then she turned back to me. "Do you like the picture of you and Maryam? My mother took it."

I shrugged. The picture was odd; I didn't have a feeling of liking it or not.

"Well, it was for you."

"Thanks?"

She came to me and tugged at my necklace. "You know this really belongs to me. You can't keep it. A woman like you would never have a necklace like this."

"Why's that?"

"Because you aren't worth anything. That necklace is mine. The minute we get ourselves out of here."

"But Abdullah—"

"What about Abdullah, lady?"

I decided not to push it. Her perspective had shifted once again, and I was on her list of reasons this particular version of herself hadn't worked out.

"Forget it," I muttered.

...

The next morning, Mohamed sat next to the pool in a white robe, smoking and looking out at the canal. I would make him his eggs first, then a date puree with juiced celery. Finally, when I had cleared the plates away, I'd present a clove cigarette alongside his espresso. I set the eggs and juice in front of him. In imaginary space, Ousha had told me to draw a diagonal line from the top right corner of the plate to the glass. This is where they should go, always.

In the kitchen, my hands grasped the jar and popped the metal clasp open. The castor beans' bitterness escaped. A single bean went into the garlic press and I squeezed its oil into the packed ground espresso beans. When the water scorched through the tightly packed mixture and the cup welcomed the poison, I found myself scratching hard at the space behind my ear, which held my anxiety. I wondered how so little liquid could feel like it was on the verge of drowning me.

I heard Dwhelli's voice in my head: *It only feels big because we are so small.*

I watched Mohamed from behind the window. When he put the last chunk of egg in his mouth, I was beside him with the espresso and extended my arm to put it on the table. My hand was shaking.

Mohamed noticed the same time I did. "You think I'm going to hurt you."

My response came to me much later, at a time when Mohamed wasn't in my life.

He lit his clove cigarette, inhaled once, and took a sip of espresso. He directed his attention away from me, which was the signal everything was fine and I could go.

Ousha stood on the other side of the window, watching. Her eyebrows arched up, her ears pinned back by the muscles of expectation. "It was fine? He drank it? He didn't notice?" I nodded as I passed her, bringing the dirty dishes to the kitchen. She followed me. "You know what this means? It'll be even easier than we thought. Put more next in time, until he notices. Wait—" She rapped her fingers on my arm. "No, no, no—do it slowly. It's better that way. I wouldn't mind letting him suffer a bit." A laugh leapt from the depths of her throat.

After I served dinner to Mohamed that night, I walked over to see Ruka. Fata asked me in, but the night air was delightful, and I thought we should walk. The fiery sky betrayed the crispness in the air.

"Are they treating you well?"

"Yes, Mama. Every day they ask about you, and they're so kind to their daughters. But they have tense words with each other at night. I can't understand what about."

"Keep to yourself and do what they ask," I told her.

"How long do you think we'll stay here?" She didn't let me answer before she pulled out a stack of folded bills and thrust it in my direction. "If we keep earning for a while, we could make a very nice life here."

I wanted to say our life was fine at home, but to Ruka that would have been ridiculous compared to what she was seeing here.

"It depends," I said, taking the money from her. I didn't want her to know we might leave quickly.

"Fata said I can stay as long as I like, and my teacher at school said the same thing."

"All good things."

Ruka slipped her hand into mine and put her head against my side. "But I do miss sleeping in the same room as you."

I had a momentary thought to ask Ousha if this was possible, but I knew she wouldn't want to deviate from her plan.

I kissed Ruka's forehead, then stepped into the elevator to bring her up to Fata's apartment.

WATERY TENSION

"Abdullah and Cynthia have invited us back to the boat. Looks like Cynthia is making this a weekly gathering," Ousha said, passing me in the entry hall.

I had an image of Mohamed getting sick on the boat and the crew casting Ousha and me overboard.

"When?"

"Tonight. We have to go."

At midday, there was a white abaya on my bed and a pair of red shoes on the floor. I put on the abaya. Separate lines of black and red sequins were spaced at the bottom, then rose and twisted until they burst in every direction of my back, like fireworks. I pulled my hair back and went to look at myself in my bathroom mirror. I didn't recognize the woman I saw; she was elegant and demure, swathed in wealth. I imagined it was easy to be lulled into the image looking back at me and ignore the grinding reality of my true self. Perhaps this was why Dwhelli had told me mirrors are unhelpful, because they show us a picture of what we want to see rather than what we need to see.

That evening, Mohamed, Ousha, and I got into the car. Mohamed winced when he bent to get into the driver's seat. Silence ruled the ride to Abdullah's house.

On the boat, Cynthia took my hand, fixated on the necklace Abdullah had given me, and led me to sit at a long table. Ousha turned on her charm and was fully invested in her conversation with Abdullah.

Jaseem came up the stairs with Fata holding his arm. Behind them, their two daughters held hands. A third face appeared, my Ruka. She wore a midnight-blue abaya, with pink flowers embroidered halfway up the arms and along the bottom. I could tell she was overtaken by everything she was seeing—amazement at a boat this big and the people who owned it.

Abdullah greeted Jaseem and Fata, then bent down to hug their two daughters. He put his hand behind him, then pulled out two silver-wrapped gifts for them.

When it was Ruka's turn, he less affectionately rubbed her arm, then produced a pink box. She glanced at me but kept her attention on Abdullah.

Cynthia led her to the seat next to me.

"I didn't know you were coming here," I whispered to Ruka.

"They told me only an hour ago and gave me these clothes to wear. Can I open my gift?"

I looked at Fata's girls to see what they were doing. They had pulled out bracelets and were showcasing them.

"Yes."

Ruka opened the box. It was a children's bracelet made of red and pink stones. I clasped it on her wrist for her.

"It's perfect for you. You must thank him."

"I will. I will." Her eyes wide, she moved her arm to catch the light.

People took their seats. Mohamed's brother and his wife sat at the head of the table and said something to us all. Across from us were Ousha's parents. They looked dour.

"Nice to see you," I told her mother.

"Why are you here? Who invited you?" she spat.

"I was invited, just like you."

Ousha glared at her mother.

"I wasn't invited," her mother said. "I was told to come. I know you're trying to take my daughter's place. I know you want Mohamed."

The accusation caught me off guard because it was so far from the truth.

"Why are you making things up? My daughter and I are trying to survive. To help our family at home."

"It's how all of you do it—come here, then wreak havoc in our lives. Try to marry into a life you have no business being in."

"Isn't that what you did?" I couldn't believe the words had come out of my mouth.

She strangled her cloth napkin two times over.

Cynthia was sitting at my side of the table, smiling politely at our conversation, as if we were talking about a new recipe and she was agreeing on the ingredients.

Ruka was still admiring her bracelet when the yacht's engines bubbled to life and the crew pulled in the lines from the dock. Mohamed's brother was still talking. The rest of the table had fallen silent. Each of their faces held a different reaction to what he was saying. Abdullah was watching with me. I felt he was taking detailed notes, while Cynthia's head continued to bob. He finished his speech, and then we headed out into the open water.

The first course of a nutty orange soup with a slice of crusty bread was served. After we finished dinner, Cynthia invited us to stand up and take in the sunset.

Ousha stood beside Ruka and me on the edge of the deck. "Did you understand what Mohamed's brother was saying?"

I knew she didn't expect me to understand any of it.

"He's taking over the company and moving the headquarters to Abu Dhabi. Jaseem is being asked to move there."

"Ruka too?" I asked.

"That's the implication. But it's not for another month."

I looked over the water; I couldn't allow Ruka to move away from me.

"This gives you all the more reason to hurry up with our plan."

"What plan?" Ousha's mother had moved in beside us.

Ousha looked startled, but by the time she turned to her mother she was beaming. "Helping Fata and Jaseem get their apartment ready for sale, of course."

"Yes, I would think that's a big job," her mother said.

"You have no idea," said Ousha.

I put my arm around Ruka and watched the last sliver of orange fall beneath the water.

In Sickness and In Health

Three identical mornings passed. I was beginning to wonder if the castor beans would have an effect.

With a grin, Ousha poked her head into the kitchen. "Shula, can you bring Mohamed his espresso and breakfast in his room?"

I held my hand up to acknowledge her. A few minutes later, I was standing at the door to his room, which was open a few centimeters. I heard Ousha talking to Mohamed; they sounded much farther in than his couch. She was consoling him. Then I heard him vomit. Gut-wrenching hurls. I pushed the door open. Ousha stood behind him in the bathroom, rubbing his back. She wiped his mouth for him, then directed him back to the couch and put a blanket over his legs and a pillow behind his back.

"Put the tray over here. I'll feed him," she told me.

I set it down; his face was gray, the slick coating of sleep embracing his head. Ousha gave him a bite of his eggs, then encouraged him to drink his coffee. Nudging with maternal encouragement, sip by sip, she nodded as he drank while rubbing his back. They didn't look up at me, but I couldn't watch, so I turned away and headed to the kitchen.

When he was done, I was called back to retrieve his plate and cup. He was sleeping, and Ousha had placed a wet washcloth on his head. The espresso cup was empty. I had put a double dose of oil in it.

Two days later a doctor was called. He left the house with a puzzled look on his face.

On the sixth day, Ousha came to me in the morning before I woke and shook my shoulder.

"He's really bad today. Give him a double dose. He won't know the difference even if it tastes bad. He's been in and out most of the night."

There were only three beans left. I squeezed two of them into his smoothie and delivered it. My insides twisted; my mind was screaming at itself, one side that I was committing murder, the other that it was the only way out. I wouldn't consider the future of these thoughts, only that when the deed was done I would bury them so deep within me that even I wouldn't know where they were.

I stood stone-faced and watched. Ousha got behind him, propping his sweaty head into her lap, her legs cradling his body. She had moved him to her bed, where she slept behind him.

They embraced each other's evil, a serpent wrapped around a scorpion. One squeezing, the other stinging, all the while carrying each other to new destinations.

The doorbell chimed. I broke from my trance and my eyes passed over the closet. I noticed Ousha's suitcase had moved from where she usually kept it and one of the latches was undone.

At the door I found Cynthia, who wore a pained look. She touched my shoulder affectionately, and I led her to Ousha's bedroom. She didn't seem to have been in this house before. She rushed to her son and said things in rapid fire. I left them to be together. Mohamed voiced something unintelligible as I left. He sounded as if he had a brain bleed.

I went across the hall and busied myself in the guest room, cleaning. Cynthia and Ousha raised their voices, and not long after, two medics stood at the door. I saw them carry Mohamed out on a stretcher, wrapped in white blankets, with a bag of fluid held in the air by one of the medics.

I retrieved the cup from Mohamed's room and scrubbed it and the sink. I took the bag that held the beans and put it inside a plastic bag. Trash pickup was tomorrow; I would make sure the bags and the grinder I had used were gone. I cleaned with purpose for hours, polishing the metal surfaces until they gleamed brilliantly. The glass was so clean it looked as though it were missing. Then I scrubbed the tiles around the pool so they looked like fresh bone.

I wore myself weary and collapsed into bed, forgetting to call Ruka.

Ousha appeared in the night, like a visiting spirit, extracting me from my peaceful blackness.

"Shula, we're going to have to leave very soon. Are you ready?" Her fingers twitched while she played with her hair.

"I'll let Ruka know tomorrow."

"You can't tell her. She's a young girl; she won't keep the secret, and Jaseem will tell Abdullah our plans before we even get to the airport."

"But she needs to be ready to go."

"I told you I couldn't assure both of you passage."

"I won't leave without her."

"Then you might not leave." She was pacing alongside my bed. "You said you saw Inesh in here?" Her voice pitched up and she turned on the bathroom light.

The skin under her eyes was puffy and purple. Her pupils were wide too, which made her look like a certain type of monkey that lurked around our house in Balapitiya near dinnertime, looking for scraps.

"There was a picture of him. That's all. I've never seen him because he's ..." It was better I didn't say it. Not now.

"He's what?"

"He's not here," was all I could offer.

"Of course he's not here." Ousha shook her head at me as if she'd encountered someone profoundly dumb. "Well, there might be a way, a form or two to fill out at the embassy before we go. But that's on you. I'm not getting involved in any government schemes. We could be in enough trouble."

I agreed politely.

"I'll be at the hospital the next couple of days. Let's hope it happens." She made a choking sound, then disappeared into the hall. It seemed the darkness gave her power.

Against the Tide

I knew Ruka could keep a secret. When the pale-pink doors of the elevator opened, she ran toward me with her arms open.

"Ruka?" I ran my hand over her hair to put it in place. "We'll be leaving soon. Can you exit in the night?"

"Sneak out?"

"Yes."

"I think so. But Mrs. Fata has been so good to me. I don't want to leave her."

We were on the sidewalk now. The sole of one of her sandals had partially detached and was flopping against the concrete. In my mind the extra noise sent alarms off in every house we passed.

"This isn't about Fata. It's about finally going home, to your brother and our life there."

"Our *horrible* life. Where we didn't have food and everyone is dead."

I pulled her closer. "You're right. Life is tough there, but it's real. This place is lie stacked upon lie. And we're the glue holding all the lies together so our masters can dance on top of us and not hurt themselves. Don't you miss Mewan?"

I felt her head move against my side.

"For the next few days, when we go for our walk, bring your things. I'll keep them with me."

"Okay, Mama." She paused, then added, "That man was at the apartment today."

"What man?"

"That Khalid man. The one who lied to me and told me you said it was okay for me to come here."

"I don't think he means you any harm, but go to your room if he shows up again. Avoid him."

...

That night, the house was still. Ousha didn't come home from the hospital. The phone rang again and again. I avoided it and eventually stuffed a towel at the bottom of my door so the ringing would stay outside my room. I dreamed about Maryam. I was feeding her, and between suckles to her bottle she told me all the things she hoped to do in her life. She wanted to be a dancer, in front of the people of London, and also have a white dog with feathery, fluffy hair and a long lazy pink tongue. She was happy when she told me these things.

Ousha clamored through the front door just after the sun rose. I was at the dining room table, drinking tea and eating an apricot scone. Her abaya was heavily creased, and she listed when she walked, cruising past but never looking into the dining room.

She went to the kitchen, then slipped through the side door and sat across from me. She mirrored what I had, but her tea sloshed over the edge of her glass mug and the crumbs from the scone bounced over the tabletop.

"He's gone." There was emotion in her voice.

I noticed an angry knot on the side of her head jump out with every bite.

"Will you attend the funeral?" I asked.

She ignored my question. "Are you ready to go now?"

"Home?"

"No, we're going to London. You can find your way from there."

I had to take a deep breath. "If Ruka can come."

Ousha took another bite, then threw the rest at me. "She can come. She can come. Stop asking me the same question." She had a deranged essence to her. "Mohamed always told me you weren't that smart."

She wasn't looking at me now; she was focused on the chair where Mohamed usually sat; her eyes were welling. I moved slowly to avoid breaking her trance and backed out of the room.

. . .

When I met Ruka for our usual walk, this time I turned her around and we went back into the elevator.

"Fata is home?"

"Yes."

Inside the apartment, Fata graciously smiled and gave me a light hug of welcome.

"Mohamed has died," I told her.

Both hands went to her mouth.

"It was sudden. I don't think there was a way to save him. He was at the hospital."

"How is Ousha doing?"

I hadn't anticipated that question, though I should have.

"She's not good. I was wondering if Ruka can come stay with us for a day. It might cheer Ousha up."

As soon as I said that, I knew Ruka would understand what was happening.

"Yes, yes. Anything to help. I'll tell Jaseem when he comes home. I'm sure Abdullah and Cynthia are devastated."

A few minutes later, we walked out of Fata's apartment onto the sidewalk.

Ruka looked up at me. "We're leaving, aren't we?"

"As soon as we can."

At the house, Ousha was in her room. I took the bold step of going upstairs without request. She was deep in her suitcase, mostly packing it with pictures and jewelry.

"I'll take that necklace now," she said.

"Not until we get to London and I have tickets onward."

Feeling the deep tension, Ruka stepped out of the room.

"You'll give it to me now." Ousha rose and pulled off her abaya, revealing a black Lycra suit underneath.

I secured the necklace with my hand. Ousha was smaller than me, and her frame lacked the hardening effects of manual labor. I didn't want this to devolve into a physical fight, but I had to secure my one item of value.

As she swiped at me, my mind cascaded through options to settle her.

"I have something else."

"What could you have?"

"I know where Inesh is."

It was a cruel move, one I instantly regretted.

Her face melted, and her body sagged. "Really?"

"After the tickets, after safety."

"Why would you?" But she knew why I would.

THREE TICKETS, SINGLE JOURNEY

It was a quarter to midnight, and we stood behind the front door.

Ousha looked at us both. "Not a word. I'll do all the talking."

We took four taxis to the airport, and Ousha paid in cash for all of them. When we were in the last taxi, she opened her purse and pulled out a passport for Ruka. It had a counterfeit name and a face that looked close enough to hers.

"I'll take mine back now," she held her hand out.

"Where did you get this?" I was happy to hand hers over.

"With money all things are possible."

The gate agent put our three passports on the counter next to the three tickets and never once looked at us. We sat in the first three seats of the plane. Ruka stayed close to me, unsure if any of this was going to work. She held my hand over the armrest of our seat.

When there was no one else around, Ousha leaned over the aisle. "Please tell me now."

I wagged my finger at her. The act of saying no to her was immensely satisfying.

She ground herself into her seat and snapped her headphones on.

She was asleep when Ruka whispered to me, "Do you really know where this man is?"

"Yes." I would have to explain to her later what I'd done and hope she would forgive me.

I watched Ousha and tried to imagine everything that had led her to this place. Had it been her father, her marriage, or the strong arm of Abdullah? Was she as out of control of the situation as I was?

. . .

The UK passport control wasn't so easy. The dour white man in his black uniform demanded that Ruka step out from behind me. Then he pointed at both pictures in the two counterfeit passports and at me. I knew what he was saying. He made a phone call, and then we were all pulled into a room together. They left us alone.

"This isn't working," Ousha said.

"I just want to get to Sri Lanka." I didn't care about entering the UK. This was all Ousha's fault for dragging us here.

"You made me come here."

"Tell them you took the wrong passport. Say you made a mistake."

The man returned with another young man from my country. He was slight, his gray jacket hanging off of him.

He smiled and sat next to me. The original officer escorted Ousha out of the room.

"Are you in danger?" he asked me. His eyes were sincere.

"No. I just forgot to bring her passport and I grabbed both of mine. We rushed out." I wasn't sure if that was the right thing to say.

"Why were you rushing from Dubai?"

A million excuses zipped through my head. I kept seeing Mohamed being taken out by the medics.

"We are just here for a visit with her parents, and then we are going to Sri Lanka."

"Do you have tickets onward?"

I shook my head.

He stroked his chin, then wrote something on a pad of paper.

"You were working in Dubai, for her?"

"Yes."

"And then she brought you here to visit her parents with a promise to send you home?"

"Yes."

"Are you in trouble?"

I flushed.

The man called back the other officer and spoke to him in English.

Then he addressed me directly. "We will give you and your daughter a five-day entry permit. But you must leave on time." The officer left, then returned ten minutes later with words and numbers on a card next to a picture of Ruka.

He leaned into me and handed me a card with a phone number on it. "Just in case you are in trouble."

...

We stood on platform seven of Paddington train station after stepping off the Heathrow express. The lattice of metal and glass overhead shielded us from the weather, but more important, from what I felt was the ever-watchful eye of those who controlled all that was. The Abdullahs and Khalids. Those who controlled the seas and the hulking jets pushing through the skies, carrying out the wishes of their great masters.

Ruka and I had followed Ousha this far without question.

"The Sri Lankan embassy isn't far from here. You can go there." She began walking.

"What about our tickets?" I asked.

"You don't get those until you tell me where Inesh is and I have the necklace."

What game was she playing? And why did the necklace matter so much? I suspected the jewels and money she had packed would carry her for years if not a lifetime. She approached a police officer and spoke to him in Mohamed's language. She then circled her neck and pointed to Ruka and me.

The officer said something in a different language and waved his hands in front of him, not wanting to get involved. He looked closely at us as we passed him but took no action.

We were outside now, standing near a line of taxis and smokers.

"Last chance," Ousha said.

"You must buy us onward tickets. We'll be stuck here otherwise. I thought this was our deal."

"Give it to me." Ousha threw herself at me, pawing my neck. I pushed her away. She screamed, throwing her hands up, then pointing at me. I turned red as the other train riders diverted themselves around us. The officer was back, helping her up. Another man who understood what she was saying approached us. When they were done talking, he encouraged her to move on. I couldn't help but chuckle. We all looked the same here; these Londoners wouldn't pay any more attention to us than any other person.

"You're making fools of us," I told Ousha.

"You've stolen that necklace from me and I want it back."

Ruka stayed behind me; I could tell Ousha's erratic behavior scared her. I took a step toward her. "You know, we can help each other. I can help you find your love and you can help us return home. We need each other." It seemed she had forgotten our deal and at moments only her animal instincts drove her. Inside me a knife twisted.

For that breath, Ousha seemed to come into exquisite focus. "You're right," she said.

...

We broke into the sunlight together and climbed the ramp out of the station and onto Praed Street. The morning was crisp and our desert clothes let the cool air chill our skin. The human sidewalk traffic was building, something not present in Dubai.

"I'm going to meet my parents here," Ousha said after we had gone a block.

She pointed to a café. There, she bought Ruka a hot chocolate and us tea and croissants. She took a sip of hers, then added a packet of sugar. When the last granule dissolved, she reengaged.

"They aren't far from here, but they can't know you're here with me."

"Why?"

"Because it will create questions, and my mother thinks you're a savage." She lowered her voice. "She thinks you killed Maryam."

I looked at Ruka; she was staring out the window of the café with chocolaty steam drifting into her nose.

I was starting to feel the thin connection between Ousha and me open. "Why don't you just tell her the truth?"

"My parents view truth as a reminder of what they're not," she said simply. "They try to avoid it at all costs."

"Where does that leave us?" I thought it was an honest question.

"How about I meet you here tomorrow at the same time?" She got up and walked to the counter. She gave the man behind it a wad of bills and said something to him, then rejoined us at the table. "You can stay here until they close and eat two more meals." Her suitcase bumped over the threshold of the door, and I watched her merge into the city.

"Let's see the city," I told Ruka. I wasn't going to sit here all day waiting for Ousha to return. I wanted Ruka to be a woman of action when she grew up. I wanted her to know the act of moving in and of itself could lead to solutions.

I watched the faces of the people we passed on the sidewalk, wondering if they'd condemn us for the color of our skin or what we were wearing. I had grown accustomed to such remarks over the last few months, but it didn't hurt as much because they weren't my people.

We stood in an expansive park. The trees were bare, with beds of wilted plants stuffed into the soggy beds, and the grass made a slurping sound when we walked on it. As Ruka danced around in the open space, brown droplets splashed onto her legs. She returned to me, and we continued on Oxford Street, under the illuminated angels hovering above the road, their colors bleeding onto us, their light merging with our own.

In the few cities I had been to, I noticed a character in each, an agreement the residents had forged regarding how they would live in concert with the city. But this place was unique. It was a jostling closeness of difference. And no one seemed to mind. If it was up to me, this was a place I wouldn't mind staying. It was a long time since I had felt a piece of something that wasn't trying to spit me out.

We kept going, my fingertips and nose refrigerated by the air, until we traced our steps back to the café, where we could warm up and eat.

When the night had fully settled in and the customers stopped coming, the man behind the counter rang a bell and pointed to the door.

"Where now?" Ruka's eyes were sleepy, and I felt lumps in my stomach. I got two more hot drinks for us. I gave one to her so she could wrap her hands around it, and we stepped onto the sidewalk. I wrapped my clothing around her, and we walked to the station, for the benches and shelter. The wet coldness of this city made my mind seek shelter in the memories of home.

I was lying on the wooden floor of our house. The neighbor had brought his wife to guide my labor. Pramith had left yesterday, to work a job in the next town. Ruka was next to me, kissing and rubbing my head. Mewan was coming. The heat of the exertion left me drenched, my sweat gathering in small pools on our floor.

Vela, our neighbor, was between my legs. She had brought a clean mat for me to lie on, as well as water from the well. "Push, Shula. Push."

A mountain of pain struck through my opening body, and I thought my insides might seize up in retaliation. I gritted my teeth and focused on Vela, on doing what she told me.

A short while later, a pillow was propped behind me, and a new baby was in my arms, Ruka's head nuzzled close as she admired her new brother.

Dwehlli appeared at the door, her wooden bowl heaped with steaming food and a smile that made her ears sit high on her shaved head. She set the bowl on our table, then came and wrapped her arms around all of us, speaking soft blessings over us for a full and comfortable life. I hadn't seen her since Ruka was born. She had fled to the north of our country; before she went, she had told me the wounds of the war still needed healing and she had been called to attend to them. But she had come back somehow; words of our whereabouts had found their way to her. A few hours passed, and it was time for her to leave. She stood over us again, her empty bowl under her arm. "You're a beautiful family," she said.

TO TAKE

There is nothing easy about a cold night on the streets of London. The police moved us out of the station at midnight, informing us it was closing. An officer pulled the gate to the ground after we stepped out. Ruka swayed with sleep, still tucked tightly in the folds of my dress as we walked. I heard some men approach from behind us; they were barking loudly and a bottle smashed near them. They said something else, pulled at my head covering, and slapped my butt, then ran past us howling with laughter. There were three of them, all university age. If others had been around, I might have felt humiliated, but now in the lonely night, it affected me as much as a subtle gust of wind.

We hadn't strayed far from the café where Ousha was going to meet us in the morning. I sat on the concrete, against the dirty crevice of the building and the sidewalk. I balled up the extra dress I had and laid my head against a pipe. Ruka was in my lap. The last thing I saw before I fell asleep was the dirt pushed up under my nails as they rested against a flattened piece of chewing gum on the sidewalk.

…

There were rough hands under my head covering. It wasn't Ruka. I reached for them, and they pushed mine away. I opened my eyes; the morning had come, and a man I didn't recognize was yanking at me.

I backed away from him. A grunting yell left my lips. My eyes hadn't been open enough to know if there were other people around me.

"Stop. Stop. Stop." I swatted at him. He put his hands on me again. Ruka shrieked. Her emergence from my clothes caught him off guard, and he stepped back and fixated on her. I took her hand, quickly stood up, and ran for the end of the block. Ousha's face was looking around the building from an alley.

"Ousha, help!" I called to her.

The man caught me and pulled me back. I fell backward and landed in a sitting position. He dragged me, then ripped off my head covering, and his hands dove under my neckline. I clasped his wrists and pushed, but he was too strong for me. Ruka wailed at such a pitch that I wanted to cover my ears; she was standing back from me, pulling at her hair, immolated. I stopped fighting and let him do what he was going to do. His hand caught my necklace, and he pulled hard until the gold hook relented. When he had it, he took off running.

Ruka sank to the ground. Her crying tore at me—that she had to witness such an act of violence against me when both of us were powerless to fight back. Ousha was there. Still watching. And then it made sense. She had orchestrated his. I patted Ruka's head and bolted upright, charging at Ousha.

"What do you think you're doing to me?" I fired at her.

She tried to back into the shadows, but I rounded the corner and caught her. I spotted a stone, which I picked up and pelted at her. The vehemence of what I wanted to do to her now inhabited me and made my rational mind mute.

It caught her in the back of the head and drew blood.

"Do you think you're going to wear me thin until I snap or give in?" I screamed at her. "Or maybe you'll frighten me into submission so I don't expose the truth of who you are?"

She held the back of her head and limped forward, trying to get away from me. Her fingers turned red. I caught her and jumped in front of her. She recoiled as though I were going to hit her again. And everything in me said to knock her dead.

"You know what you are? You're the softened scum of Dubai. Never a hard day to brandish a callous or strengthen your spine. But I've stood in greater tragedy than this. God knows you'll never break me, because if even you strike me down, I'll rise and strike you twice. Believe me, Ousha, I have the strength of ten of you, and if you walk away from me today alive, it's only a testament to my daughter that she doesn't see me murder someone. Because if we were alone, I don't know what I might do."

"You'll never get it back," she hissed.

"And you'll never get Inesh back, because he's dead. That's where he is, burned to the heavens. Go live with that, Ousha. I hope the riches you sold your conscience on comfort you with that truth."

Her fortitude against me collapsed under the weight of the revelation. Then tears came. Ruka had caught up to me and touched my back. Her cool hand reminded me that I was an inferno of anger.

I took my daughter by the hand and left her in the alley. We were moving, and I knew we'd eventually find our way home.

THE EDGE

The edge of civilization is where you stop being seen. Ruka and I walked for the day, wandering through the streets. I didn't know what it was I was looking for, and my mind kept exploring avenues I should have taken, ways that wouldn't have led me here. None of it mattered, though; we stood firmly in our present. As we walked into the night, I saw women sitting on the ground with cups in front of them, pleading in languages I didn't know, every person passing them as if they were a trash bin to be avoided. I wondered how many days away from that we were.

"I'm hungry, Mama."

"I know. Me too."

The rain began to fall, and we stood against a cosmetics store, under the awning. Across the street a bakery was closing. I watched the workers inside. The warm glow bounced off golden pastries and long baguettes. One counted the money in the register, while the other pulled out all the baked items and put them in a black bag. The rain came down harder, ricocheting off the sidewalk and soaking our feet. They walked out, locked the door, and threw the black bag onto the curb.

"Did you see that Ruka? All that food?"

When they were out of sight, we crossed the street and I opened the bag. A few people walked by us, watching as I devoured a fruit muffin and Ruka chomped through a pie only the size of my hand. The rain soaked us, but our stomachs were full.

I tied the bag, then carried it with me; there was enough food in here for a few days. My feet were wet and cold; my sandals, perfectly suited for Dubai, were a curse here. A grate in the sidewalk blew up glorious warm air, and we stood on it and let it heat our bodies and dry our clothes. Then we found a small corner, a dry piece of ground, and pushed our bodies into it. We huddled into each other and settled in for the night. Ruka was asleep within minutes, while I drifted in and out. Each time I heard footsteps or a car blow its horn, I straightened, looked around, and then my eyes would lose the battle with sleep.

Suddenly there was a crack inside my head, like summer thunder. I opened my eyes, then the pain came, at the side of my face. I put my hand to it; I couldn't touch it, but I knew it was starting to swell. I was going to walk to one of the windows and look at myself. Our bag was gone. I uncovered Ruka so I could stand up.

She woke and looked at me. "What happened to you?" She was pointing to my face.

"I don't know. What does it look like?"

"It's blue and puffy." She looked around us and out to the street. A cyclist whizzed by in a skintight yellow suit.

I stood up and felt dizzy; the ground tilted and I held on to the wall next to us. "Give me a minute, and then we'll keep walking. We won't accomplish anything sitting here."

I wondered if those women I'd seen on the street had this same resolve in the beginning and then the city had chipped it away until they were muddled heaps.

I had lost all bearing of which way we were walking. I had no idea what the city looked like or how far it extended.

Eventually we found ourselves at the big park again. The rain had stopped and the morning light was coming over the wall of buildings.

We stayed at the perimeter. I kept walking; I didn't let Ruka know I had no idea where we were going. When we had freed ourselves from the mud that day two years ago and walked through our stunned village, I had told Ruka only to "keep walking." My job right now was to keep her hope burning. With the park on our right, Ruka remained focused and led us. I was proud of her for leading. She was en route to being a strong woman.

Then I saw it.

REFUGE

"Sri Lanka (Ceylon) is a free, sovereign, independent, and democratic socialist republic and shall be known as the Democratic Socialist Republic of Sri Lanka."

Ruka read the first words of our constitution, two blocks from Paddington station on the other side of the street from the park. The building was white stone with four columns flanking the front entrance and my flag flying high. There were no lights on, but I knew now was the time to wait.

"Is that our flag?" Ruka asked.

"Yes, this is someplace that can help us." There was much less hope behind what I said.

A black sedan pulled up and two people stepped out and looked at us. They whisked by, up the stairs into the first set of doors. A slow trickle of other workers came next, heading through the same door.

"Can you help us?" I asked the fourth woman to pass us.

She stopped and looked us up and down. "With what?"

I could tell from her accent that she had grown up in the wealthy part of Colombo.

"We were brought here and left. We need to get home."

"Where in London do you live?"

"We live in Batapitya. But we were taken to Dubai and then here."

She put her briefcase down and sat next to us. "When was this?"

"Months? I think. I've lost track."

"Can you stay here for a moment? I'll be right back."

I wasn't sure if I should trust her.

A few minutes later, she returned with a folder filled with papers and a bottle of water for each of us. "Come inside with me."

The inside of the building was warm and filled with plush yellow and white furniture; the room had bright streaks of glittering color. I slipped my sandals off at the door, but my feet were so dirty and wet that they left black marks on the blond carpet.

"Sit, sit." She directed us to the couch and sat down in an adjacent chair. "My name is Shehara. Could you fill out these papers?" She handed me the folder.

I opened it and looked over them.

"Do you have a passport?" she asked.

I reached into my clothes and pulled out the two passports I had. She flipped through, studying them deeply. "I think these are counterfeit. Do you know the names of the people who brought you here?"

Of course I did, but I didn't want to tell her. I shook my head.

"I'll be back." She took them with her and left me with a pen. I filled out what I could. Ruka was acting strangely; her eyes didn't seem to focus on any one thing.

I reached over and touched her hair. She was hot.

"Do you feel okay?"

"No. I feel dizzy." There was something in her hand.

"What is that?"

"Food. Ousha gave it to me." It was a biscuit. I recognized the brown bits of the castor beans mixed in with it. I scooped it out of her hand.

"This is making you sick. How much have you eaten?"

"Just a little earlier."

Shehara returned. She'd taken off her suit jacket, and she looked friendlier. "What is it that you want, Shula?"

"Like I said, to go home. To finally go home."

A Beginning and an End

Shehara stepped off the boat with Ruka and me when we arrived at our village. She had been insistent on making the trip. She wanted to see the genesis of workers from our part of the country.

"It's …"

I knew what she was thinking. *Primitive.* It was a word I'd heard others from Colombo use to describe us.

Her heels sunk into the sand, and she pitched backward. I put my hand on the small of her back for balance and took her bag from her arm. She was trying to help, and so was I.

We walked through the main path. The heat of the afternoon lay over us like a fur blanket. Some of the shopkeepers recognized us and waved, while others looked back and forth between Shehara and us, assembling a story of our connection.

"Where is your house?" Her head swiveled.

"It's up the hill a ways. We don't need to go there. This way." I led her to the place where the thin red string delineated the perimeter of the tent hotel boundary.

"The man, Khalid, stays here when he comes. The third tent on the left. I can ask around and see if he's here or if someone like him is here. But if you stay long enough, you'll see him, passing out shiny pamphlets. Promising big houses when we return." I paused. "I need to go, to find my son."

"Please do," Shehara said, as though she'd forgotten the whole reason I'd returned.

Ruka already was charging ahead of me, through the coconut trees.

I stepped over the ground, which was slick with dead leaves, pounded down by human feet, careful not to fall. When I climbed the five logs we had embedded in the hillside as stairs, Ruka didn't say anything.

The place where our house was only had our roof, disassembled and resting against the side of the embankment. The building itself was gone. I could see the round space where I'd cooked meals, put our heads to sleep each night, and hunkered down during the summer drenching rains. A soiled piece of yellow fabric left over from a dress I'd made for Ruka was pinned under a rock.

Ruka started to cry. I pulled her close to me. "It's okay. We've been here before. We'll make a new house."

Kiyoma's mother appeared and I heard Mewan yell. "Come see your brother," she told Ruka.

He ran to Ruka first, with the widest grin, and hugged her. Ruka's tears stopped, and she realized her home was still here.

Lessons

Eight Months Later

We sat high up, on the front ledge of our house. We had built something substantial this time. A home where we would live, and where, if I was lucky, I would die.

The world only feels big because we are so small. What Dwhelli hadn't told me was how powerful our smallness was. That our tiny beating hearts could stretch across oceans and continents, through skyscrapers and deserts, and move us to accomplish things we never thought possible. Today, with one of my hands on Ruka's knee and the other on Mewan's, we sat on top of our empire. The thing Mohamed should have known when I shook before him was that our three hearts, lined up in Batapitya, Sri Lanka, a place of insignificants, could move the kings of the world. Empires—no matter if they're made of gold, soldiers, or waves of mud—could ever topple the power of our love. I wasn't afraid of his empire, but instead only longed for the deep power of mine. I pulled my family close, thinking of all the people before us, and knew what we did now would help all of those in our empire who were to come. In Dwhelli's words, we were a beautiful family.

ABOUT THE AUTHOR

James lives with his husband and two sons
in Fort Lauderdale, Florida.

www.ingramcontent.com/pod-product-compliance
Lightning Source LLC
Chambersburg PA
CBHW051139130726

47988CB00005B/1911